Simon Maginn   Merseyside, in   Mary's College an   ussex, where he studied   earlier novels, *Sheep* (a W.H. Smi   Talent title), *Virgins and Martyrs* and *A Sickness of the Soul*, have been published by Corgi. Simon Maginn lives in Sussex.

Also by Simon Maginn

SHEEP
VIRGINS AND MARTYRS
A SICKNESS OF THE SOUL

Methods of Confinement

Simon Maginn

BLACK SWAN

METHODS OF CONFINEMENT
A BLACK SWAN BOOK : 0 552 99708 0

First publication in Great Britain

PRINTING HISTORY
Black Swan edition published 1996
Copyright © Simon Maginn 1996

The right of Simon Maginn to be identified as the author
of this work has been asserted in accordance with sections
77 and 78 of the Copyright Designs and Patents Act 1988.

Set in 11/12pt Linotype Melior by
Phoenix Typesetting, Ilkley, West Yorkshire

Black Swan Books are published by Transworld Publishers Ltd,
61-63 Uxbridge Road, London W5 5SA,
in Australia by Transworld Publishers (Australia) Pty Ltd,
15–25 Helles Avenue, Moorebank, NSW 2170
and in New Zealand by Transworld Publishers (NZ) Ltd,
3 William Pickering Drive, Albany, Auckland.

Reproduced, printed and bound in Great Britain
by Cox & Wyman Ltd, Reading, Berks.

Acknowledgements

Thanks to all my usual informants, particularly Calum Bartlett and Hugh Fisher, though any factual errors are entirely my own. Thanks also to Nick Upjohn, my agent Carole Blake and, as always, my editor Averil Ashfield for spotting the cracks and helping out with the plastering.

Permission to quote from the following is gratefully acknowledged:

'Fake Plastic Trees' (Thomas York/Edward O'Brien/ Colin Greenward/Philip Selway) © Warner/Chappell Music Ltd, London W1Y 3FA. Reproduced by permission of International Music Publications Ltd.

Foucault, M.: *Madness and Civilisation* (Routledge)

Groves, T. (ed): *Countdown to Community Care* (BMJ Publishing group)

Greenblatt, York and Brown, *From Custodial to Therapeutic Patient Care in Mental Hospitals* (© 1955 Russell Sage Foundation. Used with the permission of Russell Sage Foundation)

'For seeing we are not masters of our affections, wee are like battered citties without walles, or shipps tossed in the sea'

Edward Jorden, *A Briefe Discourse . . .* ,1603

If I could be
Who you wanted
If I could be
Who you wanted
All the time
All the time

Radiohead, 'Fake Plastic Trees'

1533

'. . . He was put into Bedlam, and afterwards by beating and correction gathered his remembrances to come again to himself. But, being thereupon set at liberty and walking about abroad, his old fancies began again to fall in his head . . . I caused him to be bound to a tree in the street before the whole town, and constables striped him with rods until they waxed weary . . . Verily, God be thanked, I hear no harm from him now . . .'

Sir Thomas More, *Apology*

1. *We've Got Each Other*

To celebrate their fifth anniversary, Luke and Anna went to Le Cochon Gras with Paul and Lauren, their oldest friends, and spent a small fortune on dinner. Luke wore black polo shirt and black Paul Smith suit with narrow lapels. Anna was in a dark grey cashmere dress, long-sleeved and close round the throat, and her jet tear-drop earrings. They ate slowly, smoking between courses, lingering over cured meats and soft cheeses, drinking first champagne and then red wine. They laughed a lot. They stayed late. There was no babysitter to get back for, after all.

Paul and Lauren were down from Manchester for a few days, staying with friends of Paul's in Crouch End. They'd left London years ago, had vowed never to come back, but were always willing to visit. They were more Luke's friends than Anna's, though Luke confessed he was easier with them when she was there. They made a handsome foursome, like something out of a French film, Luke thought, Buñuel maybe, still young but fairly affluent, good-looking, well-educated, secure about who they were.

Luke didn't know what to do with the left-over bits of lobster claw and ended up trying to hide them under his napkin. Lauren laughed at him and piled them all up brazenly on her plate, building a haphazard mound of mottled brick-red shell, the razor-sharp claws sticking up like discarded weapons from a miniature war.

Anna proposed a toast: 'To us,' and Luke tapped his glass against the others and said, 'And all who sail in us.'

*　　*　　*

The streets were wet as they spilled out from the soft velvet cocoon. They stood on the pavement saying goodbye until Anna managed to hail a taxi. A figure slumped in a doorway started to rise as they got in, and Luke met his eye for a second. Quick, eager eye. On the way home Luke and Anna giggled and kissed in the back of the taxi like kids. Luke tried to stick a rose down her neck; she thumped him in the groin and was unmoved by his complaints.

'I mean,' she said, 'it's not as if you need it for anything.'

They tipped the driver far too much, and swayed up the garden path to the darkened house. With tips and extras included, the bill for the evening came to a whisker over a hundred and ten pounds.

'You better be worth it, Toots,' Luke said as he opened the front door, and Anna squeezed a handful of bum hard enough to leave marks.

'You better be up to it, sailor boy,' she said.

They both were. Luke, as always, luxuriated in every moment, spreading himself over and around her, his heavy, sensual body moving above her tighter, harder, more purposeful form. Sweat gathered in the folds of his belly, across his back, he dripped sweat over her as she moved, moaned, struggled under him.

Afterwards they lay entwined and listened to water dripping from the trees at the back. The house was completely still, no little sounds from the small bedroom, no door opening and shutting, no light footsteps to and from the bathroom. No sounds except the sounds they made. Luke realized after a few minutes that Anna was crying, absolutely silently, just allowing the drops to slide down her face. He caught one on his fingertip and licked it. He squeezed her with weary tenderness. She couldn't help crying, he couldn't help feeling desperate and resentful, neither of them could help how they felt. It just went on and on.

'It doesn't matter,' he said, 'we've got each other haven't we? That's what's important.'

'Yes,' she whispered, but it did matter, would never stop mattering; sometimes it seemed to matter more than life itself. They couldn't talk about it because when they did Luke became angry that the child they couldn't have seemed more important to her, more real, than he did. 'I'm here,' he would say, 'why isn't that enough?'

'We're lucky,' he said. 'We've got each other.'

Anna sniffled and then sighed, a great unsteady gulp of air. A hundred and ten pounds, Luke thought, and still we end up crying in bed. He hated the thought, hated himself for thinking it, hated the world for being so bloody impossible. What was he supposed to do about it? Always the feeling that it was his fault, that he should do, that he had let her down. Irrational, since it wasn't his fault, it was hers. Which itself was absurd of course, it wasn't anyone's fault, it was just the bloody world. Easy for you to be resigned, she'd said once, since you never really wanted a child, not *really*. This at the end of an increasingly desperate series of attempts at IVF, which itself was the bitter culmination of many, many months of having sex when neither of them wanted to, but the calendar coldly declared that it must be. He sometimes had felt that his penis, his balls had been commandeered like a car in a war zone, taken from him and used, instead of for his own insignificant little gratifications, for The Great Cause, the baby that would be. Nature! Life! The coursing, turbulent, unstoppable river! Except that it had stopped, refused in fact even to trickle for Anna, who cursed it and hated it and hated him for being part of it, hated herself for hating him. When he'd tried to interest her on infertile days she'd looked slightly shocked. But Luke, her face seemed to say, how will this serve The Great Cause? He imagined her as a Resistance fighter, a plucky, gamine soul with smudged cheeks and the fires of righteous defiance in her eyes. Blindly, uncontrollably when the moment was on him he plunged and bucked harder than ever, harder than he intended to, and she bowed under him, pulling him in, desperately, but somehow without passion. You're the bloody sensualist, she'd say afterwards as he made a nightcap joint, you have the sodding passion. For me it's just work, soldier. She was joking, of course.

Luke had watched her turn sad, angry, but all inward. Her tears crept down, as if ashamed, one at a time. It was a very pure misery, he thought, there was no compensation of pleasant melancholy or bittersweet regret, it was just a pure, hard, indigestible thing, rough to the touch, a stone. Ugly, untempered, unlovely thing, squeezing out occasional angry tears. This was what slept beside him now. Not always, but often.

He curled a finger lazily round her shoulder and across her breast. They slept, the heat from their bodies wrapping them as the house stood all around, cold and silent and mostly empty.

Bobby Parrot, covered up in his cage downstairs, scuttled from one end of his perch to the other, and adjusted his wing feathers. He made a tiny sound – coooooo – and batted one eye. He'd heard something, outside. Cooooo.

14

2. *Busy busy busy*

The next day, Saturday, Luke turned round a fraction too quickly coming out of the delicatessen and crashed into someone, sending his packages to the ground, cheeses mostly for that night. The person he had crashed into muttered a few words and disappeared round the corner. Luke had the strongest feeling that he'd seen him before.

Then later Luke stopped to cross over the road and again fell against this person. Once more the cheeses fell to earth.

'Sorry sorry. Sorry.' The man's voice was quick and high. He blushed and reached down to pick up the bags.

'Wait. Hold on now.' Luke put a hand to his shoulder and the man straightened up. He was about the same height and build as Luke, well made. Possibly a touch too excitable round the eyes.

'Once maybe,' said Luke, 'once I could believe to be an accident. But twice?' Luke smiled, raised his eyebrows. 'Are you by any chance following me?'

'Following you? Do you have any idea how paranoid that sounds?'

'I'm sure I've seen you before. Before today I mean,' Luke said, standing his ground, meeting the stranger's shifty eye, his mobile, flickering face and air of controlled panic. 'Haven't I seen you?'

'You tell me,' said the stranger, then jerked out his hand on the end of an arm that seemed unduly long and rather too sudden also. 'Declan. Declan Sargeant.'

Luke had no option but to shake the hand, which was cool and dry and bony, and strong. Declan Sargeant

15

held the grip and smiled back expectantly at Luke, his own eyebrows now raised also: and you are?

Luke flashed his habitual social smile, and said: 'Luke. Trethick.'

'Tre — Trennick?'

'Trethick. Tre-thick.'

'Trethick. OK.' Still the grip. Luke held the smile and made to pull his hand away.

'I'm delighted to meet you. Luke,' said Declan and nodded his head, meeting Luke's eye and darting away and meeting it again. 'Luke.'

'Let's hope we don't bump into one another again. At least,' Luke amended frantically, as Declan's eager face crumpled and the arm shot back to his side, 'at least not today. Twice,' he continued, 'is surely enough for one day. Wouldn't you say?'

'I haven't been following you,' said Declan, giving great and careful emphasis to 'following'. 'You come round here, I come round here, we're both here, we see each other, but we never speak. Why should we? I don't know you.'

'No indeed,' said Luke, smiling, leaving, getting away. 'Quite right.'

'But we could. There's no law says we can't. Is there? People should get to know each other. Shouldn't they? We don't have to be alone all the time. God didn't make us so we'd just shuffle by and not look and never speak. God didn't want that. He wants us to talk to each other and laugh and enjoy each other. We shouldn't be so embarrassed. We've got nothing to be embarrassed about. Have we?'

Luke, blushing furiously at this encounter, agreed, oh yes, nothing to be embarrassed about. He was actively seeking ways of ending the conversation. Declan, on the other hand, was doing almost anything to continue it. It was an impasse. Luke got the impression that Declan didn't actually know how to end it, was panicking slightly because he couldn't stop carrying on. Carrying on, thought Luke, and imagined the stern nurse who had undoubtedly been at Declan's side often throughout his life saying, now Declan, don't let's start carrying on shall we? There's a good boy.

There was something else as well, there was something about the way Declan spoke: it was as if he were trying out versions of things, different voices, different registers. He was like a salesman showing different lines. Do you like this? No? Then how about this?

'Look, I'm sorry, I'm really rather –' Luke said, but Declan was too quick for him.

'Busy? Oh yes, aren't we all busy. All the time. I'm busy myself much of the time. Busy busy busy. God himself would weep if he had any idea how *busy* we are.'

'Sorry –'

'Maybe he's weeping now. Do you think? Up there, all alone, crying his bloody eyes out. God's a lonely man, don't you think? Maybe he wants to come and talk to us but he's too embarrassed, thinks we're all too busy –'

Luke backed away and said, 'Look, I'm sorry but I have to get on. Do you, er –' He meant, do you need any money? Luke knew that a small amount of cash, administered judiciously, could stave off many if not most of life's ills. Like, for instance, embarrassing encounters with the mentally ill on street corners.

'Why, do you need to give me some?' Declan said, and Luke looked at him again, with renewed annoyance, but also with a new curiosity.

'Of course I don't,' Luke said. 'What are you talking about?' But Declan was twinkling at him all over, eyes and face and hands, everything, and Luke had to smile.

'Look.' Declan shoved his hands into the slash pockets of his jeans, which were loose and cock-eyed, all over the place. 'Look, Luke. We've met now. It's too late now. Do you see? It's brilliant isn't it? It's happened now and neither of us can do a thing about it. It's just happened, that's all there is to be said. So what I thought was, if you're not too busy that is, how would it be if I

17

came to visit you? Just to have a cup of tea, as the Irish say,' and Declan went into cod Irish, 'just a dish of tay and a bun? Huh? Why not?'

Why not.

'What, now?' Luke was startled by the suggestion, startled that he was even discussing it.

'This after. Three o'clock or so. Huh?'

Anything to get away. Say anything.

'Sure. OK.'

'Three o'clock then?'

'Three o'clock it is.'

'Luke I want to thank you. I really do. It'd mean a lot to me, you have no idea.'

'No problem, er —'

'Declan.'

'Declan. Yes.'

'I'll see you later then,' Declan said, as Luke walked away. Luke wanted to look back, to see if Declan was watching him, but didn't. He was certain that he was though.

Later it occurred to him that Declan hadn't asked him for his address. He was, for a second, sorry. It might be amusing to talk to Declan for an hour, listen to him. He wasn't stupid or obsessed or anything. He was just odd. Oh well, Luke thought, if he can arrange two collisions in one day then I'm sure he can arrange another. Luke wondered if he was let out every day or what. Or did he live out and just attend a day centre or outpatients or something? Or was he OK on his own? He seemed all right. He didn't smell, anyway. Luke, after all, had apparently seen him a few times before today and hadn't thought anything of him.

Later again, as he was developing film in the little darkroom at the back of the house, Luke thought: how many times have I seen him? and the answer was: more than a few.

*   *   *

18

He glanced at his watch: twenty past one. He moved the print around in the dish of developing fluid and waited for the moment when the image began to appear. It was always like some kind of very simple magic. Sometimes the picture was even good.

Luke's pictures were now, officially, a hobby, nothing more. Now he taught photography and media studies and just about anything else he couldn't get out of at a sixth-form college, and took some adult classes in the evenings. He no longer walked round with a brown leather portfolio or called himself a photographer. He no longer went after Arts Council bursaries or tried to get exhibitions. He was lucky to have a job that interested him. He had been told this repeatedly, usually by himself. Lucky. Most people had to sit in offices or factories or wherever and endure routines that bored them senseless, day after day. But Luke was lucky. All he had to do was teach people how to do what came so easily to him, teach the basic things again and again and again. Being so lucky, of course, meant that he had less and less time to devote to his own work: he found that instead of a camera he tended to be carrying a briefcase full of students' essays, and instead of developing pictures he was marking, filling in forms, fiddling about with paperwork. Now developing was something akin to a guilty pleasure. He really should have been doing something much more interesting, like completing assessment reports.

The print in front of him began to show light and shade, grey patches, the ghost of a picture. Luke picked up the plastic tongs and sloshed it about. He loved the smell of the fluids, he loved the red light and the darkness, he loved the anticipation. He loved being alone in the cramped little darkroom, thinking only about pictures.

And suddenly there it was, fully formed.

He'd taken it a few weeks ago, he just hadn't had a chance to develop it. It was a picture of Anna, walking by some derelict buildings. The buildings were a blur in the background, and Anna, head down, with the hood of her coat up, was just a shape, but the picture was good. It had the quality that was the most difficult thing to achieve in a photograph: mood. Usually all you got was a simple, if accurate, record of something, an event or a person or a scene. This though was a good picture, it was more than a visual account of a person walking, it was a picture of an emotion, almost a picture of a life. He had thought it would be, but it was impossible to tell until you developed it. He stood looking at it.

Anna.

This wasn't the only picture he had of Anna, head down, walking. It seemed sometimes to be her most characteristic look. There were few pictures of her laughing, dancing, even talking animatedly. Few recent ones anyway. But many of her walking, head down.

The other thing that there were no pictures of, of course, was a baby, a toddler, a child. Oliver and Sally had books full of pictures. Alice and David had two lots of pictures, one for each child. Little faces, tiny red screwed-up faces amidst billows of white blankets and pillows, furious faces peering out from under woolly bonnets. Little girls in polka-dot romper suits, little boys in striped dungarees and bootees. Smiling, crying, throwing up, falling down, shoving things into their mouths, reaching out for the pretty rattle, climbing over things, climbing over each other.

Luke the photographer, though, he had no baby pictures. Funny that. All he had were pictures of Anna, striding along, head down, with empty buildings behind her.

The picture blurred as his eyes misted over. Then suddenly words seemed to come out from inside it: *I am come to bring you honour and to honour your family*.

Luke blinked rapidly and reached for his cigarettes.

It was a line from *Revenge of the Crab People*, the book that had started writing itself in his head six months ago and which, one way or another, seemed to fill up more and more of his waking time. He would sit in a staff meeting and think, we need a scene there between Annya and her mother. Or he would find that he was running lines of dialogue round and round in his head, that his lips were forming the words, that he had completely stopped listening to what was being said to him. There was, as testament to this, a car accident, only a very minor one, but an accident none the less, the first he'd ever had. One moment he was thinking, *she swung away from him and disappeared into the frozen forest without a sound*, the next there was a Bedford van coming up on the inside on a roundabout, and then there was a bashed-in wing mirror. Nothing worth losing your no claims over, but it was sobering.

The main characters in *Revenge of the Crab People* were called Luc and Annya, but that didn't mean that it was a book about him and Anna. Not at all. He had no idea where the idea had come from, but come it had and there seemed to be no stopping it. Sometimes he thought it was ridiculous, sometimes he thought it was brilliant, most often it seemed to be simply forming itself without him thinking anything at all. Like a dream. He sometimes worried that it might be a symptom of some kind of internal problem, a stress reaction maybe, but he hugged it to himself ferociously anyway. He was secretly terrified of it being found out. He couldn't imagine any of the people he worked with furtively tapping away at secret novels about crab people. They would surely see it as a sign of derangement. Anna didn't know about it. Merely the thought of telling her made him squirm. He wished it would just go away.

There was one other person who knew about it, but the memory of that conversation was etched into Luke's head with such painful, visionary clarity that he knew he would never tell anyone else.

A wine bar called Piggy-Wiggy's, pitchers of Budweiser, ashtrays spilling out over the table, cashew nuts underfoot. Cartoons of pink, fat-bottomed pigs everywhere. Waitresses in striped aprons with curly tails at the back. Hot, crowded, hideous. Luke was there with Oliver Barclay, whom Luke had known since his teaching degree and who had started work at a nearby school a few months after Luke. Oliver's wife Sally knew Anna, and the four of them used to see each other once or twice a month. This was before Oliver and Sally had had a child, a little boy, Ryan. Since then, what with one thing and another, the four of them hadn't managed to arrange anything.

Quite how the subject had come up, Luke couldn't remember, but Oliver had started talking about Sally's sudden passion for making papier-mâché bowls and stencilling on them. A perfectly innocent diversion to be sure, but the question that interested Oliver was: why.

'She's pretty good at it. I mean, they're not all lumpy or lopsided or anything, and the patterns are reasonably *symmetrical* and all that. They look OK. I'm not saying they don't. When I tell her I like them, it's no word of a lie. I like them. I can't fault them. The point is though: why does she make them. Why? It just seems so unnecessary. It's fiddly, it's messy, it takes hours, and when they go wrong it upsets her. Even when it goes right, I still *cannot see* what it is that she's getting out of it.'

Luke emptied his glass and regarded Oliver, who was flushed in the face, and who suddenly seemed to be going bald. Luke was astonished that this should be the case, he had never noticed it before. But Oliver was unquestionably thinning out on top, his hairline was unmistakably moving up his forehead. Shit, thought Luke, that can only mean that I am as well. Shit. And along with the baldness, Oliver also seemed to be getting greyer, squarer and more and more like a caricature of an early-menopausal city teaching drone. Even his suit looked boring. He wasn't actually wearing Hush Puppies or horn-rimmed glasses, but he might just

22

as well have been. Luke found that the person sitting before him, across the rubble of beer-mats and cigarette packets and fag ends was turning into exactly the kind of dull, humourless berk that Luke most feared becoming himself. It was almost like looking into a mirror and seeing, not what you are, but what you will be if you don't do something about it pretty bloody smartish. Do what, though? Do what?

'The trouble with you, Ollie,' Luke said, conscious that his tongue was thicker and slower in his mouth than he might have wished for, 'is that you've got no imagination.' He intended a joky scolding tone, but it didn't get past his blundering tongue, and what did come out didn't sound joky, particularly.

Ollie looked startled, as well he might, and said, 'What's imagination got to do with bloody stencils?'

'She wants to create something, she wants to leave some kind of a mark on the world.'

'What, a bloody stencil mark?'

'Any kind of bloody mark. So what if it isn't the Sistine Chapel? At least she's trying.'

Ollie conceded that she was trying, yes, sometimes she could be very —

'Don't you ever think about that?' Luke had demanded, woefully conscious that he was three-quarters of an inch drunker than he wanted to be. 'I do. I want to leave some kind of bloody mark. I don't care what it is, it could be anything, could be a, I don't know, a book or something, anything.'

I will attend you there.

Drunk, earnest, confiding. Luke winced at the recollection.

'There's something I'm working on at the moment actually . . . '

Don't continue. *Do not* —

Ollie had watched him. Ollie suddenly seemed sober, Luke couldn't imagine how that had happened. Ollie sat back and watched him (soberly) as he described the

23

book, the ideas, the *concepts* behind it, the thrill of it forming itself behind his eyes.

'Sounds fairly weird,' Ollie had said, and had ordered another pitcher of Bud. 'They must be working you pretty hard these days.'

'What do you mean?'

'You look tired, mate. To be honest.'

Luke, drunk as he was, had got the point and shut up. With some difficulty, because now he'd started, he wanted to explain the whole thing, every detail, how it had grown from a single little idea into this big, complicated, beautiful shape. A complete world! He wanted to talk about the crab people, poor malformed creatures, with their great bony claws, driven to violence simply because it was their nature, and the war between them and the others, Luc falling in love with Annya. The whole thing. But he'd shut up and let Ollie talk about holiday plans. As they were saying goodbye at the tube, Ollie said, 'Take it easy,' and Luke had known exactly what he meant. He'd sat on the tube home and blushed at what he'd said, blushed for the first time in years. Hoped Ollie would be too drunk to remember it all. Hoped Ollie would have the decency not to go round telling everyone that Luke was secretly, quietly losing it.

Was he losing it? How could you know if you were losing it? You could be quietly disintegrating from the inside for years and never know it. Anna would surely know, but what if she wasn't paying attention? What if she was thinking about something else?

Luke looked down: the picture in the tray was darkening rapidly, no longer a figure against a background but a blob in a fog, then before he could grab his plastic tongs and pull it out, a picture of a thick black shadow at night in a locked filing cabinet. He took it out and regarded it. Terrific. Maybe you could call it avant-garde. Experimental, like. He sighed and lit his cigarette. Start again.

He was still developing pictures when the doorbell

24

rang. He looked at his watch: three o'clock, to the minute.

Couldn't be.

He stood watching the second hand as it ticked off the seconds, watched until half a minute had gone by. The bell rang again, a harsh buzz. More seconds. Then a voice, rising up from the front of the house.

'Luke? You there?'

It was Declan, of course. He knew where Luke lived, of course. He was going to have a cup of tea and a bun, spend an hour or so. It was going to mean a lot to him.

Luke waited another forty-five seconds, watching the hands on the dial. He had become fascinated by the sweep of the second hand, it was mesmerizing.

'Luke?'

He wasn't going to go away. Luke remembered bunking off school, lurking in the house, not daring to answer the phone. This felt like that. Nothing to be worried about, Luke thought. Anna wouldn't be back till six at the earliest. He wouldn't have to explain. He could just give Declan his cup of tea and send him on his way. Better to do that than to have him making a racket outside the house. In this neighbourhood that kind of thing didn't really play too well: Neighbourhood Watch were undoubtedly twitching their nets right now. Luke and Anna had been the recipients of more than one discreet tap on the door late at night. We were just checking that everything was all right, the middle-aged neighbour would say, looking inquisitorially at these drunken, flushed young people and their astonishingly hefty stereo system.

'Luke! Are you there?'

The police would be round. Explanations would be required. Luke sighed, waited till the second hand reached the hour, then clicked off the red light and went down to the front door. He stopped on the stairs and ducked back to the room he called his office, took the disk out of the computer, slid it into his pocket. Then he went to let Declan in.

*　　*　　*

Declan had no sugar, no milk. Luke had offered both, of course, and had received the impression that Declan had refused them purely out of some notion of courtesy, as if it would be rude to ask for anything. He had changed since Luke had last seen him, into loose off-white trousers and a white shirt. He had slicked his hair back and shaved. He looked entirely different. Luke made Brie and salad sandwiches with Marmite on the bread and mayonnaise. The Brie hadn't improved by being dropped repeatedly. Ripe was one thing, but mushy was quite another. Still, Luke reflected, good enough for Declan. Declan refused politely, but Luke insisted. He ate neatly, methodically, and when he was finished he pushed his plate to his left and shook his hands, as if shaking off loose water.

'Lovely house,' he said, though he had hardly looked at anything. 'I envy you your house, Luke. I could never have a house like this.'

'Thanks,' Luke said, 'it used to be Anna's grandparents' house. They, you know, left it to her. We'd never be able to afford something like this ourselves, not in a million years.' It seemed important to emphasize this to Declan.

Declan nodded at the kitchen window.

'And a garden.'

'If you can call it that,' Luke said, gesturing with his head to the undug borders and the untrimmed low hedges of lavender and rosemary, the brick paths that needed Weedclear, the nettles at the heap down at the far end.

'Isn't that what you call it?' Declan said, puzzled, and Luke laughed and said, would you like a little something in that tea? Declan looked scandalized and said, 'Well, it's a bit early for me, but if you're having a drop it would be impolite of me –'

'Yes, a house like this, well –' said Declan, after Luke had dribbled a drop of good whisky into Declan's mug, and a bigger drop into his own. He felt as if he needed it.

'Children, a dog, a wee wifey to come home to,' Declan said.

'No children,' Luke said. 'No dog. Sorry.'

'No?' Declan said. 'Oh well, you're young yet, you have time. A man could be good in a house like this, do you know what I mean? He wouldn't have to worry all the time. Now take the place I was staying at recently, for instance, it's not like this, Luke, if I can speak frankly, not at all, not really. You had to watch all the time. Say for instance I had a nice drop of something like your wee bottle there, I couldn't just put it on a shelf and dip into it from time to time, have a drop today and another drop tomorrow. If I were to turn my back on it for a moment, I mean if I were to not actually be *holding* it for a minute, then someone would have it away from me. Do you know what I mean? I had a radio, you could have FM on it and everything, listen to the cricket and the things in Parliament and all, it was a nice little thing, had an earpiece and everything. I used to listen to it at night. This is London,' Declan said, imitating exactly the tone, 'This is London. Then you got the news and all. I don't remember how I came by it. But I was called away once for a phone call. My solicitor. You wouldn't think I had one of those now would you Luke, eh? but I have. And he had to speak to me and so I goes to the bloody phone and I comes back and have I got a little radio now? I have not. Some other bugger has. I mean all happiness to him and I wish him joy and all. But you have to watch.'

Luke tipped the bottle again into Declan's mug. The sun had come out, and the garden looked warm and unruly and friendly again.

'Shall we sit outside?' Luke said.

Anna came back at six, as she'd said she would, and Luke and Declan were back at the kitchen table. Declan looked just slightly the worse for wear, and she could

27

smell at once that both men had been drinking. Luke went to her and kissed her and put his arm round her. He twisted her round to face Declan.

'Anna? I want you to meet Declan. Declan – Anna,' he said, and Declan stood and took her hand.

'Anna,' he said, and kissed it. She twisted inside, and pulled her hand away, but tried to smile anyway.

Declan left at seven o'clock, exactly. He had to get on, he said. Luke tried to give him a couple of quid, but Declan wouldn't hear of it, he had money enough. He could always get money, he said, that was rarely a problem. Thanks though. It was a generous thought.

*c.*1780

'. . . he was attached by a long chain that ran over the wall and thus permitted the attendant to lead him about, to keep him on a leash, so to speak, from outside; around his neck had been placed an iron ring; this latter slid the length of a vertical iron bar fastened to the floor and ceiling of the cell . . . a man was found who had lived in this cell, attached in this fashion, for twelve years . . . '

Samuel Tuke, *Report on the Condition of the Indigent Insane*

3. That'll Be Quite Something, Won't It?

Declan and Muriel sat, together, under the colonnade. Rain dripped steadily from the parapet. The air was colder, damp raw gusts cutting in from outside. Muriel had her arm round Declan's shoulders. She was speaking, quietly, incessantly.

'No-one's going to do anything, we're not going to do anything, everything will be like this, we will stay here and nothing will happen.'

Declan faced out, not responding, not returning the pressure of Muriel's body against him. People passed by, not many because of the rain. Those who did glanced in at Declan and Muriel, looked quickly away. One or two smiled, tightly, defensively. Mostly people lowered their eyes or looked away or up or ahead or anything, anything. Declan occasionally wanted to get up and follow one or another of them, see where they went, what they did, whom they spoke to. But Muriel said that he and she would stay here, so he couldn't move. He sighed; she felt the movement of his chest and shoulders.

'It'll be quiet, like this, no-one will come, no-one will come here . . . '

He couldn't remember where he had first met Muriel, but he had known her a very long time, ever since he had come out of Rain Fields and into the bedsit. Years now, at least two years. Two winters, two summers. In the summers Muriel didn't smell good. In the winters she said less.

Declan knew they didn't want him to be sitting out on

31

the street, with Muriel and Fat Billy and the rest of them. They wanted him to stay in his bedsit and go to their day centre three days a week. Just so they could make sure he was all right. Why can't I go back to Rain Fields, he'd asked them, I've always been at Rain Fields? He'd been so persistent that to his surprise he had finally managed to get an interview with a consultant, who had spoken of care-management priorities and resource implications.

'But why can't I go back to Rain Fields?' Declan asked, a puzzled smile on his face. He was embarrassed to still be asking this. The consultant was a busy man, important. Declan was being a nuisance, he knew it. If he was too much of a nuisance they might make him go back to the other place, the place before Rain Fields. The consultant could send him back there. Declan smiled apologetically.

'But why can't I . . .'

'Mr Sargeant, there have been some changes recently, as I'm sure you know. Now. The Rain Fields facility has been recategorized. It is no longer in the primary sector. The budget for its running has been transferred from the Health Authority. The clients who were receiving services from Rain Fields, such as yourself, have been reassessed for their care-provision requirements, and where appropriate new care programmes have been drawn up so that the resource implications are based strictly on clinical priority. Do you follow? Now.'

The consultant raised his fist to his mouth and lowered it again.

'Because of the nature of your disorder your care programme has been drawn up in such a way that residential management, such as used to be offered at Rain Fields, has been rendered needless. Your new Statement of Need stresses that residential care is, not only not necessary, but probably not even the most beneficial path for us to take with you now. Do you follow?'

'Yes.'

'Good man.'

'But why can't I . . .'

Now isn't the time, the time won't be yet, it will be later, we'll have it, but later, it isn't now . . .

Muriel's gentle voice meandered on, low and consoling, meaningless.

'Look,' said the consultant, 'don't you think it's exciting?' He had smiled at Declan, and Declan had smiled back. 'Eh? This is the start of a whole new life for you, Michael.' He glanced at the file, turned a few pages. 'Rain Fields, that wasn't much of a life for a fellow like you now was it? You need your independence.'

'Yes sir,' said Declan, leaning in excitedly, 'yes sir but what I don't understand is why can't . . .'

'Of course you do. It's perfectly natural. You're a young man, you've got your whole life ahead. You could have a full and, and, er, a full and, er. You'll make new friends. You'll meet new challenges. It won't always be easy, life isn't always easy, for anyone. You'll have an opportunity, to grow, to develop. One of the things your care team will be looking at is getting a job for you. Have you thought about that? What you might like to do?' Big smile.

'No sir,' said Declan, who wanted to go back to Rain Fields. He had things to do there. Why couldn't he?

'And they'll find you a place of your own to live. Your own flat. Or room. Eh? That'll be quite something, won't it? Your own place.'

'Yes sir, but . . .'

Whatever he said, they weren't going to let him go back to Rain Fields.

He'd sat in his own room for four days. It had been quite something. No-one had come. The papers had got lost, no-one knew where he was. It only struck him afterwards that the absence of visitors was hardly surprising. Who would come? Still, he thought someone might. He didn't eat: he didn't have anything. He thought of going next door and asking for something, but the people in the next room had funny music with shouting in playing loud all the time and shouted over it, and the woman on the other side went 'uh' every four or five seconds, and in the end he didn't. He was supposed to stay in his room, wasn't he? He didn't know if he was supposed to go out or not. Someone presumably would come and tell him. He waited.

On the fifth day he had gone out anyway and met Muriel and Fat Billy and Pascoe and the rest. They'd shown him how.

'I won't go and you won't, we'll stay, I'll stay with you, I'll stand by you . . .'

The rain dripped on. It was early afternoon. Little gusts played with the lines of rainwater falling from the parapet, pulling them backwards and forwards. Declan put his arm round Muriel. She seemed to be nodding off, but her voice continued. He stroked her hair. He knew she liked that.

She stood up after a quarter of an hour or so and motioned Declan to follow her. He stayed where he was though, and she wandered away, into the thin rain. He watched her bowed head as she swayed out of sight.

4. *How Lovely*

Anna considered the little bowl in front of her. It was as big as a large ashtray or a small dinner plate. It was a deep, beautiful azure, and around the outer rim was a thin gold line and a circle of pointed stars. At the bottom was a complicated Celtic-cross design also in gold. The inside felt rough, like an egg box. It was beautifully made, patiently made. Carefully made. Sally had given it to her, not for Christmas or a birthday, just given it to her. They'd been due to meet at the Tanners at nine o'clock, but Sally hadn't arrived until twenty-five past. Anna had tried to be less annoyed than she felt. She hated waiting around in public.

Sally had a carrier bag with her, all folded up, and was holding it tightly. Anna had gone to the bar and when she came back Sally was still holding the bag.

'Whatcha got, Sal?' she asked, and Sally said:

'It's that bowl I told you about.'

Anna hadn't been able at first to remember what bowl or when they'd talked about it.

'I thought I'd like to give it to you. I thought it would look nice on that table in your front room.' She held the bag a moment longer then passed it over. Anna unwrapped it and looked at it.

Her first thought was: what is it? What's it for? She recovered instantly, though, and said:

'This is beautiful. You didn't – you didn't *make* this?'

'Uhuh. Well, it's a stencil, you know, the cross. I didn't draw it or anything.'

'It's lovely,' Anna said, 'it's such a lovely colour.'

'I just thought, because your room is that lovely green, this would set it off.'

'Yeah,' said Anna. 'How lovely.'

Anna had never been able to think of anything to put in it. She'd tried spare keys, but they always found their way back to the kitchen drawer. Anna suggested that Luke put his loose change there when he came in, so it wouldn't fall down the back of the sofa. He wouldn't, though, and she realized later what an idiotic idea it was. Pot-pourri? But then you wouldn't be able to see the stencil. And there was something so depressing about pot-pourri anyway. So she just left it empty.

Three months after she'd given her the bowl, Sally was pregnant.

Anna stroked the rim. She could feel again the awful clench of her stomach as Ollie had told her. She had gone round immediately, to find out if it was really true. Sally looked wide-eyed, yes it was true, oh my God! Anna had felt so unbearably cheated that she had had to go home at once, and had cried in the bathroom. Cheated! Bloody Sally had taken her baby! Bloody cheating bitch!

Anna put the bowl down and was about to go upstairs when Bobby Parrot called something, she couldn't make it out. Have a nibble, most likely. Thanks Bobby, she thought, I'll certainly bear that in mind.

His cage needed cleaning. It was something she tried to put off as long as decently possible, but it had started to smell and it was such an *old* smell that she couldn't bear it.

Bobby Parrot had been watching her even as she opened the door. He did that. His face was always twisted away from you so that one eye or the other was watching you. It was just the way his face was arranged, but she wished he would sometimes look at her straight.

She slid the tray out and took it to the kitchen, screwing the newspaper up and depositing it in the bin. A headline caught her eye, 'Fire Guts Empty House'. The paper was covered with Bobby's waste in bright yellow and white splats, and a great deal of seed and seed husks, bits of apple which Luke gave him, though he almost never ate it, splinters of wood.

Was Bobby happy? She had no idea. She couldn't imagine what happiness might mean for a caged parrot. She kept him clean and well-fed, and tried to play with him for a few minutes every day. Luke tried to teach him new words sometimes, but he was an old parrot and she sensed that his learning days were over. He kept himself looking good, and was endlessly preening. He didn't peck at himself. He always seemed to have plenty of energy. He was healthy. What more was there for him?

'Hi!' she said as she replaced the tray with its new newspaper. 'Hi Bob! Hiya!'

He watched her and pecked shyly at his perch. He fluttered his wings a little.

'How ya doing?' She had a special voice for Bobby, animated, high-pitched, singy-songy, declarative. Only very rarely did she get anything back. He seemed to say less and less these days. She guessed he was bored.

'Poor Bob,' she said, 'poooooor Bobby, pooooooo-oooor . . .'

She stood up straight again and cleared her throat. What if Luke was listening? Talking to parrots was old-lady stuff.

She pushed a new millet spray through the bars and wiggled the end of it at him. He looked fastidiously away. She felt ridiculous and allowed it to drop onto the fresh paper. She did a quick tour of the room, picking up a cushion and straightening some flowers. She sometimes worried that she cleaned too much, but she also worried that she didn't clean enough, so it all balanced out. Certainly the house was in infinitely better shape than most of their friends' homes. When people came round, they'd sometimes say how nice it was, how orderly, how quiet. Not like their own chaotic horrors! She had heard often how impossible it was to keep the house straight with children around, and what a pleasure, what a joy it was to come somewhere where the chairs weren't piled up with heaps of clothes and books and spaceships, and where you could confidently put your foot on the floor without worrying about stepping onto something crunchy or sharp or, worst of all, *squashy*.

Nothing squashy here, she thought. No sir.

Saturday evening. Later Cath and Rosa were coming round for dinner. Rosa had been trying to get pregnant for nearly two years, spooning in what she referred to as 'dollops' from male friends. They had to be prepared to have an Aids test first, which narrowed the field just a little bit. She had apparently offered two hundred pounds to the producer of the successful dollop. Nothing had happened yet though. They just kept on trying.

Later, Luke and Anna shut the door on Cath and Rosa and carried on drinking, first in the kitchen, then upstairs. Luke drank whisky, Anna stuck to wine. Luke got amorous but was sidetracked into a discussion about whether he would be prepared to give Cath and Rosa a 'dollop', and what he would charge. For two hundred quid, he decided, they could have three and a signed statement that he would never want to as much as look at the outcome. He would need a guarantee, though, that there would not be, at any stage of the proceedings, any physical contact between him and Rosa, or, for that matter, Cath. Nor could he be held responsible if the child turned into something awful, like an MP.

Later still, tanked-up and convinced that the over-the-road neighbours were up and taking a dim view of the noise he and Anna were making, Luke opened the window and, with Anna pulling him back, accused them, with some energy, of spying on him. He threw books out of the window. The neighbours, if they were indeed awake, elected not to respond.

Later again, and Luke and Anna were crawling round the back garden looking for Anna's watch, which Luke had thrown out of the bathroom window, whilst pretending to flush it down the toilet. She had bet him he wouldn't dare. When they finally did get to bed Luke started muttering darkly about going rates and cash up front, but Anna was sleepy and told him to go peddle it elsewhere.

Anna woke up at four o'clock or so, dry-mouthed and with a trip-hammer heart. She padded out to the bathroom for a drink of water and, looking at the little shelf by the sink, saw at once that something was missing. A small metal fish, with brightly painted eyes and tail, a gift from Sheila. It went between the narrow blue glass vase and a small-leafed fern. She went to use the toilet: Luke's shaving brush and razor were not in their usual place on the cistern lid, they were beside the taps on the sink instead. The lid of the cistern was slightly askew. She lifted it up to reposition it, and as she looked inside she called out in surprise at what she saw. Resting at the bottom of the cistern, a small painted metal fish.

5. *You Call That Nothing?*

The grey dawn filtered through the branches, throwing long, sinuous shadows through the forest, turning the black limbs of trees to bronze and then soft silver. Luc slept, as the forest stirred, shaking off the night, putting on the day. The light found him, as he lay curled beneath the tree, traced the lines of his face and the contours of his body, fell onto his eyes.

'Luke.'

Something moved outside his range of vision, he turned round to see it, but it had gone, sending the branches waving in its wake, he heard a sound, the sound of the creature's claw as it swung through the air, wsssssk . . .

'Luke? Hey!'

He opened his eyes. He had fallen asleep in a plastic garden chair, Sunday lunch-time, still hungover, now it was mid-afternoon, he was awake and someone was standing nearby. Declan.

'Declan?'

Luke stood up and Declan smiled, took a few steps towards him, then stumbled against the wall. He was holding his hand to his side.

'Declan? What are you doing here?'

There was a stain round the hand that was held to his side. His shirt was stained, dark brown and black.

'Sorry,' Declan said, 'I didn't know what else to do, sorry.'

'Christ, what – what've you been doing? Are you OK?' Stupid questions. He was bleeding, thus he was not OK. Quick quick, what do you do about someone who's bleeding? Quick now. Luke stood looking as Declan righted himself, the hand seemingly glued in place by the brown and black stuff that had stained his shirt. There were a few spots on the concrete of the patio as well now, bright shiny red. Luke watched as another drop fell. Quick!

'Anna!' He ran past Declan, ran into the house, galloped up the stairs to where Anna was doing something in the bathroom, she had stuff all over her face. 'Come quick. He's bleeding.'

She goggled at him as he dashed back down the stairs, then was following him, the mud pack cracking as she yelled, 'Luke! Wait!'

She ran out of the back door, and saw Luke kneeling beside a slumped figure on the patio. There was a small trickle of blood running away towards the grass. Good for the roses anyway.

She stood in the doorway. The two men were folded together, she wanted to leave them there and not have to get in close. They were like figures in a photograph, she felt that she had no place in the picture.

Then she was beside them.

'Luke? Let me have a look at him.' Her voice was moderate and certain, and Luke was happy to move aside and let her in. She knew first aid. She had done a twelve-week course, half a day a week, including burns, electrocution, asphyxiation, broken and sprained limbs, concussion, even heart attacks. She was one of the few people she knew who actually had a fully equipped first-aid box. Asking for trouble, Luke had said, just begging for it, and perhaps he had been right. She reflected as she touched Declan's hand and tried to get him to move it away that he had come to a very good place to be injured.

Part of her training had been to know just how much could be done without expert attention, and it was very little. The advice sessions always ended with: seek qualified medical attention immediately. Do not attempt to – whatever it was, set the bone, stitch the wound, move the head. Don't try to be clever, you'll only do something wrong and make it worse. Know your limitations. Be aware that you could be held legally responsible in certain circumstances if your attempt to help goes wrong. It was brutal but that was how it was. There was a rule before that, but she couldn't think of it.

His hand was hot and clammy. He was holding it into his side, bracing his forearm against his ribs. His fingers were sticky with blood, some of it clotted, some still viscous: it was crusted under his fingernails, and there was a slow drip coming from under his wrist. She couldn't be certain what it was that was bleeding, hand, wrist, palm, the cut could be almost anywhere. She couldn't be sure if it was an arterial cut or not: if it was, and if that was why he was holding his arm pressed into his side, then if she made him move the arm away it could start spurting.

'Luke? I've forgotten his name, what was it?'

'Shit, I can't – shit, no, it's gone –'

Anna was all too aware of the panic in his voice.

'Try to remember, Luke.'

'What do you need his name for? He's bleeding for Christ's sake, what does it matter –'

The name popped into her head.

'Declan? Can you hear me?'

'Yeah, no problem,' he said, but his eyes were closed and his skin was white and waxy.

'Can you tell me what happened Declan?' She made her voice be steady, be firm. That was important. An injured person needed reassurance and the promise of competence as much as they needed bandages. They needed to be able to believe that you could help them or they wouldn't co-operate. The urge to drag yourself away into some corner and lick your wounds alone could be overpoweringly strong. Any kind of injury, even a comparatively minor one, could turn an ordinary rational person into a vulnerable, frightened animal, ready to defend itself in any way necessary. The first rule, the rule she hadn't been able to remember,

42

obediently came: make sure that you yourself are safe. Be aware that your patient could be violent, even dangerous, and always make certain of your own safety first. You can't help anyone unless you are yourself safe.

An ordinary, rational person. What about someone like Declan?

'Declan? Can you answer a couple of questions?'

'Yes.'

'Where are you cut? Where exactly?'

He put his head slightly to the side, pulled his mouth into a line, frowned, as if getting ready to explain something of great subtlety and complexity. His other hand moved up to join the first one.

'Here.'

'Is it your arm? Declan, is it your arm that you've cut?'

'No Anna, it's down here,' and he started to move his hand away. She made herself look down as a smell came up to her. His hand pulled slowly away from the discoloured shirt. She saw that the cotton was slit neatly, down near the hip, from roughly where the belly button would be, round the side, and halfway across the back.

'You see?'

'OK,' she said, as she saw the lips of a deep, ugly wound, purple and black, whitening on the inside. She wasn't certain, but she thought she could see an outline of bone. Pelvis, presumably. 'OK, I see. You can put your hand back now. Don't you worry, it's nothing.'

She stood and went over to Luke. She spoke in a loud voice. 'It's nothing, but maybe we should call an ambulance just to be on the safe side.'

'Nothing? You call that nothing?'

'Luke.' She held his eye. 'It's OK. Go and ring for an ambulance.'

'Er, Anna, could I have a word before you do that?' Declan's voice, sweetly reasonable. 'Just a quick little word.'

She left Luke standing where he was, paralysed,

leaning against the wall. He was incapable of doing anything. He had seen the lips of that wound too.

'I don't need an ambulance. Don't call an ambulance. OK?'

'Declan?' She knew she mustn't alarm him, but he seemed to have no idea how nasty the wound was. 'Now you're not too serious, but I don't think I can do everything you need here. I really do think we need an ambulance. I think that would be best. Just as a precaution. OK?'

She nodded at Luke, who stood still for a moment longer, then pushed himself away into the house. Declan rose to his feet and called out:

'Oi!'

He shoved Anna aside, and went lurching after Luke. He showed no sign of being incapacitated, quite the opposite in fact, and he caught up with Luke as Luke reached the phone in the hall, wrenched it out of his hand, shoved Luke against the wall.

'I said no!'

Anna was right behind him, speaking his name, trying to soothe.

'Now Declan, steady now, don't let's have any –'

'You call an ambulance and I'm out of here. You want me to bleed to death out there?'

'Nobody's going to bleed to death –'

'I need you.'

Anna looked at him.

What was it about him? How was it that he could say something so banal, I need you, and she should feel herself twist inside? How did he know how to do that? She hated him for it.

'Anna. I can't go to the hospital. Don't you see?'

'OK,' she said, and motioned to Luke, who was still holding the phone. 'It's all right Luke. Put the phone down.'

She took Declan by the less bloodied arm and led him to the sofa in the front room. There were spots of blood all over the place, on the hall floor, on the phone, on the

44

table. Luke had smears of blood over his jeans and on his face.

Anna sat beside Declan on the sofa.

'Tell me why you won't have an ambulance. I won't do anything you don't want.' She spoke quietly, calmly, almost indifferently. It was the right tone, she knew. You didn't want to show fear, neither did you want to be over-sympathetic. You had to try to be normal, everyday. She was amazing herself by how good she was at this.

'Why not?' She made herself stroke his hand, fighting fear and revulsion at the ghastly, pallid tear in his skin, the whitening lips of that gash.

'They'll take me back. To the other place.'

'What place?' But even as she spoke she knew perfectly well what place. The Bin. Loonyland.

'Declan? Do you mean the mental hospital?'

His eyes filled up and he began to shake.

'Why would they send you back there?' But again, she already knew why. He had been released because he was considered capable of making it in the outside world on his own, he was no danger to himself or others. But it was probationary, contingent, and if he brought himself back to their attention, bearing scars that showed he wasn't quite capable of making it, that he was at risk – 'vulnerable' would be the word they used – they probably would want him back again. She was sure they would. He was almost certainly right about that.

'Luke,' she said, and Luke came in from the hall. He was looking worried and upset. She guessed that he was furious at being pushed around by Declan. He needed something to do.

'Would you mind getting my first-aid kit? It's on the back shelf in the pantry. And Luke, would you mind making him a cup of tea?'

'OK.'

'And Luke? Don't put anything in it.'

'Huh?'

45

'No whisky.'

'OK.' He disappeared, and Declan leaned back on the sofa and said, 'Ah God.' Anna stroked his hand.

I need you.

Two questions: what had happened to him? And after it happened, why had he come all the way out to their house? She remembered how quickly he had gone after Luke, and watched him closely.

'Can you hold it like that?'

'Here?'

'No, can you get a bit further in –'

'Christ –'

Luke's stomach lurched. She wanted him to reach down Declan's side and hold the lips of the wound together. I mean, Christ!

They were all three on the sofa. She had taken Declan's shirt off, and laid it under him in the hope of soaking up some of the blood. It hardly seemed to matter, there was blood all over the place. She was dabbing at him with pieces of cotton wool and warm water from a bowl. There was a small mound of them, brown and red and black, on the floor by her feet, and she kept dropping new ones down there. She had persuaded Declan to move his hand away, and now Luke had to take over the job of holding everything in place. He wasn't certain, but he thought he had seen a little flash of white, it must have been bone. The thought of Declan's bones surged up in him, interfering with his breathing, making him sick and giddy. He looked up at Anna, working away, oblivious to the mud pack she had applied in calmer circumstances less than an hour ago. He tried to be calm and helpful and dependable. Maybe it hadn't been bone. Wouldn't bones be deeper under the skin than that?

Then Declan moved, just an inch or two, jerked away from Anna's probing fingers, and the lips parted and Luke saw some grey, fleshy substance, blubbery, wet, and he thought it's intestines, oh Christ, and was

46

suddenly standing halfway across the room, looking at the mantelpiece.

'Luke? Are you OK?'

'Oh yeah.'

'Luke, you have to hold the wound together, just until I can get it strapped up.'

'Yeah OK, I'll be right over,' he said, as if he had some minor errand to do first, post a letter perhaps or make some bread.

Declan's hand found the wound again, and Anna tried to restrain him. She didn't want him fiddling with it. She had tried to clean his fingers but his fingernails were still black with clotted blood.

'Luke, can you give me a hand please?' This was delivered with the same almost indifferent authority she had found earlier, and Luke had to submit to it and come back to the sofa. He put his hand on Declan's side and Declan winced away from him.

'Easy now love,' Anna said, and Luke gently closed his hand over the wound where it started to disappear round the back and allowed his fingers to squeeze, as delicately and slowly as he could manage. Squeeze it, don't jerk it soldier. Got a kick on it like a mule. He closed his face, his mouth twisted with grim distaste. Intestine. For Christ's sake.

Anna kept on dabbing, on and on, until Luke was desperate with her slowness.

'Isn't that enough?' he said, and she looked up at him and smiled.

'The only important thing is to clean it completely. Unless I clean it out completely now there'll be all sorts of trouble later on.'

'OK, I just thought –'

'And then I'll strap it, and bandage him up. Then he should probably try to sleep for a bit. It's going to hurt like anything soon.'

'It won't –' (*intestine*) '– it's not going to open up again?'

'No, I'll put an elastic dressing on, and it'll be OK, for now at least.'

'What about a doctor?'

She looked down at Declan. His eyes were closed, and his breathing was deep and easy. Was he asleep? She met Luke's eye and shrugged. 'We'll have to wait and see.'

Anna dabbed and eased the blood away, making tiny, accurate movements, thinking only about what she was doing. Declan seemed to have absorbed the authority she had invented, and had relaxed against her. She could feel his head heavy against her breast. His hair was untidy, but perfectly clean, and the shirt had been clean too. His body was lean, and his nipples stood out starkly against his white skin. He seemed to have only the exact amount of flesh that was strictly necessary, no more, no less. His stomach was flat and hard, which would probably make the wound all the more painful: a slack, flabby gut would tear easily, but tight muscle would resist.

There was no possibility that it was an accidental wound, none whatsoever. It was too neat, there was no jaggedness. Declan had obviously been viciously attacked. There were no other marks, apart from a few old scars, so it didn't look as if there had been a fight, it looked as if someone had come up to him and simply slashed him. It was terrible, she thought, that he should be out there, exposed to this kind of thing. Just terrible. He looked like a fully-grown man, but there were areas in which he was still a child. He couldn't be expected to look out for himself the way someone else would, he just wasn't capable. It wasn't fair. And even if he had been better equipped, he would still be living out there, nowhere proper to sleep, not eating right, mixing it with all sorts of people. She shook her head as she worked. She could feel his heartbeat, slow and steady now. She glanced up at Luke, who had seemingly forgotten what he was doing and was staring out at nothing.

'Luke? I'm just going to get a bandage out. Keep hold there for a minute will you?' He nodded, nothing to it. She eased herself away from Declan, lowering his head onto the sofa. He opened his eyes sleepily, and she said, shhh, it's OK.

Luke and Anna lay in bed later, as Declan slept in the spare room. The guest room. Her bandaging was as tight as she dared, and she was hopeful that there would be no leakage. The spare room was the room in the house that she had spent the most time and psychological energy decorating, and she would prefer, if it were at all possible, that it not become daubed with Declan's blood. Luke was no use at all at decorating, favouring magnolia emulsion and, in emergencies, woodchip paper to cover up the damp. His idea of preparing surfaces was to fill the little holes with paint, then keep on painting over them until it looked flat. She bought beautiful, glossy books, full of creamy pictures of reno-vated barns, unexpected colour combinations, stained wood, unusual textures. She liked things to look rough, unconsidered, just-as-they-were. It was an extremely difficult look to achieve, and the spare room had been her laboratory. Luke had more or less stopped commenting after a while, whatever he said she just changed it again a few months later. Currently it was shades of umber, lavender and dusty pink, with bold, thick stripes down one wall. She mixed her own colours a little at a time, allowing each batch to vary slightly and overpainting, so that the walls seemed to undulate, bellying in and out. She had gone for an effect on one wall similar to what would happen if the paint had been bleached by exposure to strong sunlight. She had mixed plaster in with some of the paint, to get a grainy texture.

She had laid Declan down, amongst stiff white linen, with a great white sash of bandage around his waist. Yards and yards of bandage. His head lay on thin pillows, in washed-out shades of turquoise and pale green. His arms were wrapped tightly round him. Luke

49

had rebelled and put a splash of whisky into Declan's tea. A drop of whisky couldn't hurt. Luke thought Declan needed it. He had been remarkably compliant throughout, apart from the business about the telephone. Hopefully, a drop of whisky would help keep him that way.

Luke couldn't sleep. He was thinking about the way Declan had looked, as he slid against the wall, arm braced around himself. He thought of the look that Anna had given him as she cleaned out the wound, her face absurd in the remnants of her mud pack, but her eyes full of energy and light, dancing. Excited. He couldn't remember the last time she had looked like that. It worried him that he hadn't noticed its disappearance from her life, from his life. And, inevitably, he caught little flashes of the grey, slippery, loathsome material under Declan's skin. Couldn't have been intestine, couldn't have been, intestines must surely be deeper in than that. It must just have been whatever there is underneath the skin, whatever slimy, gooey, slithery . . .

Anna stirred beside him. She was levering herself up.

'I thought I heard something.'

'Did you?' Luke hadn't heard anything.

'I'm just going to look in on him,' she said, 'I won't be a minute.'

'Do you want me to go?' Luke said, and she said, 'No I'll go.'

She slipped out of bed and crept away to Declan's room. Luke was dropping off when he did hear something, a low, gentle sound, rising and falling. He got out of bed and stood at the doorway listening. It was Anna, singing to Declan, something about the animals in the zoo.

1803

'The law justifies the beating of a lunatic in such manner as the circumstances require.'

Dr Thomas Percival, *Medical Ethics*

6. *It's all shit*

The house was full of sunlight, coming in from all over the place. You could hear birdsong from the back. Declan went round opening and shutting the windows. In the kitchen he fingered the row of pans hung on hooks from a rail: they were good pans, heavy, shiny, pleasingly alike though different in size. He opened drawers, examining folded cloths and rolls of foil and film, candles, guarantee cards for washing machines, Christmas cards. There were recipe books: he turned the pages, past pictures of food that looked too shiny and well-lit, curious words, tabouleh, tofu, mascarpone. He liked pie, rice, sausage, peas. Maybe you could have mascarpone pie. Maybe he would learn to cook. He read one of the recipes: you needed shallots, bouillon, tagliatelle . . . Declan knew how to make three things: Spaghetti bolognese, shepherd's pie, and savoury mince and peas. They were all essentially the same, but also a bit different. You could grate cheese on top sometimes. He could also do breakfast: beans, tomatoes, fried egg, bacon. That had always been enough. Mostly other people had cooked for him anyway, so he'd never bothered too much about it. He turned the cookery book over and stroked the spine. Jabs of anxiety bit through him and he screwed up his face and said it's all *shit*, all *shit*. He stood quiet for a minute until the waves subsided and the light and birdsong came back. He felt better.

He walked quickly round the garden, measuring with his stride, but he didn't like it out there. It was too open and too enclosed and too messy, too much of all sorts of things, full of busy little creatures and sly, secretive plants he didn't know the names of.

He went back through the kitchen and into the dining area, which looked unused and artificial, chairs neatly arranged round a scarred mahogany table with turned legs, Anna's grandmother's, and a light with a fringed shade over it. He stroked the fringes.

Along the hall to the front room. This was a good room, with a real fireplace and a window at the far end with a seat built into it so you could sit and watch the raindrops fall. The carpet was white and woolly. Declan reached down and stroked the pile, one way and then the other. There was a sound from the room on the other side of the hall; Declan paused for a moment, then carried on. He knew what it was. All in good time.

There was a complicated, expensive stereo, but Declan could see at a glance how it all worked, machines were usually easy.

The television and video were in another corner, stuck out of the way, not up on the wall so that everyone could see.

Over the hall, and into the other front room, the room they'd taken him into last night to dress his wound. Another fireplace, a great big leather sofa, more fluffy white carpet and a fringed rug. Declan tried not to look at the other thing, the thing that set this room aside, but it squawked and he couldn't just ignore it. He walked over to the cage by the window and the parrot scuttled to the other end of its perch and looked at him sideways. Declan ran his finger along the wires of the cage, and the parrot lifted a leg up and twisted its head round, blinked. It made another sound, and Declan said:

'It's all shit, all shit.' He waited for a response, none came. Again the parrot made its little idiot sound, and Declan said it's all shit again.

They watched each other for a few minutes. Then the parrot made a sound that could have been ogckie-*raark*, but which Declan knew was Bobby Parrot, its name. Luke had told him. Bobby Parrot. He said:

'Bobby Parrot,' and the parrot said *raaark*, ogckie-*raaaark*, stood on one leg, blinked, whistled. Declan tapped on the cage, and the creature ruffled some feathers on its wing and pecked at the perch.

'Bobby Parrot,' said Declan, but Bobby Parrot had grown shy and declined to be drawn any further. Declan watched it for a few more minutes during which the creature ignored him totally, but continued whistling, blinking, standing on one leg.

'It's all shit,' Declan said finally, and the bird said, sui, sui. 'Shit,' Declan said again, leaning in further.

'Shit.'

'Gawk. Wheeeeeeeeeeee.'

'Shit. Shit.'

'Have a nibble, wheeeeeeeeeee.'

Declan backed away. He hadn't heard 'have a nibble' before.

'Sui. Wheeeeeeeeee. Sui.'

Declan made a quick tour of the room, touching a big splashy abstract picture in a glass frame and a brightly patterned bowl. There was a glass cabinet with bottles in. Lots of bottles. Luke and Anna liked a drink sometimes in the evening. Declan didn't drink. It made you shout and break things and be sick, and it fucked you up with your medication. He couldn't see the point. One last stop, at a sword that was hanging on the wall by a small circular window with nobbly glass. He ran his finger the whole length of the blade, twitched the tassel hanging from the handle, then he was out of there, leaving the room to Bobby Parrot.

Up the stairs, into the bathroom.

The combination of glass bottles and white porcelain made him uneasy. Anna had a lot of glass bottles, full of cotton-wool balls and little soaps the shape of pebbles. The painted metal fish was back on the shelf.

He ran the taps and flushed the toilet. There wasn't anything else you could do in there, so he was straight out, standing on the half landing beside the big wicker laundry basket. He walked past the door to Luke and Anna's bedroom, merely glancing in.

He pushed a door open: a small room with metal

shelves beside the window. There were boxes and folded-up plastic bags. He took them down, carefully, and opened them up. They were full of tiny little garments, socks and all-in-one suits and dungarees, all in miniature, with embroidered teddy bears and ducks. He held one of them up to his nose, it had a sweet, sad, musty smell. One box was half full of stuffed toys, Paddington Bear, teddy bears, dolls with clown faces and pigtails. He stroked the hair of one of the dolls a few times, jerkily. He put everything back where he found it.

Another room. This one was also small, with a computer on a table and a chair. Declan rummaged about in drawers looking for disks. The ones he tried were very boring; he felt certain there must be better ones somewhere. Luke must hide them.

Luke and Anna were both at work. Anna had woken him up that morning with a cup of tea (she'd put milk in it, but he'd drunk it anyway, it wasn't too bad) and asked him how he was feeling. He was fine, he said. She'd wanted to look at the dressing, and he'd pulled the duvet away to show her. It looked all right, she said, was he sure it didn't hurt too much? It did hurt, but he said no it was fine, because that was what she wanted him to say. You did a good job, he said, you really did. She told him to have anything he wanted, there was bread and stuff in the kitchen. He should just let himself out, he didn't need to lock up or anything. She hoped he would be OK. She left some money by the bed, fifty pounds, in tens and twenties, new money, crisp and fresh-smelling. She hoped this would stop him from stealing anything, but she didn't think he would anyway. He was good as gold, she was sure.

'You really better had try to see a doctor about that, Declan,' she said, 'it's a nasty cut.' She had hesitated. 'Don't pull the dressing off until you see someone. Leave it alone. OK?'

'You saved me,' he said.

Suddenly she wanted to stay with him, find out who

had attacked him and why, find out how he had ended up roaming the streets. She wanted to listen to him, advise him. She hovered by the bed.

'Good luck then,' she said, and pulled the door shut behind her. He could hear her standing by the door for a few moments, then her footsteps moved away.

Luke had also looked in, quarter of an hour later, and said some of the same things, about not needing to lock up, and good luck. Doors were slammed and cars started up, then quiet.

Declan let himself out of the side door and took a stroll round the front. He left the door on the latch. It was a big house, old-looking, with a knotty tree in the front garden that shadowed over the wall and the windows, and a short twisting path to the gate. The front garden was dark and surrounded by a shoulder-height stone wall. There was a side passage round to the back, where Declan had come the previous day looking for Luke, bleeding. He peered over the wall to the next-door garden, which looked completely different, pink and white cement slabs and small square patches set in with roses and things in them. He liked this one better. He let himself out of the gate, though, and went to visit next door.

Anna hoped she was wrong, but she was getting the strongest apprehension about what she would find when she came back home that evening. She wasn't certain that Declan had really understood her, that she expected him to be gone when she returned. She had no way of gauging how good his understanding of anything was.

Nor did she have anything except a feeling (he's good as gold) to protect her from the possibility that she would come home to the scene of a burglary, everything that couldn't be stolen damaged and thrown around.

Anna encountered a lot of people, men and women, every day, though not in the most propitious circumstances. They came to get the results of their tests, positive or negative, mostly positive if they had been referred to her. It was her job to 'counsel' them, a task which she found varied greatly depending on gender. The men came through the door, their tails between their legs, unable to meet her eye, clutching their referral letters as if they were personal insults. Mostly the condition was minor, an NSU or syphilis, easily treated. But anything that affected them *down there* (coy, but it was the term she found herself using most often) had a disproportionate effect on them, and her job was to soothe, advise, lecture when necessary, but above all reassure. Nearly every man who had walked into her office over the last few years had walked in convinced that his time was up, that this time it was The Big One, that he had pushed his luck too far. It was funny sometimes, particularly if all they had was a dose of clap. They walked out happy, relaxed, cocky again, and in most cases, she knew, went back to their old ways, convinced anew that they were lucky, chosen, immortal. The women, on the other hand, tended to be furious with the dick-happy bastard who had chosen to favour them with the products of their philanderings, but otherwise matter-of-fact. Women, she reasoned, were so much more used to the idea of being probed and scrutinized and fiddled about with by medical professionals.

She liked men, but they could be so transparent. She found it difficult sometimes to think of them as anything except big children.

Declan was different, because he wasn't even trying to be taken for anything except what he was. He was transparent, because there was no defence. Did that mean he was good as gold though? It seemed less and less certain as the morning went on.

She came back from lunch and phoned home. No response. She was abruptly certain that she must go home immediately. The shifty, embarrassed men would have to stay shifty for a bit longer. She had to leave *now*.

58

She made apologies to the doctor, and drove home at speed.

Mrs Keyes sat in her kitchen and waited for the police to come. Meanwhile she gave Declan tea and chocolate biscuits from a tin. He had just arrived at her kitchen window, tapping at the glass, smiling, and she had been so startled that she had thought he was the window-cleaner, even though the window-cleaner was thirty years older and came on Thursdays. Declan, she had thought, must be a new window-cleaner. She had opened the kitchen door, and Declan had come in, smiling, chatting, complimenting her on her garden, and just sat himself down. She realized at once that he was a nutter or whatever you were supposed to say these days, and, on the pretext of letting the cat back in had gone to the phone and rung the police. Then she had come back to make tea.

'I'm just visiting, next door,' Declan said. 'Do you know them next door? Luke and Anna?'

'Oh yes,' said Mrs Keyes, surprised that he should know their names. 'We're neighbours, you know.'

'They're very good people. Don't you think?'

'Well of course,' said Mrs Keyes, who had known Anna's grandparents very well, and who had known Anna since she was a diffident little girl, sitting at this very table solemnly drinking her Ribena. 'Yes they are.'

'Which one do you prefer?' Declan asked, 'him or her?'

'Well,' she said, 'do you know, I've never really thought about it. Of course I've known her longer.'

'I prefer her,' Declan said. 'He's fine though.'

'Yes.' Where were the police? 'Let me top you up there dear.'

Anna tried to unlock the door, then realized that it was unlocked already. She called out 'Declan!' she chased

59

round every room of the house and round the garden. No trace of him anywhere. He had gone and left the door wide open. Thank God she had come back! How could they have been so stupid? What had they been thinking of! She slumped on the sofa, furious with Declan, furious with herself and Luke.

She became aware of a car door slamming next door and the sound of a two-way radio squawking. She peeked through the window: police at Mrs Keyes. We've tracked you down at last Ma Keyes, the jig's up. What could she have been doing?

Then there was Declan, on the pavement, pointing at the house, turning from the police to Mrs Keyes and back again, giving an account of himself, protesting. At any minute he might undo his shirt and show them the bandage, and then it would be she who would have to account for herself, and was she ready to do that? Why *had* she doctored him, kept him from the police and the other agencies? Didn't it all look a bit odd in the light of day?

She couldn't just lurk in the house, that was for certain. She went out and, to the unhidden astonishment of Mrs Keyes, claimed Declan as a bona fide guest: not a wandering lunatic, not a disorderly or disgraceful vagrant, not a criminal, but a perfectly respectable person, a friend, who had every right to be there and who was no threat to anyone. The police went away, after much standing about and murmuring into their squawking radios, to make reports, and Mrs Keyes said she was sorry if she had caused any trouble, she had just thought –

Anna ushered Declan, still protesting, back into the house. He looked flushed and defiant. Anna told him that he could stay today, but that he mustn't go wandering off. He would only get himself into trouble. Just today, then he would have to leave. She stayed with him for an hour, until he had simmered down and stopped going on, then asked him if she could trust him.

'Declan? I'm being very serious now. Can I trust you?

If I go back to work will you promise to stay here and not get into any more trouble?'

'Yes.'

'Do you promise?'

'Yes.'

'You know what a promise is?' She spoke gently, but clearly. Firm but fair.

'Means you've got to.'

'That's right. OK. If you promise, then I'll go back to work and see you later, and we'll talk about what needs to happen. OK?'

'You made the police go away.'

She looked at him.

'Yes I did.'

'You saved me again.'

She laughed. Saved him!

'I just want –' She stopped in mid-sentence. What did she want? 'I just want what's best for you.'

Declan watched her from the front-room window as she drove away. Then he went into the back garden and pulled out one of the plastic chairs and sat himself down in the sun. Mrs Keyes came out an hour or two later to take in some washing and Declan waved and called 'Hello'. She smiled back uncertainly and disappeared inside again.

7. *Number Eleven*

That evening Anna managed to persuade Declan that he must go to the hospital to have his wound looked at. She fed him stories of infections and swellings and unimaginable agonies. He blustered and refused then submitted quite readily, as she'd known he would. The dressing was holding up well, but there were traces of black blood beginning to show through, and she didn't want to risk taking it off to check on the progress of the injury. She had done her amateur best, now it was time for the professionals to take over.

'We'll say you're my brother. What name would you like?'

Declan looked uncomfortable, twisted about.

'How about Bernard?'

Declan smiled, as if despite himself.

'Yeah. OK.'

'Just remember. You're my brother Bernard, and you cut yourself falling against a jagged railing.'

'Railing.'

They got into Anna's car, and she pulled out into the wet night traffic. Lights and reflections smeared against the windscreen.

She knew that the story about the railing wouldn't stand up. Anyone who knew anything about injuries (like, for example, a casualty doctor) would see at once that Declan's gash was non-accidental. Which was to say, deliberate, malicious. An assault. A police matter. She would be suspected of involvement, questions would be asked. This wasn't going to be as easy as she was making out. But she was sure she could carry it off. As long as Declan stayed calm and didn't go into one of his rants they would be fine. She wondered whether to try to dope him up a bit, feed him alcohol, but decided not to. The result was too unpredictable. They would have to take their chances.

Anna knew doctors. As long as they were covered and there was no risk of a case coming back to haunt them later, they would be only too willing to be relieved of the responsibility if she assumed it with enough seriousness. They were busy. If Declan did catch anyone's attention, if the question of his mental competence came up, then there would have to be delays in treatment, a social worker would have to be scrambled from God knows where and the whole process could take hours. It was just the kind of thing they hated. They liked wounds, broken limbs, head injuries, areas of simple clinical judgement that could be resolved with X-rays and blood tests. They wouldn't want to be trying to make tricksy guesses about borderline personalities, they didn't really have the time. Declan could slip in and out unremarked, and if anyone did say anything, Anna could fend them off. She was a responsible adult, a relative (as far as they knew) and a clearly trustworthy person. It didn't hurt, she thought wryly, that she was middle-class, articulate and professional.

Unless they were particularly unlucky and someone recognized him, they would be OK.

It didn't occur to her to doubt that Declan was better off out of hospital than in. The little she knew about the insides of those places was enough. Declan was entitled to be in charge of his own life, he had been given the chance to make it on his own and he deserved it.

She grimaced as she thought about the treatment she had herself received from doctors in the past. Months of the most ghastly, intimate fiddling about, all sorts of promises, tests and samples and probes and fumblings. She had had five attempts at IVF, each one a major surgical procedure, under a general anaesthetic, each one a total failure. She wasn't going to have any more. Her inability to conceive naturally, she had been told, was a result of scarring to her Fallopian tubes because of chlamydia. She thought she had heard wrong. Chlamydia? But that was just a little thing, almost nothing at all, cleared up so easily, hardly even worth mentioning. And it had been *years* ago. How could a tiny little infection like that stop the baby that she knew was out there waiting to happen? It didn't make sense, it wasn't in proportion. It wasn't fair.

The horrible, humiliating attempts at IVF not only failed, they damaged her further. She learned the word 'iatrogenic', illness caused by medical treatment, and stored it up bitterly inside herself. It had a bitter sound to it. If her tubes were scarred before the treatment, afterwards they were like a field of poppies after a First World War battle. Poor Luke, huddled in a cubicle in the hospital with his little plastic bottle, labouring away manfully to produce the 'sample', trying desperately to feel some kind of erotic charge in the antiseptic toilet surroundings, and finally spurting his meagre juice with the rim of the plastic bottle cool and rough against his belly. All for nothing.

Doctors.

She glanced over at Declan, as they were waiting at a red light.

'Declan?'

'Yeah?'

'It'll be all right, I promise.'

'Yeah.'

'I know how awful it must have been, living in those hospitals, I do, really.' Actually she didn't, but she thought she could guess. Not necessarily cruel or vicious or even callous, but intrusive, humiliating, degrading. She knew the days of recording every bowel movement were gone, but still there could be no real privacy in that place, everything was available for scrutiny, comment, nothing would be truly his own there. No privacy, not even privacy of thought. Every little thing dragged out, teased out, gloated over, tested, measured, charted, named. She knew some of their

64

names. Dreadful, twisted words, seeming to have gone through some kind of nightmare mangle and come out deformed, writhing. Words they thought suitable, she thought, for the tormented things they described.

'Jargonaphasia,' Declan said, as if plucking the thought from her head. Anna jumped and broke sweat. 'It means I don't talk properly sometimes and I make words up that aren't real words.' The light changed, and she stalled pulling away.

He adopted a nasal, authoritative voice, with a pronounced Home Counties accent.

'Spontaneous speech fluent with neologistic and semantic jargon, with a great deal of pressure of speech,' he intoned. 'Raven's Colored Progressive Matrices score only 21, AQ of 22.3 per cent, falls into Wernicke's category. Shows a poorly defined left parietotemporal infarct.' Then his own voice.

'Talking bollocks, basically. I only get it a little bit. When I'm tired. That's just a little problem though, really. The main thing, you see,' cautious here, precise, eyes downcast, 'is that I have a personality disorder. The two things are not necessarily connected. They couldn't tell what kind of personality disorder it was at first. There are eleven.'

'Which one are you?' Anna asked dryly, and Declan said, 'Number Eleven. Passive-dependent.'

Anna thought she detected a grim trace of humour in his voice, which surprised her.

'It means I don't do things right. They told me I did everything wrong. They said I shouldn't always be trying to be like someone else, I should just be myself, but I didn't know how to, and they didn't know how to tell me. And they said, he said, you shouldn't let people make a monkey out of you, you don't have to please people all the time, you should please yourself. But they wanted me to please *them*. They wanted me to be like them, not like me, and they wanted me to do what they wanted, not what I wanted, but they told me the opposite. So it was them trying to make a monkey out of me, wasn't it? I got confused. What's wrong with the way I am, I asked them, what's wrong with me, am I mad or something or what? They said, well it's not an illness. You're not really ill. Well what am I then? I asked them. They told me, you've got a personality disorder. I said, is it my fault then? They goes, no it isn't your fault, but it isn't an illness either. Not like schizophrenia.' He sounded bitter now. 'If it was schizophrenia or something I'd be ill, properly ill.'

'It doesn't matter what they say,' Anna said, and patted his leg.

'They still gave me injections though. Every month. Depot injections. They give me enough in one go to last a whole month, it just comes out slowly. I still have to have them now. I said, what are you giving me that stuff for if I'm not even ill, not properly? Huh?' He seemed to be addressing the question straight to her, furiously.

Anna drove slowly in the rain, wet tyres squishing past every so often.

'Huh?'

Anna patted his thigh again. He was surprisingly solid down there. He was quiet for a moment.

'When I got the aphasia though, I couldn't help it, it just came out when I was tired. She'd say, they'd say, aren't you going to finish that pie Declan and I'd say well you see it's never like *that*, he's up in it, on the things, just all over. Sometimes it wouldn't even be proper words. On da. See it? Hakka all it I'm forjik.' He laughed suddenly, and Anna laughed too. It just sounded funny.

'Finega solly forse fay fargazus mingslaw,' he said, in a high, quick voice, as if he were giving directions. 'Buk. No. Doh yes, uh guh bo ver za.'

They laughed more, Anna laughed so much her eyes were streaming and she had to slow down to wipe them with her sleeve. They were still laughing when she pulled into the hospital car park.

*　　*　　*

She stayed with him every inch of the way, talking for him, explaining, smoothing the path. She answered the questions at Reception, spelled his invented name, her brother's name, gave herself as next of kin. Address? She gave her address. Declan hovered at her elbow, a sick smile on his face. It was that hospital smell, she guessed. What must it remind him of? They took seats in the waiting-room, which was filling and emptying all the time, a slow steady dribble of walking wounded, holding some bit of themselves with exaggerated caution, and relatives with compassion fatigue. The ones who were waiting sat glazed with boredom in the chairs and watched the monitor screens. There were some children messing around with the drinks machine. A parent came to pull them away. There was absolutely nothing to do. It would almost be preferable to be injured, she thought, at least it would give you something to think about. Accident and emergency ranked very low as entertainment, in her opinion. How come it made such good television?

A young man came through the swing doors, supported by two others: his face was running with blood, his clothes were soaked in it. The receptionist asked him something and he laughed. Everyone in the room seemed to be watching him, but guiltily, as if they were ashamed of relieving their boredom in this way. The less flagrantly injured looked admiring but also slightly resentful, as if he were stealing their thunder. Was there any need to be quite so showy about it, their faces seemed to say.

Declan sat unquietly beside her, fidgeting, throwing off occasional, unconnected comments. Look at that there. Christ, did you see her? Anna got him a cup of coffee, forgetting again that he had it black. He looked nervous, as if he might make a dash for it any minute.

Within half an hour, though, she noted that he had taken on the slumped, apathetic, slack-jawed immobility of all the others. His face had seemingly been drained of all the energy and fizz that was usually there, and to replace it there was this bovine indifference. She was surprised by the transformation. She thought it boded well, though: the quieter and more tractable he was the better things would go.

Suddenly it was their turn. They were ushered into a little cubicle, and a busy doctor performed a quick examination. Anna watched as Declan's lean white body was exposed to the doctor's cool efficient fingering.

'This is a good dressing,' he said as he cut through the bandage.

'Thanks,' said Anna. 'I did the best I could, but I'm no expert.'

The last loop came away, and suddenly there was the wound, whitened from the pressure of the dressing, but also a deeper angrier red and more swollen. The lips were moistened now, beaded, slightly puckered, a raw, damp moue. The smell came up again, a day older now, not freshly torn tissue but something that had been locked away in a room with the window shut for too long. Anna felt a surge of dismay as she saw how it had deteriorated over just twenty-four hours.

'How long have you had this?' the doctor asked, asked Declan, but it was Anna who spoke.

'He did it yesterday. He fell against, he fell down in the back garden and there was a broken bottle in the grass, and it cut him.'

Declan looked up at her, the first time he had taken his eyes off his ripped belly since they had come into the cubicle. Railing, his face said, railing.

'Must have hurt,' the doctor said, kind and indulgent to Declan, from whom he clearly expected something. Declan gave him a pale little smile, not one that Anna had seen before. She hoped the change of story wouldn't confuse him. He looked bothered. Tired. Oh God, she prayed, don't let him be tired.

'Oh he was very brave,' she said, 'weren't you Bernard?'

'Yeah,' he managed, and his smile widened for the nice doctor. Anna tried to see the doctor's face, but couldn't.

'Well, young man, you were lucky that this lady was around to help you. You really should have come in straightaway,' he said, to Anna now, 'something like this needs immediate treatment.'

Anna hunted for an answer to the unspoken question, but none came, and she stood, watching, as the doctor touched and stroked. Declan was staring straight ahead now, eyes clamped wide open, staring at air a few feet behind the doctor's shoulder. The doctor satisfied himself and went away. Declan didn't relax, though, if anything he seemed to be stiffening. Anna took his hand and squeezed it, but she got nothing back. She stood awkwardly beside him for a minute.

A nurse came, wheeling a little trolley, and started to tear open sterile paper bags. Declan's awful damp-soil smell fought with the accusing, righteous smell of the new dressings. Blood and a thinner, paler fluid, like tears, were mopped away. The nurse anaesthetized and stitched and wrapped.

'This looks awful nasty,' she said after a few minutes, 'however did you do it?'

'It was a railing,' said Declan, and Anna gripped his hand harder and said nothing.

The nurse smiled with easy sympathy and kept on with her work. They're all very busy, Anna told herself, they're too busy to worry about something like this, much too busy.

The nurse's dressing looked gorgeous, tight and secure and tidy. It inspired absolute confidence. She told them that they should have the outside stitches taken out by Declan's GP in ten days or so. The inner stitches would melt away on their own. They didn't need to come back to Casualty, she said, addressing Anna now, since Declan seemed to have drifted away, his eyes glazed over.

'Don't let him take the dressing off,' she said,

69

automatically taking Anna to be responsible for Declan now. It was just something about his manner, his quietness, his tractability. She's going to ask me about him, Anna thought, any second.

The nurse finished off, clearing away the debris of paper bags and plastic implements into an open bag hanging off the side of the trolley.

'Has he had his tetanus?' she asked, and Anna said oh she was sure he had, definitely.

The nurse was still fiddling about with her trolley, like some kind of deranged air hostess, Anna thought, when she said:

'I see he has a few other scars, they look quite recent. Is he often injuring himself?'

'Oh no,' Anna said, 'this is the first time. For ages,' she added quickly. 'Ages and ages.'

'You said he fell down,' the nurse said, holding her palm to Declan's forehead. 'Does he fall often?'

'No.' Anna, prepared for anything, found herself again without the necessary words.

'OK, well that's all we can do for him now. He's going to be fine, you don't need to worry. He mustn't do anything that might pull the stitches, so no heavy lifting, no athletics, that kind of thing. OK?' She addressed herself directly to Declan, who blinked rapidly, but said nothing.

'I'll see he doesn't,' Anna said, looking round for Declan's shirt. 'I'll keep a good eye on him.'

'Bye Bernard,' the nurse said, patting his hand and looking directly into his face, which was a thousand miles away by now, up beyond the clouds, up among the satellites and the constellations and the space debris.

The nurse kept her hand on his for a moment more, as if trying to feel her way through to him, then took it away.

Busy, Anna thought, busy busy busy.

'Right. Let's get you home Bernard,' she said, and couldn't believe how false her voice sounded, how absurd and arbitrary 'Bernard' seemed. The nurse must surely notice something. Anna wasn't used to lying. She was used to hearing it though. She sounded like a liar.

She got him out and into the car. She had to press him down into the seat. He had gone.

Luke was slumped on the sofa when they came in, smoking. There was a can of Guinness by his side.

He sat up guiltily and turned the television off as Anna opened the door. She sat Declan down and went to make him a cup of tea.

'How'd it go?' Luke asked, and Anna called from the kitchen, 'OK.'

Declan sat looking at Luke.

'You look like you could do with a drink,' Luke said, and Declan grunted, not moving at all.

Luke went to the kitchen to get him a drink.

Anna watched him as he took two more cans from the fridge and went back to the sofa.

Luke slumped down again.

'Anna says it went OK,' he said, but Declan had nothing to offer. He opened the tin and watched it as the foam spilled out onto the carpet.

'Do you want some of this?' Luke said, offering the joint to Declan. Declan took it.

Anna came in and gave Luke a look: is that really wise, do you think? It was no more than a tightened lip and a crease round the eyes. Luke ignored it. Declan inhaled, twice, deeply, and sat a fraction less stiffly. His face showed traces of animation again, the death mask that he'd walked in with starting to slip away.

Anna went up to bed. Luke and Declan sat together for a while: Luke turned the television back on.

'Well, you know where everything is,' Luke said when the joint was finished, and left Declan alone.

Luke undressed in the dark while Anna explained about Mrs Keyes. Luke humphed. Their neighbour had never made any secret of her lack of enthusiasm for him.

'If I hadn't shown up,' Anna went on quietly, 'the police would have got him. God knows what would have happened then. God only knows. I think they'd have tried to have him readmitted.'

'For Christ's sake,' Luke said, 'what's the matter with people? Anyone can see he's harmless. You only have to look at him.' I didn't tell him my address but he knew anyway, Luke thought quickly, and I've seen him quite a few times before. The thought carried no particular charge, it was just an item. Anna didn't know about it. Luke saw no reason to tell her. She'd only get stupid about it. There was any number of ways Declan could have known the address. Any number.

'Well at least he's had that injury looked at now. The doctor said mine was a good dressing,' Anna said.

'You were admirably cool,' Luke said, slipping in beside her. 'You're a good man in a tight corner. No really, I was impressed, I really was.'

She was warm and solid beside him.

'I wasn't particularly cool in that bloody hospital,' Anna said, 'I'd completely forgotten how totally bloody horrible those places are.' Luke moulded his body against her, nuzzling into her neck. 'And that's just to visit. Can you imagine living in one?'

'Enough to drive anyone mad, if you ask me,' he said, and she snorted in acknowledgement of the small joke.

'Can you imagine waking up every day and smelling that smell and seeing those bloody little women in those putrid little outfits, and having people poking at you the whole time?'

'Is that what they do in those places now? Poke at the mental patients?'

'You should have seen him, Luke, I'm not kidding, I thought he was either going to just make a run for it or, I don't know –'

'Go mad?'

'Start acting up or something. He looked trapped, you know. It was just terrible, I hated seeing him look like that. It felt like I was part of it. I think he thought I was going to let them take him away again. And we couldn't even keep the stupid *story* straight. It wouldn't have taken a genius to see that there was something not right.'

Luke nuzzled her again, and wriggled in a bit closer. He was dropping off to sleep.

'Luke, what are we going to do?' she said, but he just patted her leg and sighed. She wondered how many joints he'd had. She thought, fondly but sadly, that he was perhaps *not* a particularly good man to have in a tight corner. She squeezed his hand and adjusted his leg so that his ankle wasn't digging into her foot. Pictures turned over in her head, of Declan's dreadful smile at the doctor, of the beading on the lips of that wound, of Luke passing him the joint. She jolted awake at the sound of footfalls on the stairs, then the opening and closing of the spare bedroom door.

She was almost asleep again when she recalled the nurse's words – he has other scars. Is he often injured?

Anna thought: I don't know. I know nothing whatsoever about him. Less than nothing.

8. *In the Big Forest*

Anna woke late the next morning and had to rush out, no breakfast, nothing. She didn't even have time to use her facial scrub and spent the whole morning feeling gritty and unfinished. She rang home several times, but there was no answer, and she was busy. She would try to get home at lunch-time.

Luke also woke late, later than Anna. He was muzzy and slow from too much Guinness and dope the previous night. He tiptoed around, anxious not to wake Declan. He assumed Anna had spoken to him, he didn't want to have to confront him. He got his things together and closed the front door as quietly as it would go. He would ring Anna at work.

Declan slept through to eleven o'clock. At twelve thirty he spoke briefly to Mrs Keyes, who was going to the vet with her cat. She'd finished her antibiotics but she still wasn't eating properly. In the afternoon he slept on the sofa with the television on, the sound turned off. The phone rang a few times. No-one had remembered to uncover Bobby Parrot: he spent the day moving from end to end of his perch and mumbling to himself.

Luke came in that evening, exhausted and pissed-off and still late. Tuesday evening was his evening class. Photography for Pleasure and Profit. He usually had time for a bowl of cereal and a can of beer in front of the news, then he was out again, crawling through the late rush-hour traffic to the other end of town, where he presided over a group of a dozen or so men, and the very occasional woman, whose main interest always seemed to be in photographing the nude. They had to go to other, less salubrious, courses for that, but Luke was required to comment and advise on the results nonetheless. He was rarely anything other than appalled. The men were obsessively technical. They devoured magazines, and not just the ones with the scuba-diving babe on the front cover, but deep, dark, terrible journals. They always knew about the new cameras and films and accessories before Luke did, knew the specifications, the availability, the price. They were the kind of men who would hang round photographic shops just to catch the staff out in something.

The other thing about Tuesday evening was that on Wednesday afternoon Luke had a Communications and Cultural Studies double with a large group of seventeen-year-olds, and they needed a film. Whatever spare time there was on a Tuesday evening was spent cursing through stacks of videos which were imperfectly labelled to find that tape of *Metropolis* or *Boys from the Black Stuff* or whatever. It didn't really have to be anything in particular, since the Wednesday afternoon sessions were mostly open-ended and discursive in character, or, as the technical term went, 'a doss'. But it had to be something, and that something had to be located and checked for picture quality. Luke was very familiar with that teacher's dream of coming unprepared to a lesson, or coming prepared with the wrong thing. Like a video that, halfway through, turned into something else, something not quite appropriate, something bizarre. In front of a class of bored, clever teenagers, the recollection of such dreams could be powerfully unmanning. There was a particular feeling, a moment of loosening that accompanied the dreams, which was only ever held back, held down, with some effort. It crept up sometimes while he was teaching, ambushed him in the middle of a sentence, so that he stopped and looked around, meeting their eyes, at bay. He pushed 'play' on the video remote control sometimes with eyes clenched shut, terrified at what might come up on the screen. Tuesday night could be tricky.

He sat on the sofa, five minutes to go before the news, and pulled open a can of Guinness. He longed to change his clothes, but the effort involved was simply too great, it would take hours. He had barely eaten all day, because his dinner hour had been swallowed up covering bridge-club supervision for someone. Bridge-club supervision meant making sure they weren't really playing poker. The beer triggered the mechanism that started him wanting a joint. He lay back, waiting for the news.

The programme began, followed by the local news. A shipyard that had been deprived, quite unreasonably, of a Ministry of Defence contract. A murder. An assault, a broken shop window. Rumours of chaos. Old people outraged. He flicked through the channels impatiently, a second or so for each one, only barely enough time to register the image. He went round several times, just for the hell of it, isolated words and pictures flying out at him like shrapnel.

He became aware of something behind him, at his shoulder. He turned round and up on the sofa, a difficult manoeuvre, and met someone's dead eye and his shoulders and chest. Behind the sofa. He panicked, levered himself upright, he half lifted himself from the cushions, before he recognized who it was. Then he froze.

'Declan?'

Declan what are you doing here? I thought Anna had told you to go away to – wherever it is you people go to, I thought we were free of you, what is it that you want here?

'Declan?'

Declan was behind him, behind the sofa. He came round and sat himself down in the chair. The chair that Anna usually took when she was sitting down in front of the telly.

'Still here then?' Luke tried. His voice was light and high.

Declan gestured minutely at him and settled down, his limbs seeming to mould perfectly to the contours of the chair, his eyes fixed on the television.

'I've got to be away in a minute,' Luke said, then, 'have you seen Anna?'

'I don't think she's back yet,' Declan said, 'I haven't seen her. Doesn't she have something late on a Tuesday?'

'Oh yeah.' She did indeed have something.

'OK well look, I have to turn the telly off to look for a video. I hope you don't mind?'

'I don't mind.'

Luke went over and crouched by the stacks of videos, lurking neatly in the corner. His sense of what he was looking for was eaten away by the presence of Declan in Anna's chair. He just couldn't think what he wanted. He skimmed over titles. *French and Saunders*. Ice skating (sport as mass culture), re-runs of *The Tube*. None of it seemed to have anything to do with him suddenly.

The French Lieutenant's Woman. He'd recorded it a few weeks back. That'd do. Sex scene at the end? It was all right, as far as he remembered. History of sexuality and stuff. No problem.

It couldn't be far.

Declan made no sound behind him. Luke powerfully wanted to stand up and tell him to go. Just go! OK? But he didn't, he knelt in front of the piles of tapes, and felt Declan's gaze somewhere behind his back. He imagined beams criss-crossing the room.

His eyes met a tape, he was sure it was *The French Lieutenant's Woman*, though that wasn't what it said on the spine. It said all sorts of things on the spine, different coloured inks all crossed out and things scrawled over the top, it was also numbered '14' and '8', but he felt certain he recognized it. He grabbed it up and a whole lot of other tapes fell down, knocking his hand and making an astounding amount of noise.

He came back to the video machine without facing Declan, still half on his knees, a most ungainly posture.

He fiddled with the machine and ejected the tape in it. Racing from weeks back. A friend who knew how to place complicated bets called Yankees and Americans and so on had made more than £500 on the afternoon. They had sat in front of the screen screaming and emptying beer cans, and when Boney's Delight had come in they had both jumped and danced about, hugging each other. Luke had watched the tape several times since, amazed that there could be a thrill in watching races when you already knew the result. It made him feel lucky.

Hard to imagine screaming and dancing about with Declan sitting there dead-eyed and blank. Erased, like a blackboard. Or like a video with no racing and no old Marx Brothers film and no *French and Saunders* on it.

Luke rewound the tape, listening to the sound of the mechanism whining, and sat back on the sofa. The tape clunked and stopped. He pushed play on the remote control. Flickering pictures and some warp on the soundtrack, then the opening titles. He stood up to get another can. The first one had made barely a dent.

'Do you want a drink, Declan?' he said from the kitchen, and Declan called in yes.

He was pulling the can open as he slumped back down on the sofa when he saw that the picture on the screen was not a scene from *The French Lieutenant's Woman*. It was the brightly-lit interior of an American hospital, and a group of men were sitting in a semicircle, with a smartly uniformed nurse at their centre.

Luke knew instantly what the film was. The style and atmosphere were immediately recognizable, unmistakable. His eyes widened. *One Flew Over the Cuckoo's Nest*. He must have taped it over *The French Lieutenant's Woman* and forgotten. An unfortunate choice, he thought, and froze with embarrassment. He couldn't just turn it off, but it did seem a grotesquely inappropriate piece of entertainment in the circumstances, it did indeed.

He sneaked a glance at Declan: he was merely sitting,

with his glass eyes fixed on the screen. The camera panned round a ring of faces, which expressed bewilderment, incomprehension, inappropriately fixed smiles, fear. They were all mad people.

Loonies.

Shit thought Luke. Shit shit shit.

One of the loonies did something, gestured wildly, and Declan looked round at Luke and laughed.

'Christ, did you see that?' he said, and laughed again.

A row was developing between two of the men, then another joined in. Soon they were all shouting, shrieking, jumping up and down, and black guards or orderlies or whatever in bow ties came to restrain them.

'Jesus, did you see that?' Declan said, and threw himself backwards, yelling out like one of the loonies:

'It's all a lot of baloney!'

Luke snorted into his beer, and Declan laughed again.

'Christ, did you ever see such a bunch of nuts!'

Luke had forgotten what a good film it was. He forgot that he was supposed to be rushing out to go to his evening class and sat in front of the screen instead. He had soon finished his can (his second) and, abruptly, felt the impact of both the cans together. How could it be surprising when it was so predictable? But there it was: he was now drunk. He was, therefore, absolved from certain obligations. He could not now, for instance, drive through London's congested streets to his evening class, allowing cars and Luton vans to feed in from side turnings, stopping at zebra crossings, any of that. It would be possible to get a bus or even a taxi: possible but not, somehow, very likely. He was back at the fridge before he'd even thought of going there, coming back with two more cans. He would have to ring up and say he was sick. Pitiful, but that was what he would have to do now. His woeful little flock of amateur nude photographers would have to go without his inestimable wisdom and experience, his generosity of spirit, his enthusiasm, his sheer know-how. Sad for them. He imagined them, in a raggedy single file, trailing back dispiritedly to their cars, offering each other lifts, turning their front-door keys to their barren cells, their stacks of camera magazines, their expert accessories and padded cases, their artful nude portraits.

Opening the third can also absolved him from the obligation not to have a joint just yet. He went to find his papers and matches, leaving Declan to soak in the spectacle of the loonies and the terrible nurses.

Thus, when Anna got in from her Tuesday evening supervision group, she found, not a quiet orderly house but, apparently, two drunks sprawled in front of the telly smoking, and laughing their socks off. How could she object? She couldn't. She needed a drink herself. And it was good to see Luke enjoying himself, he didn't seem to do much of that lately. Was it good to see Declan? He had flickered through her head a couple of times during the day and evening, his messy hair and quick eyes, his confusion and helplessness in the hospital. Yes she was glad to see him if that was the alternative.

She took a can from the fridge and joined Luke on the sofa. He tried to sit up straighter but slipped backwards and she clouted him one. She drank quickly. She had some catching up to do.

By the time the water cooler was being thrown through the window they were all three well on the way. The film ended and Luke cheered, while Declan looked from one to the other of them and laughed and smiled. Luke put on a record, Elvis Costello, loud, and borrowed Anna's driving glasses to imitate him. He was good. Anna and Declan applauded. Anna did her Annie Lennox, pulling ferocious faces from behind her sleeve. Declan watched her, dumbstruck, while Luke rolled another one.

'Your turn,' she said to Declan, and he stood, smiling hesitantly at each of them in turn.

He stood, swaying. Then he seemed to change, his

posture, his shape, his smell almost, everything. He stood differently, less tall and gangly, more sturdy, more hunched. His face changed, became feral and mad, flushed, crafty, frightening. Anna stared at him, still, silent, and her stillness and silence made Luke look up from his rolling. His hands stopped moving as his eyes met Declan's new mad eyes, new shape and size. Declan towered over them, impossibly different.

Then he flung up his arms; Anna and Luke ducked down reflexively, and Luke spilled the unfinished joint onto the carpet.

'I want my cigarettes! Give me my cigarettes!' he yelled, and Luke and Anna, cold, took an endlessly long few seconds to understand. Then Anna shrieked.

'From the film! Luke!'

She nudged him in the ribs and he slumped over again.

'That was brilliant! Declan!' She stood up and held his shoulders, then hugged him. He grinned awkwardly, his arms to his sides. She let him go and sat down again. He stayed standing for a moment longer, then threw his arms up again, and she shrieked again, and Luke toppled over again. The joint, when Luke finally finished making it, just made them all worse and Luke turned the record up for his favourite track, which was slow and lugubrious but very noisy. Declan stood up to dance and Luke joined him, though it wasn't really a dancing track. Their two shadows reared up and formed one deranged composite on the wall. The next track was a favourite of Anna's, 'A good year for the roses', and she sang along, a mournful, penetrating, dreadful sound like a poor wounded creature alone in a forest. Luke tripped over an ashtray and banged his head. The doorbell rang.

Nobody moved. The record blared on, suddenly deafening. Anna looked at Luke, who was lying on the floor pulling a stupid face. She would have to go.

She tried to feel sober and sensible as she smoothed her hair and aimed herself at the door, but she wasn't.

81

It was the dope more than anything, it just made her stupid. She wanted to waggle her head round and make baby noises.

She opened the front door to Mrs Pelling with the slighter, balder figure of Mr Pelling just behind her.

'So sorry to trouble you dear,' said Mrs Pelling, 'we just wondered if everything was all right?' Sweetly enquiring.

'Oh,' said Anna. 'Yes.'

'Only we heard a noise, we thought there might be a burglar or something.'

'Oh no, nothing like that,' said Anna, terribly conscious of what her face was doing, which wasn't quite what she wanted it to do.

'Would you like to come in? Just for a moment?'

'Oh no dear, it's a little *late* for us,' said Mrs Pelling, but Anna had the devil in her and was insisting, holding the door wide, gesturing them in. Mr Pelling gave her little frightened looks as he slunk in behind his wife.

She was conscious of movements as she opened the door to the front room. The music had stopped. Luke and Declan were sitting up nicely, on sofa and chair respectively. The cans seemed to have vanished. She couldn't see any ashtray either, though the smell was strong.

'We were just having a drink,' she said, as she pulled Luke up from the sofa and plumped cushions for the Pellings. 'Can I get you something? Ted, anything for you?' Ted was torn, he glanced at his wife, who was steadfastly refusing everything.

'Got any lager?' he said, and Anna said 'Lager,' and went to the kitchen.

Luke had nowhere to sit, so he leaned against the wall by the fireplace. His smile slipped about. Declan was ramrod straight.

'Have you met Declan?' Luke said suddenly, as Mrs Pelling was whispering something to her husband, and she turned and smiled hugely at Declan.

'No, no we –' She stretched her hand out, and Declan stood and took it, shaking it very gently.

'Irene,' said Mrs Pelling, and Declan held her eye and said Irene. And this is Ted. Ted, said Declan, and held Ted's hand too, without letting go of Irene's. He didn't smile, he forgot.

'We live just over the road, number forty-six, with the copper beech in the front,' Mrs Pelling said, pointing out of the window to where her house lay.

'It's a very handsome house,' said Declan, and Mrs Pelling said yes it was, and wasn't *this* a lovely house too, and hadn't Anna done a lovely job on it.

'How's it going Ted,' Luke said, and Ted said fine, yes, not so dusty. Neither Anna nor Luke usually called him by his name if they spoke to him at all.

'Don't you want to take off your coat and er . . .' Luke asked Mrs Pelling. She had on a tartan wool jacket and an off-white crocheted or *macraméd* cap or beret. Luke didn't know quite what to call it. Would you like to take off your stone or ecru macraméd skullcap, Mrs Pelling? He twisted his face up in an effort to keep it straight.

'That's all right, we're not staying,' she said, and sat a little forward on the sofa, to reinforce the point.

'No, we just popped in . . .'

Anna came back with Ted's lager, interrupting her.

'I know you won't think me a terrible old nag,' Mrs Pelling said, 'but Ted has trouble sleeping at the best of times, and our bedroom's right at the front, I really wouldn't mention it –'

'Oh the music,' said Anna, relieved, and turned to Luke. 'She means the music.' She'd assumed it was something to do with Declan.

'Sorry, did you say dreadful old nag or dreadful old hag?' said Luke, and Mrs Pelling turned to him, astonished. Mr Pelling gawped over a lager-froth moustache. Anna glared at Luke. When was he going to grow *up* for God's sake. Why did he have to show her up like this all the time?

'I'm terribly sorry, Irene,' Anna said quickly. 'I had no idea it was so late, it must have been an awful nuisance.'

'I do hope you don't think me an old bore.'

'Of course not, don't be silly.'

'Only it *is* rather late.'

Yes! Yes! Don't go on about it!

'Really, I couldn't be more sorry.'

Mrs Pelling decided to be satisfied, and sat slightly less rigidly.

'So. What's the celebration? Someone's birthday? We haven't missed your birthday dear have we?'

'Sorry,' Luke said leaning forward, 'sorry, did you say old bore or . . .'

'Have you met Declan,' Anna cut in quickly. 'He's staying with us for a few days, just a little stay. He's, ah, he, you know, blimey! he knows my brother. He's a friend of my brother's. Have you ever met my brother Bernard?'

'Bernard,' said Declan, and Mrs Pelling said, no, she didn't think so.

'Bernard,' said Declan.

Anna looked at Mr Pelling's glass. He was plugging away at it. It was no-brand lager, it was probably terrible, Anna thought. She tried to think of something to say.

Then Declan stood up. Anna screwed her face up tight, clamped her eyes shut, she was sure he was going to do his cigarette thing again, she was certain. If he does that, she thought, I'll spill Ted's lager on him and they probably won't remember about Declan in the fuss. She was all ready to do it, but Declan just said:

'Excuse me, I have to go to the toilet now,' and left the room. She relaxed again. Luke was still leaning against the fireplace. His head was wobbling a little. He also seemed to be trying to think up things to say. Ted sipped his lager.

'Well, maybe we should be making a move?' Mrs Pelling said, and Ted nodded, swallowing the last inch and a half or so in one go. Anna took his glass and stood

up to see them out. Luke smiled in farewell, still trying
to come up with something naughty to say.

Declan was coming down the stairs as Anna opened
the front door.

'Excuse me,' he said, and they all turned and looked
at him.

'Excuse me.'

He seemed to be addressing Mrs Pelling. Anna waited
with a fatalistic dread in her heart.

He came up to Mrs Pelling and shook her hand again.

'I do like your hat,' he said. She was lost for words.
Luke could be heard cackling from the front room as she
took her hand away. Anna closed the door on them.

Anna went up to bed at one o'clock, instructing Luke to
please keep the noise down, which he did, apart from
some unfortunate crashing about in the kitchen and an
accident with the bathroom door. Oh and some
shouting.

At two fifteen Luke, all spit and urgency, was leaning
in to Declan, who was still sitting very upright, and was
saying:

'But you must think about it.'

The 'it' in question was sex, of course. Luke wanted
to know what you did about sex in a mental hospital,
and Declan had given the deeply disappointing answer
that he never really thought about it.

'But I mean you have – I mean you're not, you know –'

Declan raised an uncomprehending eyebrow.

Are you chaste? Our law demands no less.

'You must have fantasies, you know?'

Declan returned Luke's overheated gaze with his own
quick accurate (sober) eye. He wasn't quite getting it.

'I mean I do. All the time. You know, it's nothing to
be – you know, everyone –'

Still no flicker of understanding. Luke glanced up at
the ceiling, leaned in closer.

'You see someone, some girl, and you think – you
know? I don't mean you'd ever do it, but you still think

of it. I could,' voice a notch lower, 'have her. I could tie her up, for instance, tie her hands behind her back or behind her head, I could beat her with a strap, I could turn her over –'

Declan maintained his look of polite interest in what Luke was saying. Tie her, beat her, yes, I see. And?

'Of course you have to keep it to yourself. Obviously. Keep it under your hat, you know? Keep it up your sleeve. It's not the kind of thing you go round broadcasting, you know?'

Declan regarded him soberly. The idea of keeping something hidden, of dissembling, of *lying*, this was new and astonishing. Declan could see immediately how much power it could give you. He would watch Luke more closely, he decided. He would learn how to do it.

Luke was thrashing on, in a voice that was viscous with insinuation and knowingness.

'You must think things like that sometimes? Didn't you ever think, when you were in the hospital, what you could do with one of the nurses, say?' Luke smiled a crafty smile, and Declan smiled back.

'I mean, I'm – you know, I'm not frightened of my, whatever you want to call it, my dark side, if you like. My shadow. Everything in the universe has a shadow. Except the sun. You know what I mean?'

Declan pulled up a corner of his mouth, turned his head slightly.

'My wild side. You know what I mean? I'm not frightened of it. I'm not frightened of it. It's part of me, part of *me*. It's all just there in my head, just churning round, in my head. All the time.' Luke was dimly aware that his voice was in operation, was somewhat conscious of what he was saying, but was unable to call it to heel. It was like a frisky dog in a park, barking, chasing, yapping at children. Heel. Heel, boy! His wild side.

'I mean *you* – I don't mean because you've been in an asylum or anything. Or not just that. But you must have a bit of a wild side yourself. Am I right? Huh?'

'I never did anything.' Declan's voice was quiet, his manner still.

'No no Declan, I didn't mean – Christ, I didn't mean anything like *that*, I wasn't saying you'd ever actually –'

Luke couldn't express himself forcefully enough on this point. He made it several times more. Then:

'All I'm saying, you're probably in touch with your, your whatever you want to call it, your shadow. You know what I'm saying? Your shadow.'

Declan had no response to make. Luke watched him intently. Then he leaned in again.

'Hey Declan. Do you want to see some pictures?'

They tiptoed up to Luke's darkroom, Declan making almost no sound, Luke making much. Luke flicked on the red light, though he wasn't thinking of doing any developing just then. It was just a habit. It was also a precaution: if, by any mischance, Anna should discover that they were in there, she would hesitate to come in if she saw the red light under the door. It was a rule.

Luke got down on the floor and started rummaging about underneath a cupboard. He pulled out boxes of paper and bottles of fluid and plastic bags full of odd-shaped plastic things. Declan stood in the cold room, looking at the pictures on the walls.

They were mostly black and white, grainy paper, rough-edged. They were of broken-down cars and derelict buildings and scruffy children on waste ground and so on. There were some of Anna, she looked serious, as if she were thinking hard about something. She looked very unhappy.

'Here we go,' Luke said, and dragged a cardboard box out into the light.

He pulled out files and envelopes, squinting at them in the dim red glow until he found the one he wanted.

'This is it.'

He stood up straight.

'You'll like these,' he said, and winked. He slid the pictures out of the envelope and onto the counter. He tapped the little pile into alignment, then handed them to Declan.

'What do you think?'

Declan examined the first one very carefully. It was in black and white too. It was a picture of a woman, but not like the pictures of Anna. This woman didn't look serious or unhappy, and she didn't have so many clothes on either. She was heavier than Anna, taller, older. She wore different clothes, expensive-looking, but ripped, and there were ropes. She was tied up, tied to things. She was bent and twisted into all sorts of positions. The light was stark, and the woman cast strong shadows. In some of the pictures she wore a mask over her face. In some of them she had marks across her back and legs, like whip marks. In a few of them there were trickles of blood coming from her mouth and nose, and little puddles of it around her head. You couldn't see her breasts or anything like that, Declan thought, and she wasn't smiling. She had long black hair. Declan examined them one by one.

'I took them a couple of years ago. They were part of a portfolio I was putting together for an Arts Council bursary. Sort of "Images of Women/The Perverse Eye" kind of thing, you know.'

Declan looked up, smiled, but his face was worried.

Luke looked at the pictures in Declan's hand.

'They're not *real* – you know, she was an actress. A model.'

Declan looked at him, eyebrows raised, and Luke, drunk as he was, winced at his own stupidity.

'Well of course you knew that. Sorry.'

'Good aren't they?' Luke said, watching Declan's reactions. Declan nodded knowledgeably.

When he'd looked at them all he looked at them all again, then he gave them back to Luke, who hid them again. There was no reason to stay in the cold little darkroom any more. Luke stumbled back downstairs, with Declan at his heels, though Declan was thinking it was really time to go to bed now.

As soon as he got into the front room Luke seemed suddenly to think so too, and drooped all over the sofa. Then he stood up and said, 'I'm going to bed.'

Declan was relieved and stood up too.

'Tell you what,' Luke said as Declan opened his bedroom door. Luke seemed to have forgotten that he was supposed to be going to bed. He swayed in the doorway, licking his lips. 'Tell you what. I'll tell you a story.'

Declan had the pillows bunched up behind his head, a mixture of soft greens and blues and indeterminate shades in between. His hair was tousled, sticking up in odd places, and his bare arms and throat and shoulders were white and surprisingly thick, sinewy, gristly. He had his knees pulled up, forming a mountain range between him and Luke. The duvet, also in blues and greens, with traces of dusty pink, settled around him, in folds that looked too perfect and sculptural to be accidental. They looked like the frozen stone folds round the loins of a Michelangelo slave.

Luke sat on the futon, not a simple matter since it was so low, and felt as if he had parts of limbs poking out all over the place, knees, shoulder-blades.

He was speaking, his voice was quiet but insistent: from outside the room it would sound like a drone, a rumbling reverberant thing. He was completely drunk, stoned, off his face. He wasn't thinking about tomorrow and the double Communications and Cultural Studies session in the afternoon. He wasn't thinking about anything. His voice seemed to be working on its own initiative. He was telling Declan the story of the crab people.

'It all happened thousands of years ago, see, before anything was written down. There weren't so many people around then, and there were these huge spaces where no-one lived.'

The sound of his voice pleased him as he hung the story onto it. It seemed to make so much more sense spoken aloud like this, rather than the furtive life it had on computer disk and screen. The disk was so small, the screen so flat! His words felt cramped and harassed there, all tidied away by the computer. But aloud, in the free air, they seemed marvellous, magical, true.

'People lived in tribes, about a hundred and fifty or so. They would build a settlement, little huts made of tree branches and leaves and mud . . .'

It was delightful also, he thought, that as he spoke the story seemed just to be inventing itself, spinning itself out, not every word laboured for and corrected and worried over. Declan watched and listened, taking it all in, wide-eyed. Luke had been too drunk, too preoccupied, to notice that Declan had barely drunk anything, and that he had held the joints more than smoked them.

'The men were strong and handsome and the women were beautiful. All of them. There were no exceptions to this. None whatsoever.

'When Luc was about eight or something his tribe had settled beside an enormous forest. It was a good place because there was plenty of running water and grass for grazing. It was high up, so they could see if anyone came near. And the forest would be good for wood, for burning and building, and there would be little animals in there, wild boar and big clumsy flapping birds. And plants to make medicine.'

Declan had his eyes fixed on the wall, over Luke's shoulder. He blinked infrequently, slowly, like a cow. The only sound he made was an occasional swallow. Luke was anxiously alert for any signs of boredom, but detected none. Declan seemed completely rapt, though he was clearly becoming sleepy now.

'When Luc was little everyone told him not to go into the forest, because he could get lost and they might not be able to find him and he would die. Also there were monsters, terrible things. Luc would go a few steps in with two or three others and look round, expecting to be snatched up at any minute, his eyes bulging out of his head, and his little legs trembling and running with sweat behind the knees.

'Then one day someone disappeared from the village. No-one knew where he had gone. A few months later another person disappeared. Everyone got together and they decided to go into the forest to see if they could find him. The forest was the only place he could have gone to. A dozen of them went in, with big sticks and clubs and torches, you know, burning branches, shouting and calling and thrashing at the undergrowth and the branches. They were gone for three weeks.

'Then one of them came back. He looked old suddenly and terrified and sick, and he was wounded, all across one shoulder. They gave him medicine, but he quickly died. Before he died he told them that there were people in the forest, people who weren't people, not like the villagers, but different ones. Their faces were different, bonier, and they had a terrible huge claw on one arm, that could lash out and slice you in half.' Luke slashed at the air, a great slicing movement, like a tennis forehand. 'When they ran they ran slightly sideways, because of this claw. You couldn't always see the claw because they could pull it back into the body and hide it. They were called the crab people. They had killed all the villagers who'd gone searching into the forest, except this last one. He had only escaped from them by hiding in the tops of trees where the crab people couldn't climb.'

Declan's eyes were drooping more now. His head lay slightly sideways against the pillows, and his breathing was slower. He was nearly asleep. Luke went on, conscious of the gentleness, the rhythmic drone of his voice. He didn't know for sure if Declan was still really listening, but it made no difference. The story rolled out into the air regardless.

'When this last survivor died, he was burned on a huge pyre forty feet high and the burning went on all night. Luc was eight years old. He told himself that when he was a man he would go into the forest and look for these crab people, see, and fight them. He would stab them with a big spear. He would bring back a claw to show everyone, and he would be a hero. He dreamed for weeks afterwards of battles and chases and things like that. He couldn't wait to grow up.

'No-one went into the forest after that, only the very near parts to collect dead wood. Luc didn't tell anyone about his plan. He just waited to grow up.'

Declan's eyes were completely closed now, his head was sunk deep into the pillows. He looked sad, almost pained. His mouth was half open. As Luke watched him a shudder passed through Declan's body, then he was still again. Luke watched him for nearly fifteen minutes, though he could by now barely keep his eyes focused. The story ran on in his head, even when he finally managed to crawl away to his bed.

1807

'There is hardly a parish in which may not be found some unfortunate creature, chained in the cellar or garret of a workhouse, fastened to the leg of a table, tied to the post in an outhouse, or perhaps shut up in an uninhabited ruin; or sometimes he would be left to ramble half-naked or starved through the streets or highways, teased by the scoff and jest of all that is vulgar, ignorant and unfeeling . . .'

Sir G.O. Peele, letter to the Secretary of State for Home Affairs

9. *You're a Good Girl, You Always Were*

Anna felt as if she should be wearing dark glasses as she opened the front door the next morning. The sunlight seemed excessive, overdone. She ducked her head and pulled the door shut behind her.

'Anna dear!'

Mrs Keyes, bobbing her head above the garden wall, waving.

'Dear, do you have a minute?'

Anna sighed and went over to the wall, treading over grass that was cool with dew.

'Would you like to come in? Just for a moment? I do hope I'm not holding you up dear, I know how busy you are.'

Anna could see no decent way of refusing. She said OK and walked round to Mrs Keyes's glossy green front door. There was a carriage lamp. Luke had had a great deal of basically malicious fun about this carriage lamp when he had first come to live with her. Anna had always liked it, she remembered it from when she was a little girl. It had always seemed grown-up and desirable and settled. When I'm grown-up, she had told herself, I'm going to have a carriage lamp too.

They sat in Mrs Keyes's kitchen, with the sun pouring in from the garden where small birds pecked optimistically at half-empty seed feeders.

Anna said thanks for the coffee. It's about Declan isn't it? She had never had to beat round the bush with Mrs Keyes. Mrs Keyes sighed.

'Oh I know everything's different these days, and

95

we're all supposed to be very *caring* and not call them *names* and all that. And that's quite right, of course it is. My sister's husband had to go to a hospital, this was before the war of course, and I used to go with her to visit. I'll never forget it. We used to sit on the bench at the tram stop and hold each other and just cry when we came out it was so awful. The smells! Worse for her than for me, naturally. Worst of all for him, of course,' she added quickly. 'He looked unhappy, always. Never happy. He used to cry, he'd say Edie, get me out of here can't you, for pity's sake? It was terribly upsetting. How could he not be unhappy, shut up in that dreadful place with those others? It wasn't fit for people like him to live in. For anyone really. The staff tried to be kind, but often they weren't. It wasn't really their fault, they did their best I suppose, but it just wasn't possible in that place.'

Anna had noticed how, as she aged, Mrs Keyes spoke more and more in long, remembered anecdotes, which seemed to be located further and further back in time. This was before the war of course. My father had a cart pulled by a horse. It was as if she were tidying everything away, getting it into good order before she died. Anna, gradually and reluctantly, had come to doubt that everything Mrs Keyes said was completely accurate.

'There must be better ways of treating them. I'm sure there are, much better ways. But Anna, dear,' Mrs Keyes leaned forward and covered Anna's hand with her own wrinkled claw, 'are you being wise? What do you know about him?'

'He's not staying, he's just here for a few days . . .' Anna began to say, but Mrs Keyes cut in:

'You don't know anything about him, do you? He could be anyone.'

'There's nothing wrong with him, not really, he's just –'

'But how do you know?'

'Because I've talked to him. Really, he's perfectly all right. That's why they let him out. They wouldn't have let him out if he was a menace to society would they?'

'Anna dear, the stories you hear these days –'

'You think, just because he's been in a mental hospital he's going to break into your house and carve you up with a bloody steak knife in the shower, or stab you in a tube station . . .'

'Now dear, no-one's saying . . .'

'They're not all bloody psychos you know!'

'Pray calm yourself dear.' This was an old weapon of Mrs Keyes's, a cool, disdainful tone of voice and a call to self-possession. It had always worked.

'Sorry,' Anna said stiffly. 'Sorry I said that. I know you don't think that.'

'He may well be perfectly harmless. On the other hand he may not be. All I'm saying is that you should find out which. Am I being unreasonable?'

'I didn't say you were being . . .'

'Am I being unreasonable?'

'No. You're not.'

'All right dear. We won't say any more for now. I don't want to make you late for work. I know you're a busy girl.'

'Yes. I should be getting on.' Anna stood up. Mrs Keyes held onto her hand.

'It's you I'm worried about my dear. I should never forgive myself if anything happened. I wouldn't say anything otherwise.'

Mrs Keyes had suffered with Anna through the IVF, had known at every stage what was happening, or not happening, knew what it had all cost, emotionally, financially. She knew how desperate Anna had been for that baby.

And now, suddenly, Anna had taken in this mental patient. Adopted him, seemingly. Of course there was nothing sinister in it, Anna was a good girl. She would never do anything to hurt anyone. But it made Mrs Keyes distinctly uneasy. She had a friend who had had a little girl, severely retarded, her brain damaged. She had become entangled in her umbilical cord at the birth, had been partially strangled for a few dreadful moments, not much but just enough. Her mother had been advised that the little girl ought to be placed in a residential hospital, but she had refused. She looked after her herself, had devoted practically her whole adult life to it.

'I couldn't bear for her to be in strangers' hands,' she'd said. But later in the same conversation she had admitted that her little girl (now a plump, implacable woman in her mid forties) was her only consolation, and having her there was like having a baby, only she never grew up. Who was there to judge the rights and wrongs of it? Mrs Keyes felt odd about it, that was all, and every time she imagined life in that house, with a forty-year-old baby and a mother devoted solely to her welfare, she wondered whose interests were being served and at whose cost. Things had been simpler when she was younger. Mrs Keyes looked at Anna.

'And I think it's marvellous you think so well of people, I do, really. There should be more like you around. You're a good girl, you always were.'

Anna squeezed the hand, cool, dark, with little brown spots like overgrown freckles, and pulled her own away. She hesitated at the front door.

'Your sister's husband. What happened? In the end?'

'You mean, did he die in there?'

'Yes.'

'Yes.' Mrs Keyes stood in the hallway as the cat wrapped herself round her feet. She pictured the glimpse of the body she had caught accidentally, before they were ready for her to see it, a grey rubbery form laid out on a table, hair shaved, wearing only a nappy, a label tied round its ankle.

'Yes he did dear.'

Luke woke up at eleven, wishing he was dead. He felt as if someone had been pummelling him with a medicine ball all night. His mouth tasted of filth and vileness, things washed up under the arches of bridges, old, dead. He was going to be sick, but not, he knew with horrible accuracy, not quite yet. Not *now*. No, he would have to wait a while. He lay, desperate for more sleep, but there was no more sleep, he knew. The light was absurd, even through the curtains he could see its insane intensity, as if it were particularly pleased with itself today for some reason. Come out and play, it said, in a nasty, mocking kind of way, jump out of that horrible stinky old bed and come out and play with the other children. Dance! Sing! He pulled the duvet over his head, but there was no escaping it, he was going to have to crawl somehow to the bathroom to piss and drink water and wait to be sick and want to die. He kicked the duvet away.

Hungover on a school day. A few too many of those lately. It really wasn't *fair* on his *fellow workers*, his *colleagues*, he thought in a sour, censorious, staff-room voice, it really wasn't. His fellow workers. He considered them as his thick, malodorous urine fell into the toilet bowl. God bless them each and every one. He sluiced out his mouth under the tap. The water tasted dead too. He thought about getting under the shower but it seemed too much like hard work somehow and he dragged himself back to bed. He clamped the pillow over his head to keep the light out. He tried to sleep. He was too hot. The birdsong was deafening and merciless, unremitting.

Declan sat in front of the television. Beer cans and ashtrays, torn-up cigarettes and bits of card were strewn around. Records were lying on the floor, out of their sleeves. The room was rank with the smell of spilt beer and stale smoke. He hadn't opened the curtains. He didn't think of it.

His eyes were fixed on the screen, as he changed the channel every few seconds. His thoughts were scattered. Bits and pieces of Luke's story flitted through his mind, just phrases here and there, 'she is not of our kind', 'our ways are old, older than you know', 'you do well to stay at arm's length'. Sometimes they seemed to come out of the mouths of whoever was on the television.

The day had come and gone for his appointment, his depot injection. He was supposed to go to Outpatients once a month for a jab, they'd told him many times how important this was. Now they weren't going to be around any more to keep an eye on him, they were going to have to depend on him to make sure he kept his appointments. Could they depend on him? they'd asked seriously. He'd nodded, also seriously. Everyone agreed that it was a very serious matter.

'What's it for?' he'd asked.

'It'll keep you feeling tip-top,' the nurse said, and ruffled his hair. 'It'll keep you feeling on top of the world.'

He was now three days on the wrong side of it. He felt fine. He didn't feel so stiff and boxed-in, he felt freer, looser. Stronger. He flexed his arms, sending them in great circles round his head, warm-up exercises. Then one arm shot out, a fast, sudden swing, low, like a tennis forehand, unplanned, unintended. Declan brought the arm back and held it.

'Go now, while you are not yet enemy.'

He heard movements from upstairs, Luke going from bedroom to bathroom. He looked up at the ceiling, then back at the screen.

Mrs Keyes saw Luke leave the house at one fifteen. She noted the greyness of his face, the sunken eyes. She observed that his clothes were crumpled, stained. She watched him shield his eyes from the sun, screw up his face; she watched him fumble with the gate latch. She had of course heard the commotion last night.

None of Anna's young men (she didn't like 'boyfriend') had lasted this long. Never, before this one, Luke, had the question of babies come up. She remembered Anna introducing her at the gate one evening, explaining that Luke was someone's friend, his girlfriend had inexplicably gone off somewhere, details very scarce, and he was just staying for a while. Mrs Keyes smiled, but she had never liked him. She just didn't like the look of him. She'd looked on helplessly as Anna and he had grown closer, first like brother and sister, doing the garden together, decorating, then in the other way. He was drunk a lot and noisy. Exuberant. She thought a young man should be steady, sober, quiet. But Anna was happy, for a while, at least until the baby thing started up.

She watched him return a few minutes later with a newspaper and a carton of milk. She watched him go back in.

No-one else went in or out for the remainder of the day. She didn't see that other one, though she knew he was in there. No-one opened the curtains all day.

10. *That's enough now*

Declan was shaving. He'd been in the bathroom for twenty-five minutes. Luke was timing him. Anna was fidgeting in the kitchen. Bobby Parrot stretched his neck and said 'corrrrr', very softly.

They were due to meet Ollie and Sally at the Tanners at nine thirty. It was twenty past now. Anna popped her head round the door and caught Luke's eye: he shrugged. He was cross-legged, jiggling a foot. He was getting desperate for the toilet.

Thirty minutes. Luke heaved himself up and went up to the bathroom. He leaned into the door. He could hear little noises, water running, tiny unidentifiable sounds. He stood for a moment then tapped gently on the door.

'Declan?'

'Minute,' Declan called, his voice tight and muffled.

'Any chance of getting in there for a second?' Luke called, louder than was strictly necessary.

'I'll just be a minute,' Declan said after a few moments' pause. Luke sighed heavily, shifted his weight from foot to foot.

'Well. We're about ready when you are,' he said, and trod gracelessly back downstairs.

He went to the kitchen and stood behind Anna, rubbing her neck.

Four more minutes. Five.

He strode up the stairs two at a time, was back at the bathroom door, tapping.

'Declan? We're going to have to have you out of there. You nearly ready?'

Declan said something Luke couldn't hear.

'What?'

No reply. Luke stood back from the door, then grabbed the handle, rattled it.

'Declan?'

No reply.

Luke knocked, louder, and was about to try to push the door open when Declan's face appeared, ringed with shaving foam, his eyes slipping away from Luke's. There were patches of red amongst the white. There were drops of bright red blood on the white porcelain of the bowl, and on the black and white tiles.

Declan let Luke in and went back to the mirror over the sink. Luke went straight for the toilet.

'Cut myself,' Declan said, and Luke agreed that it certainly looked that way.

'I don't usually cut myself,' Declan said, scraping away diligently at the foam. 'In fact I never do.'

Luke, his equilibrium restored by the relief of his bladder, was unable to miss the anxiety, the tightness in Declan's voice. He made himself be patient. He sat on the rim of the bath and played with a bottle of Anna's skin conditioner.

'Everything all right?' he asked, 'I mean, about tonight?'

'I won't say anything.'

Luke sat back and regarded him.

'You mean later? In the pub?'

'I'll just, I won't say anything.'

'Why not?'

Declan wet his razor, pushed his nose to one side.

'Declan? Are you nervous about tonight?'

Declan stared hard at himself in the mirror. A fat drop of blood gathered on his chin, then fell down into the basinful of water.

'Sometimes I say stupid things. Only when I'm tired. But I do. If I thought about it first like he said, like they said, then I wouldn't say them, but they just come out, and everyone laughs, even though I haven't said anything funny, so I laugh as well even though it isn't funny.'

'Declan, no-one's —'

'So if I just don't say anything no-one will laugh.'

'No-one's going to laugh. Why would people laugh at you?'

Declan shook his head, and his eyes misted over. Luke hesitated, then came and stood behind him. He put an arm round his shoulders and squeezed.

'Just be yourself, that's all. That's all you have to do. Everyone's going to like you, just like Anna and I do. We don't laugh at you do we?'

'Maybe you do when I'm not here.'

'Declan. Listen now. You know and I know that you're not the same as other people. You've got this — thing, this whatever they call it.'

'Personality disorder.'

'OK. That's what they call it. But that doesn't mean that you're not as good as anyone else. You mustn't think that people laugh at you behind your back. It just isn't true. If Anna and I like you, and we do, then why shouldn't our friends? They're just like us.'

'Maybe just say a little bit then, if no-one else wants to.'

'Say whatever you like. Just try and enjoy yourself. OK?'

'OK.'

'And if you feel uneasy you can just get up and go whenever you want and no-one will think anything about it. Deal?'

'OK.'

'OK.' Luke administered another squeeze. He offered up a prayer that no-one *did* laugh at something Declan said. Luke tried to imagine feeling that people were laughing at you when your back was turned, but couldn't. It was such a childhood feeling, such a school-yard feeling, it was too distant. Poor bloody Declan.

Luke took his arm back and smiled into the steamed-up mirror.

'*Courage*,' he said. '*Courage mon brave!*'

*   *   *

104

Luke had said often, Anna thought, as the three of them walked the few streets to the Tanners, that he'd cooled towards Ollie of late. He no longer felt anything for him, he said, Ollie had become a shadow since he and Sally had had their child. Boring. Talked about boring things. Could never stay out late. Anna suspected that all he really meant was that he'd lost a drinking buddy. But there was also the fact that Ollie had proved, in the only way that counted, that he was fertile, whereas he, Luke, just had some doctor's word for it.

She didn't know how strong those feelings were in Luke, but she sensed them bubbling away sometimes, caught a peculiar hard look in his eye or felt an arm muscle stiffen when he was holding her hand. And he was drinking more, smoking more, talking less than ever. There were moments when she was certain, absolutely sure that he was slipping away from her, closing himself off bit by bit prior to leaving. Going away. In other cultures, she knew, a man who married an infertile woman would be, not just allowed, but actively encouraged to take another wife, one with more life in her eyes, more promising-looking hips. There wouldn't be the same courtesy extended to the woman, of course. She wouldn't be expected to be looking elsewhere. Why would she even want to?

Declan was walking with Luke, a few paces ahead of her. She watched the two men, so similar in basic shape, so alike. Declan had little pieces of tissue paper stuck to his neck. He hadn't got all the shaving foam from behind his ears. His clothes were clean and neat, though, and there was nothing wrong with his grooming, his hair was washed and tidy. She ticked off the components in her head, trying to put her finger on what it was that *looked* so wrong about him. Maybe it was simply that he obviously worked so hard at being unremarkable, anonymous. The trousers were too ordinary, the shoes too improbably boring in someone of his age. He looked like a Young Conservative or a member of a Christian Rambling Association or something, but even more so. Not even the ghastliest Young Conservative would have shoes like that, hair like that. He wore a jumper, brown, V-necked. Absolutely nothing wrong with that, she admonished herself. And yet.

No, he just looked odd. You knew it immediately, and you could spend hours trying to figure out why. She remembered the nasty little twist inside she'd felt when he'd first shaken her hand. He was a Young Conservative Ramblers for Christ from your nightmares. Or at least a good imitation of one. Just not a *person*.

Though he and Luke were walking abreast, they weren't talking. Declan looked tight and miserable with anxiety.

It had been she who had raised the point with Luke, since he seemed incapable of addressing it. If she and he were going to the pub with Ollie and Sal, she'd said, then what was going to happen with Declan? Would he be left behind, like Bobby Parrot, stuck in front of the telly with sandwiches and instructions on how to use the microwave?

Of course not. Luke had been hotly contemptuous of the very idea. Declan was not some guilty secret they had, they were not ashamed of him.

OK, so he was going to shave, brush his hair, come out with her and Luke?

Of course, Luke said, but in truth neither choice seemed good. It disturbed her that they were now in a situation where they were faced with such choices. It disturbed her that they were in a situation at all, though that was unquestionably what they were in. It disturbed her most of all that Luke didn't seem prepared to acknowledge it, if he even saw it.

Luke went in first, with Declan at his heels. The door swung shut before Anna could reach it; for a moment she saw Declan's face at the little window goggle-eyed with horror that he'd lost her, then he was pushed sideways by someone and she lost sight of him. When she found him again he was standing with Luke at the bar, very close, at his elbow.

They went to sit with Ollie and Sal. Luke squeezed in beside Ollie in an oddly ingratiating way he had that always annoyed Anna. She sat on a stool, very straight-backed, feeling irrationally hostile. Declan sat on a stool beside her, having been abandoned by Luke. Everyone was introduced. Ollie and Sal had some people with them, who were sitting further down the bench: they also were introduced. Declan shook hands with everyone; he even smiled.

After ten minutes Declan was surprised to discover that he had finished his drink. He had been sipping steadily, now it was all gone. No-one else had finished theirs. He nursed his empty glass, sipping from it occasionally, covering the lower part with his fingers. Luke was talking fast to Ollie: Declan met his eye, but Luke looked away immediately. Sally was leaning in, talking to Anna. Declan couldn't quite hear what they were saying; he sat back.

He caught the eye of someone sitting behind him, a man.

'How do you do?' he said and held his hand to be shaken. The man laughed and shook his hand. Declan did the same with the other people in the group, they all laughed, all shook hands. Anna became aware of Declan's voice coming from behind her, talking, laughing, heard him saying 'not a real illness' and swung round to get his attention. One of Declan's new friends caught her eye and shrugged an eyebrow sympathetically. Anna put her hand on Declan's arm.

'Declan? Everything all right?' He dropped the smile and twisted himself back round to sit facing Luke and Ollie. Then he stood up. Anna flinched without the least idea why. 'I'll be back in a second, I just have to go to the toilet now,' he said.

'It's over – it's that way –' Anna tried to say, but Declan was already heading off in the wrong direction.

He had got no more than a few paces before there was a bump, then a crash. Someone's glass had shattered against the bare floorboards. Declan was facing someone off, the person was shaking his head, brushing beer from his shirt front and sleeve.

Anna was by his side in a second.

'Declan?'

'I bumped into him, it was an accident, I didn't –'

'I'm terribly sorry,' Anna said to the beer-soaked man, 'let me get you –'

'Funny bloody accident,' the man said, not looking up, still shaking his head. 'Looked more like he was bloody going for me.'

'I didn't, it was just –'

'He just swung for me, I didn't even see it coming.'

'Declan? I'm sure you didn't mean it, did you?'

'He – I never –'

'Let me get you a drink,' Anna said, 'what are you drinking?'

'Want to watch that right hook of yours in future pal, could get you into all kinds of trouble, know what I mean?'

Anna guided Declan back to his stool. He was hot and indignant. She patted his knee, put her arm round his shoulder, cooed and soothed. Luke looked up from his conspiracies with Ollie, raised enquiring eyebrows.

'Nothing,' she said. 'It's nothing.'

Anna couldn't quite say when, but at some point she became aware of Declan's voice again. He was speaking, but when she looked he wasn't speaking to anyone, he was just speaking, odd little off-the-wall comments, like the ones she'd heard in the waiting-room at Casualty.

She turned to face him.

'You see, I never had any kisses or cuddles. When I was little.'

'Oh. Uhuh.'

'Not like you're supposed to have. The doctor said it

was my mum's fault I was like this, he said she should have given me kisses and cuddles.'

Anna felt rather than saw first Luke's and then Ollie's and then everyone's attention focusing on her and Declan. She flushed.

'Aye, all we ever got was smack round t'chops and grateful for it,' Ollie said in Emmerdale Farm Yorkshire. No-one laughed.

'Declan?' This was Sally's voice. She was leaning forward to address her question, trying to see round Anna's body. Only when Anna shifted to the side did she realize that she had in fact been protecting him, screening him from them. She sat back.

'Declan? I hope you don't mind me asking –' She flicked hair away from her face, and Anna saw that Sal was drunker than she seemed. Anna knew she didn't get out that much these days, with a young baby. Sal was definitely making the most of her freedom.

' – have you got a girlfriend?' A big coy smile. It was the kind of question an indulgent aunt might ask of a tongue-tied five-year-old. Anna clenched her teeth. Declan shook his head, said no, looked at the floor. Anna tried to distract Sally from any further attempts at drawing Declan out by starting in on baby talk. Ollie rolled his eyes.

'They took me into care, then they said I had something wrong with my head so I had to live in the hospital. Then they let me out of there and I went to Rain Fields, which was residential, and I lived there for eight years. Then they said I had to leave, they were closing it down, and I had to have a place of my own, even though I didn't want to.'

This was all delivered straight at Luke, at high speed, with tremendous energy. Luke looked as if someone had hit him. Ollie was mute beside him. Sally stopped in mid-sentence. Anna imagined a wave of silence spreading out from their table, rippling outwards, until the whole pub was silent, with Declan at the centre of it, the pebble in the pond.

'I said, why can't I go back to Rain Fields, why can't I? Huh? I didn't like having my own place, there was no-one to talk to, and there were no activities. At Rain Fields we had activities. They were supposed to get me a job but I couldn't stand for that long and my ankles swelled up.'

Ollie leaned back in his seat and met Sal's eye. Anna tried to address Luke, but Declan cut in over the top, his voice louder.

'I never, you see I never had what other people have, I just never had it, I didn't have anyone to say Declan, you know, and give me a cuddle, you know –'

'Declan –' Luke met his eye, held it.

'It wasn't my fault, no-one could ever say it was my fault, they couldn't say that, no matter what they said, what he said –'

'Declan –'

'If I'd had someone to hold my hand you know –'

Luke leaned in and put his hand on Declan's knee.

'Declan. That's enough now.'

Declan opened his mouth and closed it again. He looked shocked.

'That's enough, Declan.'

Declan became rigid: Anna could feel him stiffening, drawing himself in beside her. No-one spoke.

He stood, suddenly, knocking his stool over. The glass in his hand dropped to the floor and smashed. Luke flinched, one arm came up to protect his face. You are not of our kind, you do not understand our ways.

Then Declan was on his feet, pushing through the crush. Anna went to follow him, but felt Luke's hand on her sleeve, restraining her.

'Just leave him,' Luke said, and Anna sat down again. Sally patted her hand, and Anna breathed in, then out, deeply, slowly. She didn't like to admit it but she was overwhelmingly relieved to be free of him. All the time he'd been at her side she'd felt tense, frozen, waiting for something to happen, waiting for him to explode.

The conversation picked up again.

Declan caught sight of the man whose drink he'd spilled earlier. You are not yet enemy. Declan pushed past him.

11. *Foo-king freezing*

. . . the moonlight spattered him, the forest lay all round him, branches twisting, creaking as the wind rushed through the treetops . . .

Luke and Anna lay in bed, not touching apart from the tips of their toes. Neither was asleep. Words were spilling through Luke's mind, pictures, scenes that always led him to the same place, the sudden turn of the body, the disturbance in the air as the deformed limb-blade swung out, heavy and fast and deadly. He cringed each time it happened. Anna felt his body shudder periodically, but seemed distant and powerless to comfort him. She had visions of her own, visions of figures hunched in doorways, huddled, lonely, lost. Their eyes were Declan's eyes.

'Do you want to go somewhere?' Lee asked. He was with two other men, both much older though not much more sober. Declan looked from one face to another.

'They're not coming, just you and me,' Lee said, 'what d'you think?'

'Yeah,' Declan said, 'OK. Where is it you want to go then?'

The youth swayed, staggered back a half-step.

'Dunno.'

'Do you want to go up the allotments?'

'Could do. If you like,' Lee said. 'Yeah. OK.'

. . . Luc followed the path, the moon turning the frosty branches into glittering bones. The way was stony, littered with branches and studded at intervals with weird fungi that reared up into the blackness, their flesh contorted, blotched. Sounds reached him from far away, cries, whistles, the howl of a dog . . .

Declan and the lad Lee went up to the allotments, along by the railway line. Quite a few of the allotments were unused, lush, extravagant carpets of bramble and tall weeds taking the place of the legitimate frugal winter cabbage and sprouts.

Declan and Lee walked along the path, stumbling against watering-cans and the edges of pieces of carpet half-buried in the soil. The path was too narrow for them to walk abreast, and Declan went ahead. There was little light, the ground was rough.

Declan led the way up between two allotments, the one to the right demarcated by doors sunk into the ground on their sides. The allotment on the left was not in use, and was a chaos of piles of vegetation, heaps of wood and cushions, charred patches surrounded by bottles and cans, and the burned-out hulk of an armchair, its springs sticking up like tough, unlovely shoots. Declan swiped at a pole leaning against one of the doors. Lee floundered behind.

. . . a sudden gust of wind agitated the treetops, their dead branches creaking and shuddering. A breath of wind reached down to Luc on the forest floor, scattering leaves, pulling at his ankles, stroking his face. Moonlight spattered him through the skeletal branches overhead. Luc stumbled forward, through the darkness and the light . . .

The shed was halfway up, made of plywood sections, doors, strips and patches of felt and creosoted board. Declan hesitated outside. Lee caught up with him and pushed at a particular section of board and it gave, swung inward. Inside was no warmer, and seemed somehow damper. There was a strip of mushy carpet on

113

the floor, and a ledge. The smell was raw, suggesting rank growth and rich decay.

Lee fiddled about with something on the ledge, struck a match, and suddenly there was candlelight, absurdly romantic. Declan stood in the doorway, silhouetted now, a solid, cautious figure. He fingered the camera in his coat pocket.

Lee set the candle back on the ledge and moved things around the tiny, chaotic space until there was room to sit on the floor, and cushions for the head. He sat, stretched out his legs, folded his arm behind his head, grinned, his face alight with anticipation and lustful heat. Declan watched him from the doorway.

Lee produced cans from his pockets, and handed one to Declan. Declan sipped tiny mouthfuls, while Lee poured rivers of the stuff into his mouth, letting it run over his chin. Declan watched him, following the movements of the throat and Adam's apple, watched the muscles working, drinking him in, absorbing him. Lee finished his can and Declan offered his own, which was received and despatched in minutes. Lee had to relieve himself immediately, and stumbled outside, cursing at the cold. He'd been drinking since ten that morning.

He came back in and dropped heavily to his knees, straddling Declan, breathing beery breath on him. He put his cold hands on Declan's neck, and Declan twisted away and laughed. 'Foo-king freezing,' Lee said. Declan regarded him, the grin never leaving his face. He let his eyes travel over Lee's face and body. He reached up with one hand and took hold of the crotch of his trousers.

'I've got an idea,' he said. 'Want to try something?'

. . . suddenly there was someone in his path. He shrank back as the figure turned. Draughts of cold air sprang up around it as its cloak moved. Luc tried to retreat, but his back was to a tree. As if in slow motion he saw the figure turn, saw the great deformed limb-claw swing through

114

frozen air, felt the air part to allow it through, heard the air whisper at its passage. He flinched back . . .

Anna felt Luke tense, felt his toes curl. She stroked his ankle with her foot.

An hour later Lee seemed to be asleep. His hands were bound behind his back, his legs spread and tied to the boards, his jeans round his knees. Declan was on top of him, standing, taking pictures. The flash whined, clicked, whined again. The sounds were exact and correctly calculated. Lee came to and murmured something, and Declan said, 'What?'

'Freezing in here,' Lee said, 'freezing me bloody bollocks off,' and Declan said sorry, I'll not be long.

Before he left Declan loosened the ropes and blew the candle out. Didn't want to start any fires. Lee was out on the floor, his head twisted to one side, face pushed against the floor, trousers hitched back up. Declan patted his rump and pushed his way out of the shed, into the misty night. He brushed himself down as he walked, smoothing out creases, combing his hair with spit-damped fingers. He unwrapped a piece of chewing-gum: not knowing what he did, he made a little figure of a man from the foil, and wrapped him tightly, snugly, in a blanket made from the paper. The moon came out, lighting his way.

12. *Someone's Got to Love Him*

Declan had been gone for two days. Anna had been certain that he would be outside the pub when she went looking for him ten minutes after he'd stormed off. Then she'd been sure he'd be waiting on the doorstep when they got home. She'd called in to Mrs Keyes to see if he was there. She'd waited up till half-past two, sitting stupidly in front of the television. She'd gone out to look in the back garden, in the dark, to see if he'd somehow got in there and collapsed or something.

Luke maintained simply that he was no concern of theirs.

'He just isn't our responsibility,' he said. That was that. 'We're not a bloody social service. Anyway we haven't got the training.'

'Oh, training!' Anna shouted at him. 'Training! For God's sake! You're as bad as they are!'

'Look we just can't be responsible for him. How can we?'

'OK, so who is then? Eh? Bloody doctors? Bloody hospitals? Eh? Or just whoever he happens to find himself rubbing up against out there?'

'Whoever. It isn't us.'

'He was attacked, Luke. Someone slashed him, with a knife. You saw that wound. He isn't looking after himself. He isn't making it. It's not working.'

Luke shook his head.

'It isn't . . .'

'Someone's got to take responsibility for him, Luke.' Her voice was ragged. 'Someone's got to love him. Who will if we don't?'

'We tried, we did our best –'

116

She remembered this line from their first few attempts at IVF. He was always giving up on things.

'Oh for God's sake, he was here less than a week. Just a few days.'

'So how long do you think he should be here?'

'Until – until –'

'Anyway, I thought you didn't like him. I thought he gave you the creeps.'

'I didn't say that. I never said that.'

'Yeah you did. You said exactly that. The first time he was here, in the kitchen. Remember?'

An odd little twist inside when he'd shaken her hand, touched her. A little twist of revulsion. Was it?

She remembered his face when he'd come to her, bleeding, collapsing. *I need you.* And afterwards: *you saved me.*

'That was before,' she said lamely.

'I just don't understand why you're so worked-up about it.'

'Him! Him, not it, he's not an it . . .'

This line *Luke* remembered from some interminable bloody all-night row about the bloody IVF. *It won't be an it, it'll be a he or a she.*

'OK so what do you think we should do? Go out and find him?'

'Yes. Yes, actually, I don't think that's a bad idea at all.'

'It's a ridiculous idea. How do you think we're ever going to find him again now?' *He knows where we are anyway,* Luke thought, *and I didn't tell him, he just knew. There was only one way he could have known, and that was by –*

'There aren't that many places he could be, not round here.'

– following me. Following me back from the shops or the swimming-pool or the tube. Watching me, singling me out, then waiting for me, waiting out of sight, walking behind me, right up to the doorstep.

'You know the places they hang out.'

(Had he stopped at the doorstep?)

'Anna, he's gone. I think we should just forget about him. I honestly think that's the best thing to do.'

'Just pick him up and then drop him. Like a puppy for Christmas –'

'Oh please –'

'Only when he rips up the carpet or shits on the floor or barks all night you drive him somewhere and dump him? Is that what you think?'

Luke tightened his mouth. This wasn't going to go away, he realized. It had become an Issue. Perfect, just perfect. She had that look about her. He surprised himself when he recognized it. She hadn't had it for so long that he'd forgotten how well he knew it, that he even had a name for it.

The baby look.

13. *Do you want to see some pictures?*

Declan sat on one side of the desk, facing two policemen. A third opened the door, said something, and shut the door again. One of the two facing him stood and went out.

Declan watched the remaining policeman, saw the short hair and the hard face.

'Been a naughty boy, haven't we?' said the policeman, and sat back in his chair, shaking his head.

'Yes sir, sorry sir,' said Declan, certain that the policeman must be right but unclear as to the details. 'I'm sure you're right, sir.'

The policeman continued to regard him, picking at his fingernails. Nothing happened for a few minutes, and Declan and the policeman both jumped when the door banged open again.

The second policeman came back in, holding a cardboard file in his fist. He whacked it down on the table in front of Declan. He stood leaning over the desk, his face closer to Declan's than Declan wanted it to be.

'Been a naughty boy, haven't we?' he said, and Declan said yes sir, sorry sir.

'Do you want to see some pictures?' Policeman Two said, eyebrows raised so high that they almost disappeared into his hair. 'Would you like to have a look?'

'Thank you sir,' Declan said, feeling his way carefully with these big, overly-animated figures. 'Don't mind if I do, thanks.'

Policeman Two turned to Policeman One and licked his lips.

119

'Hear that?' he said, and Policeman One said yeah I heard him. Bastard.

'He said he wanted to look at the pictures. Even though he doesn't know what kind of pictures they are. Does he?'

Policeman One said, 'He knows all right. Scum.'

'Don't you want to know what kind of pictures I've got in my little file here?' enquired Policeman Two, stroking the cover, his voice so laced with what he intended to be menace and sarcasm that it came out sounding genial.

'OK sir. What –' Declan wetted his lips. He was picking up the rhythm of it now. 'What kind of pictures would they be then sir?'

'I think you'll probably like them,' said One, and turned to Two. 'Don't you think he'll probably like them?'

'Fucking love them. Fucking animal.' He wetted his lips. 'He'll probably come in his pants.'

Two sat down again, sighed heavily, and looked hard at Declan. Declan watched them watching him, watched their four eyes and twenty fingers as they fiddled with fingernails and files and cigarette lighters. They were fidgeting a lot, he thought. He pulled out the little foil man he'd made last night from his gum wrapper and unfolded the paper blanket. The policemen watched him.

Two sighed again, shucked his head to the side, and pushed the cardboard file over the desk to Declan.

'Have a good look,' he said, and licked his lips. 'Take your time.'

Declan glanced at the tape machine on the desk. Not on. Weren't they supposed to record things these days?

He opened the file. Inside were some sheets of flimsy, shiny paper, with pictures on, and strings of numbers and letters, date stamps, scrawled initials at top and bottom. The pictures were grainy, greyey-blue and you could see lines going across them. Declan could imagine the kind of machine that had printed them out, the whining, burring sound it would make.

He held the first one up. It was a little difficult to make out what it was a picture of, at least at first, because the contrast was too high and the right-hand edge had smeared. Then he got it: the whitish smears were flesh, human flesh, arm, back, neck. It was a picture of someone's chest and stomach. The flesh was blotched, there were patches of black and grey on it. Bruises, presumably. Many bruises, overlapping. There were also smears, splashes, discoloured patches. Blood. Anything else? He wasn't sure. It just wasn't a very good reproduction.

He looked up at Two, who was watching him, a clumsy sneer plastered over his face.

'Like it?' Two said, and Declan said yes sir, and turned to the next picture.

This was a picture taken from the back. There were several marks on the back, like on the first picture, and a ring round the neck. The head was all swollen up, darker grey. Again a lot of grey blood all around. There was a chair and what could have been part of a table in the background. The other pictures were all much the same, and Declan couldn't be sure if they were of different people. He looked at each one with great attention.

'So. *Mr* Sargeant,' said Two, and folded his arms.

'Yes. I see. Thank you,' said Declan, and folded the file up again and pushed it to one side.

'So you see, we know all about it,' said One, and looked hard at Declan.

'Well, you've got all the pictures haven't you?' Declan said, 'you've certainly got all the pictures all right.'

'Someone saw you. She saw you walking up to the allotments with someone, a boy. She saw you come back again, she estimates, about an hour later. Without a boy. So we were wondering if you wouldn't mind telling us where he disappeared to.'

'What was she doing watching me?' Declan asked, not

angry, just out of curiosity. The idea of it surprised and pleased him.

'She saw you, that's all. And she says that this is not the first time she's seen you, not at all.'

'She watches me all the time?' Declan asked, delighted with the idea. He so often had the feeling that he was being watched. It was good to have the feeling confirmed. 'Can I meet her? Do you think she'd mind?'

One laughed, and Two laughed along with him, so Declan laughed as well.

'Oh, well, I don't think there'll be any need for you to meet her. Not yet anyway. You'll meet her in good time. But right now you've got a bit of explaining to do, haven't you?'

'Yes sir.'

He scanned their faces, anxiously, trying to get a foothold into their minds, trying to work out what they wanted. They wanted something. They wanted him to say something, about the allotments and the pictures.

'Is that where you do it, up at the allotments?'

'Yes sir, that's right.'

'Always there, not anywhere else?'

'No sir, never anywhere else, just there. That's where I do it.'

'Well that's strange, because some of the people in these pictures, they weren't found at the allotments, they were found in all sorts of different places. Railway lines, ditches, squats, all over the place. How do you account for that?'

'Well, I don't know how to account for it sir –'

'You maybe move them, after you've done it?'

'Move them?'

'You could put them in the back of a car, drive them somewhere and dump them.'

'Where would I get a car sir?'

'You could borrow it from a friend of yours. Couldn't you?'

'Yes sir.' A tilt of the head, a tightening of the mouth. 'Well except that no-one I know has got a car. Except

Luke, and he wouldn't like me borrowing it, I can't drive anyway –'

'Oh come on . . .'

'I could learn though, couldn't I? I could have lessons. Just like anyone else.'

'Now Declan you don't expect us to believe . . .'

'Or maybe I can drive but I just don't know it?'

They all laughed again, and One looked at Two who looked back again, and shrugged.

'All right son.' Two had had enough, and stood, indicating that Declan was free to go. They'd finished playing with him.

'But I did it,' Declan said in a rush, suddenly understanding what they wanted from him. 'All those people in the pictures. I did all of them. Then I drove them round in my car and put them in railways and things, like you said.'

'OK son. You're a killer, obviously,' Two said, and gestured for Declan to leave. Declan stood.

'You're free to go, Mr Sargeant,' One said. 'We're going to be watching you now. Don't forget that.'

'Thank you sir,' Declan, downcast that he'd let them down. 'It was me that did it all, all of it.'

'I know son. Off you go now. On your way.'

'Or if it wasn't me, maybe I could find out who it was for you. Ask some questions?'

The policemen were ushering him out and into the corridor. One clapped him on the shoulder.

'That's it son. You go out there and find him for us.'

'Yes sir. In fact I think I know who it was already.'

'Good for you. You go off and catch him then.'

'Yes sir. Thank you.'

'OK son,' Two said and the two men disappeared into a room. Declan left the police station, thinking about Luke's car, and the crab people.

1813

'Tuke organised an entire ceremonial around these observations. There were social occasions in the English manner, where everyone was obliged to imitate all the formal requirements of social existence; nothing else circulated except the observation that would spy out any incongruity, any disorder, any awkwardness where madness might betray itself.'

M. Foucault, *Madness and Civilisation*
(referring to 'tea-parties' at Tuke's Retreat at York, to which the inmates were invited alongside staff, and watched)

14. *You Made a Monkey out of Me*

There were a few places that Anna knew about. The most likely was round the side of the British Rail station at the top of the High Road. There were some boarded-up shops and an alleyway where you often saw them. She cruised past as slowly as she could manage, peering out into the darkness. She saw some but she couldn't make out any faces, they were on the wrong side of the road. She drove up to the roundabout and came back down. They were closer now but she still couldn't be sure.

It would have been easier if Luke had come with her, but he had refused. She could do whatever she wanted, he'd said, it was her house, but he wasn't having anything more to do with it.

She parked, illegally, in front of the station and got out. She talked to three or four people, who looked up at her from their little nests, taking in her good shoes and good jacket. No-one knew anything about Declan.

It was after midnight when she caught up with him. Just a shadow in a doorway, but she recognized his shape instantly. She stopped the car and the sound of the door slamming woke him up. He craned his head out and squinted up at her, eyes bright and sharp with alarm. He showed no recognition.

She approached him, slowly; his face registered nothing.

'Declan?'

He didn't move, didn't speak.

'You better come back with me.'

Still nothing.

'Don't you think?'

He stood up, letting the seedy-looking blanket he had wrapped round him fall to the ground.

Anna reached her hand out.

'Come on sweetheart. It's OK.'

He looked at her, looked away.

'Declan? You can't just stay here now can you? Come on.'

'You made a monkey out of me.'

She tried to meet his eye.

'We didn't mean to. We're sorry.'

'Not you. But he did.'

'He didn't mean to, Declan, he meant well.'

'Yeah well.'

He was standing his ground, his eye moving to and from her face.

'He said, come and meet my friends, they'll like you, then he didn't talk to me, and then when I wanted to talk to him he said –'

'I'm sorry, I really am.'

'He told me to shut up. He didn't want me talking in front of his friends. He made a monkey out of me, and no-one, I don't let *anyone* –'

Anna took a step closer; Declan threw up a hand, as if to ward her off.

'We want you to come back. You don't have to do anything you don't want to. We really want you to come back.'

'Yeah well.'

This, she thought, was getting ridiculous.

'Look he's only human, Declan. Like you are, like I am. He's sorry.' Still nothing. 'Please. Please Declan.'

He looked, looked away.

'Please?' She smiled. 'Pretty please?'

He started to fold up the blanket, but she put a hand on his arm.

'Leave it.'

'I want it.'

'OK. OK. Come on.'

He sat beside her in the car. She patted his leg absentmindedly. He went back to sleep, still holding the grubby pink blanket.

Luke was still up when they arrived back at the house. He stood up and looked first at Anna, then at Declan.

'Declan,' said Luke, and couldn't meet his eye. 'I'm glad you're all right. We were worried about you.'

'Yeah well,' said Declan.

'I'm glad you've come back.'

'I have to go to bed now,' Declan said, and went upstairs.

'I just want to have a quick look at his bandage,' Anna said and followed him up.

15. *Melancholy Passing into Mania*

Luke sat in the middle of the darkened auditorium as the pictures flashed up on the big screen at the front. The air conditioning wasn't on: the hall was buzzing with heat.

The person giving the talk, whose name Luke had temporarily forgotten, was in full flow. He had a series of slides to show, all of which were making some point or other about the use of photography in medicine in the final decades of the last century. It was incredibly interesting. Luke was so interested that he kept waking up, jolting forward. It seemed to have been going on for days.

It was part of a three-day seminar called Looking at You Looking at Me, which, the brochure soberly said, was about photography in its social and historical context. It was organized by Luke's old college and when he'd signed the form and sent off the cheque, almost nine months ago, it had seemed almost too interesting to be true. A chance to think about something apart from exam papers and those accursed assessment forms. A chance to think about photography again.

And medical uses of early photographic techniques, particularly psychiatric uses, had seemed a good enough option for the second morning, particularly when you considered the other options for the session, which were Photography under Pinochet and Soviet Sports Photography. I mean, please. How many pictures of men with moustaches could you take? Or women with moustaches, come to that.

Inevitably he was hung-over. Late-night discussions with people who were as committed as he was to the idea of getting totally out of their minds in the subsidized bar were an essential feature of the seminar. Participation, though not strictly compulsory, was fairly inevitable.

Luke tried to wake himself up, squirmed about in the seat. He felt somewhat as if he had just stepped out of a swimming-pool and was sitting in wet swimming trunks. Sweat trickled down from groin to knee. He wondered if anyone would mind if he took his shirt off. It might liven things up a bit, who knew? Maybe everyone would take their shirts off, girls as well as boys, and they could have an orgy. Someone could take pictures. He tried to sit up straighter, tried to concentrate. He had *paid* for this, paid out good money, he should try to get the benefit.

He focused on the screen in front of him. It showed a picture of a woman lying on a bed. It was from the 1880s and had that over-developed, slightly unreal, heightened quality that pictures of the period had. It was an effect of the chemicals used at the time. The woman had a very odd smile on her face, and she was lying in a very odd way, arms held stiffly out, back arched upward, neck twisted round.

Another picture took its place: another woman, wearing the most astonishingly ferocious scowl, again on a bed, again the ungainly posture.

Luke tried to listen to the speaker.

' . . .the great Dr Charcot, the most eminent psychiatrist of his day, and one-time teacher of the young Freud, would give demonstrations of these women to auditoriums of students.'

A picture came up, of a short, pudgy, balding man with a moustache and a faraway look. The great doctor, presumably. He had some horrible piece of medical equipment beside him, all rubber tubes and metal clamps and dials.

'Of course we know now that the contortions and the bizarre facial expressions were not the result of any mental condition, or hysteria as Charcot sincerely believed, but were 'put on', as we'd say now, by the women themselves, who knew exactly what was expected of them and performed on demand. They were encouraged and even coached by their wardens, who also knew what the great doctor wanted and were at pains to see that he got it. None of this was fraudulent in the way that we might think of the term now. The photographs, which were also used as teaching and demonstration materials, were taken by photographers employed by the asylums, in this case the Salpetrière in Paris, purely for this purpose.'

Dear God, Luke thought, don't let me die in here. It was so *hot*! He stretched and leaned back, and met the eye of someone, a woman, who he recognized from last night's late boozing session. What had her name been? Debbie? She grinned conspiratorially and elaborately yawned. He smiled back.

'Each picture was labelled according to the phase of the illness that it was supposed to represent. Thus we have "euphoria", "melancholia", and so on.'

Another picture flicked up onto the screen, grey, slightly blurred. The woman was leaning forward towards the camera: her hands were clutched at her breasts and her face was lit up with an extraordinarily languorous smile, gazing up through demurely lidded eyes. She looked beautiful, ghostly, eerie. Her hair streamed out from her face in a corona. The caption underneath read: 'erotomania'.

She's like Debbie, Luke thought. Well, a little bit anyway. Round the eyes. The woman in the picture was wearing only a diaphanous shift affair, her throat and bosom were very much on show, white and smooth and oddly artificial-seeming. What would Debbie look like in a little flimsy shift, Luke wondered. The same woman, a different picture: 'ecstasy'. The lecturer went on, all seriousness, and Luke wondered how many people in the hall would be able to tell you what exactly it was he was talking about. If you shook them awake first, that is. It all seemed to hinge on whether the poor, white, ghostly women in the pictures were really mad or just posing for the pictures. Just posing for the pictures, apparently. Fine, good, that settled it then, anyone for a drink? Luke yawned again; his jaw felt as if it were about to dislocate. Anyone taking his picture at that moment, he thought, would have no problem diagnosing him as insane. Degenerative mania in his case, probably. Maybe the women in the pictures looked the way they did because they were just bored senseless.

A sheet of pictures came up, rows and rows of mug shots of women: 56 German criminals, according to the caption. Then straightaway another sheet, rows and rows of skulls, apparently also of criminals. The same ones, Luke wondered? It was all getting too bizarre. If I don't get out of here soon, Luke thought, I'm going to run amok with a meat cleaver and when I've finished there won't be anything left worth photographing. He tried to signal to Debbie that he was going, but she had seemingly become entranced by the pictures and her eye was not for catching. Ah well, he would see her later. Definitely. If she lived that long. Luke stood and edged his way along the row, apologizing as he went. People watched him enviously.

1838

'The shock of the electrifying-machine, which is often found beneficial in cases where the powers want rousing, is, in cases of determined obstinacy and bad conduct, equally useful. The terror of the machine will often overcome the vicious inclination.'

Dr Ellis, 'A Treatise on the nature, symptoms, causes, and treatment of insanity'

16. *Rain Fields*

The day was quiet and overcast. Anna drove across London, glancing over at Declan periodically. He sat solidly, hardly even blinking, his eyes fixed on the road ahead. They were going to Rain Fields.

It had been Anna's idea, at least partly.

'Let's do something today Declan,' she'd said, and the sun had briefly streamed through the kitchen window, a beautiful Sunday morning. He was eating Honey Nut Loops, and she'd felt a quick surge of affection for him run through her, the opposite feeling to the little twist she'd felt at their first meeting. With Luke you never quite knew what he was thinking, there always seemed to be things going on underneath, but Declan was so transparent, so completely *there* all the time. He was incapable of lying, of masking his feelings, of parleying one thing into something else. He couldn't sit there and have a part of himself hidden, secreted away, like Luke. He was just raw, himself. His disorder was an affliction, to be sure, but it was also, in some ways, she thought, a blessing, even a gift.

'Anything you feel like doing?' she'd said, and Declan had looked at her, still eating, dribbling milk from his spoon. 'You know, like a day out.'

Declan agreed to everything. She'd gone through her usual day-out list of ideas, the zoo, Covent Garden, Kew. Everything appealed equally, though she couldn't help wondering if he even knew what she meant.

'Do you know what a zoo is, Declan?'

'Yeah. With animals.'

'Have you ever been to one?'

'No. I was going to go once with my mum but she

137

wasn't feeling well so we couldn't. I didn't really want to go anyway,' he said defensively, as if Anna had somehow criticized his mother, 'they tried to say she wasn't a good mother, but how did they know. Huh? Just because she wasn't the same as everyone else, you know, she was different, she had her own ways.' He said this doubtfully, as if it were someone else's explanation for her behaviour. 'The doctors said it was her fault I was like this, she didn't treat me right, but I was happy. I was happy, I can remember. Sometimes we went round the shops together.'

Anna didn't speak. Declan was visibly grappling with something.

'I mean, maybe they were right, maybe she should have taken me to the zoo, maybe she should have given me kisses and that, but she couldn't help how she was, could she? They said she was "lacking in affect", well what does that mean? Huh? They said I never developed right. But I was OK. We were OK. She did her best for me, and let me tell you, I was never hungry, not ever.' Again the defiance.

'Where is she now?' Anna spoke very gently, anxious not to break his mood. She'd never heard him talk about himself like this before.

'Oh she's still in Ireland. In Ballinasloe, last I heard. Do you know where that is?'

Anna smiled, shook her head.

'Well it's in Ireland. It's not far from Galway. You know where that is don't you?'

She shook her head again. Declan looked at her as if he simply couldn't believe such ignorance.

'Is that where you were born?' she asked.

He shook his head. 'No. We travelled about a bit, you know. We were always on the move!' He smiled, and she could see him as a little boy, walking beside his stiff, distant mother, walking down a dusty track from nowhere to nowhere, somewhere in rural Ireland. 'She said we had dancers' feet, her and me, that was why we could never stay in one place.'

'Do you ever hear from her?'

'No.' He was becoming uneasy, she could see his eyes shifting about. He stood up suddenly.

'Let's go somewhere. OK?'

'The zoo?'

'Yeah. Let's go to the zoo.'

No discussion, no arguments, just yeah. Anna laughed. If you had this conversation with Luke, she thought, you'd immediately be wading knee-deep through a whole lot of shit about animal welfare or eight thousand reasons why he wanted to drive out to some bloody wasteland to take pictures of *mud* or whatever it was. She looked at Declan: he said yes, and that was it. There was no bubbling undertow or hidden meaning, there was just yes.

'OK.' She leaned back on the counter, folded her arms. 'You ever been to Kew Gardens?'

'No.'

'D'you want to go? It's really nice, you can go up to the top of the palm house and look down –'

'OK.'

' – and then these jets of steam come out and drip all over the – yes?'

He nodded his head. OK.

'Thames Barrier. National Portrait Gallery. Brick Lane market.' Yes. OK. Yes.

'Declan, I give up. Where do you *want* to go? Really?'

'I don't want to go anywhere.'

'Come on. There must be something you want to do.'

He didn't speak for a moment, then muttered something into the bowl, his mouth full of cereal and milk.

'I'm sorry?'

He kept his eyes down.

'I want to go back to Rain Fields.'

It hadn't been possible to get him to explain clearly where it was. He seemed to think it was hundreds of miles away, though he was adamant also that it was in London. North, south? No, he didn't think so. She had asked him was there anything nearby, a landmark or anything? He said there was a railway station. Oh great, she'd said, well that certainly narrows it down. Finally she had a brainwave, a directory of mental health services in London. She'd had it for years, had used it perhaps twice. Rain Fields, Long Stay Facility, Woodside Road, Wood Green. Thirty, forty minutes away at most.

He'd told her very little about his time there, but indirectly he'd told her a lot. It was his measure of how things ought to be done. Quite often he'd said something like: 'At Rain Fields, they do it like this', whatever it was. Long Stay meant sheltered accommodation, though on quite a big scale. It wasn't a halfway house or anything of that sort, it was a fully-fledged home. There would be some degree of security, and visits and outings would be organized and accompanied, but there would also be a great deal of freedom on a daily basis, and there would be occupational therapy and other things. Activities, he'd said. Discos in the TV Lounge alternate Fridays, step aerobics on Tuesdays. Cookery classes. It wasn't some grim asylum, she knew that. Declan had been in one of those before his stay at Rain Fields, and had said next to nothing about it. He seemed to have a superstitious dread of even mentioning it, in case he had to go back. She knew he had had ECT at one point when he'd become depressed. There had also been an operation, he hadn't been quite clear what it had been for, but claimed that it had given him special powers. She guessed that he had been given some such absurd explanation by the staff. What kind of powers, she'd asked him? He'd blushed and said, well they said that after the operation I could have intimate relations with as many women as I wanted to. Intimate relations, Anna thought. Their stupid coy bloody double-speak. It was almost funny. Who told you that, she'd demanded, about the special powers? It sounded like the most outrageous nonsense to get him to agree to some probably completely unnecessary operation.

'Declan? Who told you that?'

'One of the orderlies in the ward where I was waiting to go in,' Declan said. 'I've already got a girlfriend, we've had intimate relations and she's going to have a baby,' Declan had said, and the orderly had winked and said, 'Well we already know all about that. But now you'll be able to have as many girlfriends as you like.'

'What do you mean? Do you mean I'll have special powers?' Declan had asked, and the orderly had winked again and said yes. Anna seethed at the injustice of it, the *insanity* of it, telling someone with an already deranged sense of self that they were being given special powers. It was exactly the kind of belief that would have put him into their hands in the first place. Outrageous.

They chatted in the car, though Declan, fiddling with Luke's camera, seemed preoccupied. She asked him about the injury, how was it feeling. It felt OK. She suddenly found it possible to ask him how he got it, who had done it to him, had he told the police? It was an accident, he said. No it wasn't, Anna stated firmly, it was no accident. I didn't mean to, I was just trying it out, I didn't know the knife was so sharp, I wouldn't of done it if I'd known it was going to bleed so much, honest. She closed her eyes for a second, appalled. He'd done it himself. Of course. And the other scars? She didn't ask. Poor bloody Declan. Another little thought strayed into her head, and she said, apropos of nothing in particular,

'Why did you put my metal fish into the toilet cistern?'

'I never,' Declan said.

'Declan, we both know that you did. If you're going to lie to me, you're going to have to do a bit better than that. Frankly.'

He was quiet for a few moments, then he said: 'I just thought he ought to be in water.'

Can't argue with that, Anna thought, and laughed,

patted his leg. Halfway there, Anna had been struck by a thought: if Declan had been discharged from Rain Fields, then it was likely that the others had been too: it was likely that the place had been shut down. She didn't want to mention this.

They came to Wood Green underground station, and Declan craned his head to watch it go past.

'I've been there,' he said.

Anna had to grab glances at the A-Z on her lap as she drove, but she thought she knew the place. She carried on up High Road, past the police station, and suddenly there was a high wall on the right, with bushes and tall shrubs poking up above it, and a discreet roll of razor wire across the top. She slowed down to a crawl.

They came to a gateway, locked. Anna drove past, looking for somewhere to park. She found a spot round the corner, and they walked back to the gate. Declan had the camera Luke had lent him round his neck.

'All locked up,' she said, rattling the gate. 'Sorry.'

'They must all have gone out somewhere,' Declan remarked, and started walking away.

'Declan? Where are you going?'

'There's another gate round the back,' he said, and she caught up with him. She put a comforting hand on his arm.

The gate round the back was locked also, but you could see over it. The main building rose up from the surrounding grass and foliage. It looked disused. A big, solid late-Victorian Gothic pile, with turrets and even an incipient bell-tower. Declan stared at it, unblinking, and Anna came up behind him and put her arm round him.

'Declan?'

He was silent and unyielding beside her.

'I think everyone's gone. I think they must have closed it down.'

The windows looked down, empty, onto the warm overcast day. Grass and weeds dotted the drive up to the

142

great arched brick front-door surround. Anna saw that a couple of the windows were broken. There were traces of green poking out from the gutters and ledges. She guessed that if you went inside you would find little piles of lager cans and old newspaper, a strong smell of human urine, evidence of recent though casual occupancy. You might also find stackable chairs, maybe iron bedsteads, cupboards gaping open, the wood cracked and warped from long disuse. Stairwells and corridors and rooms, dark or with great splashes of sunlight falling onto them, dusty, still.

She gave Declan a squeeze.

'Where did everyone go?' he said, and Anna could only hold onto him. He took a picture, framing it carefully. She kept hold of his hand all the way back to the car. She gave him a peck on the cheek before they got in.

17. *Self-Esteem Low I'll Bet*

The accommodation was a student hall, a place that
Luke hadn't even thought of in ten years. Thus, when
Anna tried to ring him he had to be sought out and
found. He was located in a room on the second floor,
where there was something a bit like a party in progress.
Not quite like a student party because they were drinking good quality alcohol, no-one was talking about
Kafka, and they had all had at least a decade apiece of
experience in smoking dope, so were not sick in the sink
or out of the window. Debbie was there too, coinciden-
tally. She was banging on about how people always
seemed to think she should be modelling for the pictures, not taking them. Aren't you on the wrong end of
that camera darlin' kind of thing. Luke could understand why, but was sympathizing when he heard his
name being called from down the hall. He got up slightly
too fast and had to hold onto the wall for a second.

He was a touch breathless when he reached the
phone.

'Hello?'

'Luke? It's me.'

'Is everything all right?'

'Of course.'

'You're sure?'

'Luke I'm fine, Declan's fine, he hasn't raped and
scalped me or anything. Well not yet anyway. Maybe he
just doesn't fancy me.'

'Turned down by a serial rapist eh? Self-esteem low
I'll bet.'

'There's always another one round the corner. So
how's it going then? Tedious?'

'Appalling. Actually I was about to string myself up when you rang.'

'You're just miserable because I'm not there.'

'That'll be it I daresay.'

'So. Are you missing me you bastard?'

'Yeah.'

'Oh yes it really *sounds* like it.'

'I am. I mean, you know, not every *second* or anything.'

'You should be missing me every second. Strictly speaking.'

'Right. Well I'll just have to work harder.'

'Declan says hello.'

'Tell him hello back. I think he'd like it here actually. They're all fuck-ups too.'

'Luke!'

'Sorry. So. Any news?' He wanted to hurry it along just a bit actually, he wanted to get back to sympathizing with Debbie.

'Me and Declan had a day out.'

'Yeah?'

'Yeah. Poor old Declan.'

'Uhuh.'

'Oh I can tell you're really interested.'

'I am. Look, I'm in the middle of something actually. Why don't I ring you tomorrow?'

'I don't know. Why don't you?'

'I will.'

'Bastard.'

'I love you too.'

'Bastard. Fuck you then.'

'Kissy kissy. Uhm-uhm.'

'I might be out when you ring tomorrow. Out shagging.'

'Speak to you then.'

He hung up and took himself back to the room on the second floor. Debbie was now being sympathized with by someone else. Luke found someone to sympathize with him instead.

145

18.   *The Single Most Ridiculous Thing I've Ever Heard*

Anna and Declan sat in the front room watching television. Anna sat in her chair, Declan was sprawled out on the sofa. He had a can of Guinness open in front of him, though she hadn't seen him drink any. The programme was something about political lobbyists and their effect on something or other to do with some piece of legislation or another, she wasn't too sure what. It was all a blur of impossibly boring men in blue suits and young women with businesslike hair and winning ways. They were coming to complicated arrangements with each other.

Declan appeared very relaxed, though she had the strongest impression that he was monitoring her rather than the television.

'Declan? Are you following this?'

'Yeah.'

'Oh.'

She glanced sideways at him.

'Do you want to see if there's something else on?'

'All right.'

He didn't move.

'Have you got the remote?'

'Oh yeah.'

He flicked through the other channels, very quickly, no more than a few seconds for each, round and round, ended up back with the blue suits and the determined women.

'Is this what you want to watch?'

He shrugged and switched round the channels again,

landed on something different. An advert for antiperspirant.

'You want to watch this?' She was seeking information only, not challenging him.

'If you do,' he said.

'No, but what do you want to watch?'

He shrugged again.

'Whatever. Whatever you want.'

'You don't care? At all?'

'This is fine.'

She pondered this for a moment.

'That's the single most ridiculous thing I've ever heard. "Where do you want to go Declan?" "Anywhere." "What do you want to do today?" "Whatever you want to do." "Do you want butter on your potatoes?" "If you do."'

He kept his eyes on the screen.

'It's all right for you to want things, Declan, it's all right to say what you want.'

'I don't want anything.'

'Yes you do. You just won't say what it is you do want. Why is that?'

'Don't know.'

'Yes you do.'

'I *don't*.' Quietly insistent.

She watched him watching the television, his eyes flickering over the images. What was going on behind the eyes? What sense did any of it make to him? What sense did the world make?

Who are you anyway?

'OK. OK, Declan. You may get away with this when Luke's around, but not with me.'

'Get away with what?' He turned to look directly at her.

'You know what.' She steeled herself to say it. 'Being a mental patient. Being a person with a passive-dependent bloody personality balls-up or whatever it's supposed to be called. Luke may go along with it, but I'm not having it, frankly.'

147

She saw his eyebrows go up, but his eyes stayed on the screen.

'OK. I'll tell you what. You take me somewhere tonight.'

'Where?'

'Well now, I think you're going to have to think of somewhere. All by yourself. Somewhere you want to go. Not somewhere you think I might want to go or Luke might want to go. You.'

'I don't want to go any –'

'Declan, now fair's fair. Did I, or did I not, drive you several hundred miles all the way to Rain Fields earlier on?'

'It was all shut down.'

'I know, I know, I'm sorry. I really am, Declan,' she said, and her voice softened, lost the facetious, slightly hectoring tone she'd been using a moment earlier. 'But you can hardly blame me for that, now can you? Fair's fair, and I want you to take me out. Somewhere. I don't care where. Anywhere.'

His eyes were still on the screen, but she knew that he was working feverishly, trying to second-guess her, trying to figure out exactly what she wanted him to say, wanted him to be. Nothing was simple for him, nothing came easily. Identities flickered under his skin, behind his eyes. He had to invent them, second by second.

'Declan. You don't have to do all this crap. You really don't. You can just be yourself.'

Just be yourself, that's all you have to do. But what if being yourself meant a perpetual slipping and sliding in between other people's expectations of what your self was? What if you had no self to be, only reflections of other people's selves? What if there was no you?

Poor bloody Declan. It all seemed so unfair. In many ways, she thought, it was far crueller to have released him like this. In the back ward of an asylum he could have hidden, blended effortlessly in, and probably gone unnoticed his whole life. What kind of a life that would be was another matter, but what kind of life was this for him? Out here in the wide world, in the pitiless daylight, he was constantly having to try to be normal, like everyone else, without the least idea of how to do it, and every imperfect effort he made was mercilessly exposed to view, to condemnation and even ridicule. Surely it was kinder to leave him alone somewhere where he knew exactly what was expected of him and was able effortlessly to perform it. He must feel like a circus animal, she thought, fearing at every moment that he would displease his trainer and get a lashing. Constantly on display, with an audience that was waiting all the time for a flaw in the performance.

She stood and came behind the sofa. She put her hands on his neck.

'I'm sorry I shouted. I wasn't shouting at you.' Mummy isn't angry, she's just upset.

After about a minute Declan said, 'I've thought of somewhere we can go.'

Moonlight played over her hair, showing up copper threads amongst the black. It cast hard shadows over her face, exaggerating the contours, the dips and hollows of cheek and chin. Her cloak swept out, draughts of cold air and mist rising up like wraiths. Her carriage was slow and secure, with only a slight list to the side where the claw lay, hidden, coiled at her side. Luc followed her, abashed, almost ashamed at his own clumsiness. She swept aside branches and creepers, her movements the quick, certain movements of one accustomed to life in a forest. Luc followed . . .

Anna followed a few steps behind. Declan was moving fast, confidently, where she was constantly finding something underfoot to detain her. It was a very poor path, very uneven, obstructed in places by overhanging foliage and the shells of old furniture and tyres. There was maybe half an hour of daylight left in the sky. A low, full moon was starting to rise, pink, ghostly.

149

He wouldn't tell her at first what their destination was. He had directed her to White Hart Lane station, and they had parked. He walked purposefully, head down, swiping at the occasional tall plant. She had thought he intended Tottenham Cemetery, but that wasn't where they were.

'Declan? You're not telling me that all this time you've been weeding raspberry bushes or whatever you people do in these places without telling anyone?'

He strode ahead, no answer. She still wasn't completely certain of his mood. She didn't know how much she'd upset him earlier on, though he didn't seem upset exactly, he just seemed determined. Maybe she'd dented his pride and he was showing her that he could be a man, his own man. The thought alarmed her, a quick bite of anxiety like a wind in the treetops.

I've thought of somewhere we can go, he'd said. Obviously, she hadn't been expecting *La Traviata* at Covent Garden, or even a Pizza Hut, but somehow she hadn't expected this, a short drive up to the allotments. Never talkative, Declan had lapsed into complete silence, and Anna found herself, for once, at a loss.

I know nothing whatsoever about him, she thought, less than nothing. Was she about to find something out? A gust of wind came out of nowhere, and she shivered. He was a few steps ahead of her, ignoring her completely, not even looking to check that she was still following.

She caught a stray scent on the air, just a whiff of something, at first she couldn't place it. She had noticed it in the car as well, but hadn't attended to it, it hadn't seemed important. But it did now. It was Calvin Klein, Luke's Calvin Klein, the stuff he put on maybe twice a year, if the occasion demanded. He could only rarely be persuaded to use it, on the grounds that it cost a lot and had to be used sparingly. It was for best. He had been wearing it, for instance, on their anniversary dinner when they'd had lobster, with Paul and Lauren.

150

And now Declan was wearing it. Just a dab. To escort her up to some deserted allotments.

Another tug of wind, she caught now another smell, the strong damp smell of turned earth, heaps of vegetable matter composting quietly, damp wood, damp soil. The two smells came together and she almost ran, back to the car, away from this silent, unknowable man and his unimaginable intentions, back to bright lights and ordinary routines.

As if sensing her sudden alarm, Declan turned round and gave her a small, tight smile.

'It's just round here,' he said, and she had to smile back at him. 'Nearly there now.'

He left the main path and headed up the boundary between neighbouring plots. She waited at the path. He surely couldn't mean her to follow him. There was nothing up there. A bird was twittering nearby, singing the sun down. She stood, undecided, feeling at a loss. She really wasn't dressed for this kind of thing. She should have been in jeans and boots, not heels and tights and a long split skirt. She was all wrong. Really, she was thinking, really I shouldn't be here. Somewhere, it could have been miles away, she heard a burglar alarm sounding. A second bird answered the first. The ground and the sky and the trees all faded to the same colour. It was getting colder.

Declan stood beside a shack or a heap of some kind, then he had disappeared. She had lost him. She screwed up her face trying to peer through the gloom.

Suddenly there was a light, a wavering changeable thing, coming from inside the shack or whatever it was. The shed. There must be a window, she thought, and Declan must have lit a candle and it's shining out. So he must have candles, matches. He must know where everything is. He must have been here before. Often.

She thought of the car, correctly parked in the station forecourt. She wanted to be in it, with the radio on. She knew where all the switches and buttons were in the car. She didn't seem to know where anything was here with birds twittering in her ear and a fat pink moon slipping up behind the trees. And Declan, somewhere out of sight, in a shed with a lighted candle.

Was this his idea of a date?

Have you got a girlfriend, Declan?

She was about to go, just go and leave him to do whatever he wanted to do up here, but not with her, when he reappeared, a dim lumbering figure in the half darkness. He came back towards the path, where she was standing, and called out to her:

'You coming up?'

An odd little twist inside her. She had known exactly where it had been, but had refused to recognize it. It was in her womb. It was exactly the feeling she'd had when they'd done the implanting of the zygote. The fertilized egg. As she'd lain on the table under the bright light while they fiddled with their turkey baster or whatever the surgical equivalent was, she had felt it, something so small you couldn't see it. So important that it had legal status. A possible person, a little boy or a little girl, a man or a woman, who might go on to help produce further little girls and little boys. A microscopic blob of stuff, placed with tremendous, even superstitious caution, inside her, where it would start trying to do the extraordinary thing and turn into a person. And she could *feel* it there, as she lay on her bed too terrified of disturbing it to move, terrified every time she sneezed, every time she went to the toilet, every time she turned over, that she would dislodge it from its precarious perch inside her and send it tumbling down. She had *felt* it, each time, and it had been alive, for days, until she bled, sobbing, distraught, unconsoled in the bathroom. Flushed away. But it had been *alive*, and she had felt it, an odd little twist. In her womb.

'Aren't you coming up?'

They gave me special powers, I can sleep with any woman I want. Magical potency. Madness! The birds had fallen quiet as the light leached away into the ground and the sky and the trees. The burglar alarm rang on, far away, unheeded, as the huge moon ascended into the sky and she felt the flare inside as she ovulated, became fertile. Moonlight spattered her.

Luke sat at the open window with Debbie. The smoke from her joint curled up and out into the darkness. Luke took it from her, closed his eyes as he inhaled, held the smoke. They sat and talked softly. Watching the moon.

At first Declan was quick and clumsy, but she was patient and he learned quickly. She was amazed at the difference between his ordinary self and his sexual self. Dressed he was jerky, unsure, diffident: undressed, his body expressed itself effortlessly, his movements smoothed out, became relaxed, confident, even playful. He had the advantage of wanting to please and had an almost uncanny ability to discern what did.

It didn't surprise him that Anna wanted him, not at all, people had always wanted him; in all the institutions he had ever been in there had been those who wanted him, men mostly. Sometimes women. As far back as he could remember he had been trying to figure out what they wanted him to do, how he was to please them.

He had to go a bit careful because of the stitches; she traced the outline of his bandage, feeling the muscle underneath. Afterwards they lay, not speaking, on the damp floor and she looked out of the little window, then slept. Declan watched her.

19. *Right Now, Please*

Anna was dreaming of thunder and lightning. The lightning flashed, but the thunder didn't roar, or rumble or growl, it merely whirred, which, she thought, was odd. She turned to her companion, some incredibly ancient woman like Mrs Keyes and asked, was it like this when you were little? Mrs Keyes said, you were always a good girl, but look at you now. Help me with this shopping, dear, it's a terrible weight, but Anna shook her head. I don't think I can, I don't think I can move my arms, she said, and twisted about on the floor. Something was digging into her side. You'll have to get someone else to help you, she called out as Mrs Keyes went away, I can't help anyone, I can't —

A flash of lightning, a whirr of thunder.

She woke up to some kind of light, not the moonlight, but a brilliant flare close to her face, a flash, blinding her, leaving patches of colour in her vision.

— I can't move my arms.

She tried to sit up straight, found that she couldn't, because she couldn't move her arms, they were behind her back, the muscles and joints were aching faintly, her arms were numb except for a faint tingling. Something was digging into her wrists.

Her arms were tied.

She lifted her head up and squinted into the dark. It came again, a few feet away, the flash and the whirr.

She tried to remember where she was. There was a sour, damp smell, there was dampness unpleasantly underneath her. The shed at the allotments. With Declan. So where was he?

'Declan?'

She struggled to lever herself upright, struggled to stay calm, she wanted to scream. Another flash, blinding, disorientating.

'Declan?'

Someone came close to her, she could feel the heat of his body. She kicked out but her foot didn't move, her feet were tied also. She screamed.

He came in close to her.

'You all right?'

She couldn't see his face, but the voice was Declan's.

'What are you doing, Declan?' Her voice was level enough but underneath it was pure panic, scalding.

'Won't be a minute,' he said. Another flash.

'Declan. Would you mind untying me please?' She was lying on the floor of a shed at night with a lunatic who had tied her up and was taking pictures. So what tone of voice was appropriate, what register? Experienced as she was in talking to all kinds of men in all kinds of circumstances she found herself at a loss. One thing was for sure, she wasn't going to panic. Another flash.

'Declan!'

'Just a few more.'

He backed away from her, presumably to get a different composition. She was abruptly reminded of something; the movement was familiar to her, she had seen it before. The memory was confusing. She tried again to kick but succeeded only in vibrating. She could feel the sweat breaking, trickling over her. Tone of voice, she thought, tone of voice, I must speak the right words in the right tone of voice, otherwise he's going to

Thought failed her for a moment as panic cut in, boiled up, milk in a pan, she thrashed, unable to bear the pressure of the bindings round her wrists and ankles for another second, not another *second* –

'For Christ's sake – you –'

155

Flash and whirr, flash and whirr. The tone of voice she was seeking came to her suddenly, confidently, seemingly out of nowhere.

'Declan. That's enough now.' Mummy's not angry, though she might be in a minute. End of patience. 'I won't tell you again, Declan. Now I want you –' she swallowed, her throat terribly dry, ' – I want you to untie these ropes right now. Right now please.'

'I'll just be –'

'Not in a minute Declan, right now please.' She heard him pause, consider. It was working. Was it?

'I'm waiting. This minute, Declan.'

She felt him approach her. He had the camera round his neck. And in his hand?

She tried to shrink back against the wall, into the mushy floor, as she saw the glimmer of light on what he was holding in his hand. What kind of light he had in his eyes.

The voice came on again, unbidden. It was as if she had been rehearsing it for years, maybe all her life.

'I won't ask you again. Now I'm going to count to three.' He edged closer, she flinched, her eyes slammed shut and she had to force them open again. She had to see him, had to see his face, his eyes. Had to see who he was.

'And if you haven't untied me by then –' There was no second part to the sentence, she knew that. Did he? She couldn't tell. His eyes flickered. She had to try to invent someone for him to be, just by her tone, her words. She had to invent him by inventing herself. She had to get it right.

'One.'

The light glanced off the object he held in his hand. It was a pair of shears, rusty, pitted, but sharp enough no doubt. Sharp enough for what? She forced herself not to look at them, to keep her attention on his face.

'Two.'

He screwed up his face, clenched his eyes tight shut. There was some kind of battle going on. She couldn't breathe. There was no sound. He opened his eyes.

'Three.' Barely audible.

But it was enough. His face was the face of a child, his eyes a little boy's. He had to come in *this minute* and have his tea. He would do as he was told. He lifted the shears, and she flinched again, purely a reflex; he jabbed and sliced and scissored at the twine until it frayed and gave. She sat up and rubbed herself to get the circulation back. Pins and needles flared up and down her arms like fire. She started picking at the twine tying her left leg. Declan attacked the other one with the shears.

'I thought –' he said, then stopped, confused. He looked cross, resentful, sullen. 'I mean, I thought he wanted me to, I thought you . . .'

'I don't care what you thought,' she said. 'I don't want to know what you thought.'

She glanced at him as he hacked at the twine.

'It's OK, Declan, I'm not angry with you. Let's get you home. Huh? What do you say?' Her heart shook and pounded as the twine snapped and unravelled. She stood and forced herself to smile, take his hand. They walked back to the car, not speaking. I thought he wanted me to, she thought, isn't that what he said? And he had seemed familiar for a moment, he had been someone, someone whose every move she knew well. The name wasn't long coming: Luke. Luke held his camera in exactly that way, ducked back and forward in that way, did everything, in fact, exactly that way. She held Declan's hand, and it was like holding nothing, a flat dead thing in her hand. She kept an eye on him as he sat beside her in the car. She had the strongest impression of looking at something that had gone out.

They passed a police station on the way home. I should just take him in there and surrender him to them, she thought, just give him up and have done with it. I can't manage him any more.

The police, of course, might want to know certain

157

things. Such as, how had she got mixed up with him in the first place? What was she doing with him, in a shed at the allotments? And what exactly had he done to her that she was complaining about? Was she going to bring charges against him?

She pictured herself trying to explain this to Luke. You see, I went with him, alone, in the dark, to this really deserted place, where I knew there would be no-one about, and then I went into this little shed with him. Of course, I never *imagined* he'd do anything like this! Why did I go into the shed with him? Well naturally because . . . because . . . She gave up. There was no good explanation for her behaviour, not for the police, not for Luke.

And anyway, she was damned if the police were going to get their filthy paws on him, make fun of him, lock him up in one of their filthy cells. He wasn't a criminal, he couldn't be held responsible for what he did. No, if she gave him up to anyone, it would be to the social services, to properly qualified people. The same people who'd let him out in the first place. They were the only fit custodians for him. She found that she was bristling suddenly with indignation on his behalf at the very idea of handing him to the police. It would be an outrageous betrayal. No. She would get him home, get him settled, and then she would see what she was going to do.

I'll have to lock him up, she thought, and glanced over at him as he sat quietly beside her. I'll have to lock him up though. I can't take any more chances. The thought had a dismal sound to it. Neither of them spoke all the way home.

They stood in Luke's darkroom. Declan didn't know how to develop the pictures, so Anna was going to help him. It was her idea. The red light was on. She fiddled with the camera, trying to remember how to get the film out. It was a long time since she had used a camera. Luke had pretty much put her off them, with his easy expertise and serious intentions. F stops. Her idea of a camera was something small that had auto everything and a nice stylish steel case. Luke liked dials and wheels and ranks of hieroglyphics. Tiny little numbers which, bafflingly, seemed to go from one to infinity in the space of three-quarters of an inch. And his kind of camera was never easy to get the bloody film out of.

Declan watched her fiddling, with no apparent decrease in his index of her competence. She said she knew how to do it, he believed her, he didn't really know how not to.

Finally she got the film out, and placed it neatly on the counter alongside the shallow plastic trays and the plastic tongs and clothes-pegs. This was as far as she could go. The next part, she knew, involved using the enlarger, a great ugly contraption with a light and a lens and all kinds of bits that slid up and down on a mechanism that always reminded her of a gallows. She was uncertain as to its operation: she didn't know, for instance, where the on switch was.

'Oh I just thought,' she said, 'I'll have to go and get some bicarbonate of soda.'

'What for?' Declan asked respectfully.

'For, you know, for the chemical things. You know? You have to have bicarb or it doesn't work properly.'

'Really?'

'Oh yeah. Stay here, I'll just go and get some.'

She walked to the door, certain that he was going to stop her but he didn't. She went down to the kitchen, then unbolted the basement door. Somewhere down there in the small and cluttered area was a key to every door in the house. Her grandfather had been the kind of man who arranged his tools on hooks on the wall in order of size, who kept his nails and screws in tiny compartments, separated by material and size, thread-type, head-type, countersunk, self-tapping, anodized, and bent. She had been down here many times when she was a little girl. He would be making or mending or just meddling with something, and she would come and watch. He would ask her to fetch things. The big ring of keys had hung on a nail over his workbench. It was something she had coveted for as long as she could remember. Every door in the house, he'd told her. You never know when you're going to need them. A long-forgotten fantasy came back to her, of going round the house with a candle in a tall candlestick and the big ring of keys, locking and unlocking every door. Every door in the house. She was sure they hadn't been cleared out, not by her anyway. Would Luke have thrown them away? Not very likely. They must be here somewhere.

She had told Declan to wait in the darkroom and she was sure he would do just that. He wouldn't wait for ever though. There were endless amounts of things down here, and they were all disgustingly dusty, the kind of dust that gathers over years, gains substance and solidity, takes on shapes. She scrabbled amongst the debris like a lunatic at a jumble sale.

She found them in a black metal box inside another box on top of a cupboard. She lifted them out: they jangled pleasingly, like a tambourine. Each had a little tag tied to the barrel with fine string. Each label had a coloured dot to indicate the floor, and a number. She counted off the doors on the first floor in her mind. Number three. She took the right key firmly in her hand and pressed the ring against her body to dampen the rattle. She made her way back upstairs.

She pulled the door of the darkroom open, just for a second, just to be sure that Declan was where she'd left him. He was, exactly. She met his eye, trusting, patiently waiting for her to bring the bicarbonate of soda to make the pictures appear. She shut the door again quickly, put the key into the lock; it wouldn't turn. She wrestled with it, but it wouldn't work. Number three, it had to work, it was the right key, she twisted it back and forth, it wouldn't turn.

'Anna?'

She could feel the pressure of his hand on the doorknob, on the other side of the door. 'Are you all right? Did you find it?'

'I'll just be a second Declan, I dropped something,' she called out, far too loud. Her voice sounded absurd. Lies lies lies. She just wasn't good at it. She was getting better though, she thought, oh yes. Good enough to fool poor bloody Declan.

There must be a reason why the key wouldn't turn. It was the right number. Then she realized: the wrong colour. It was, after all, at least twenty years since she had had the colour coding explained to her, black for basement, green for ground floor, yellow for first, red for second. Or that was how she'd remembered it anyway. She was sure about black and green, so she must have the yellow and red mixed up. She found the red three, trying hard to stop the keys rattling, but there was quite a racket anyway. She kept her left hand on the door handle, she could feel Declan's grip on the other side, though he didn't seem to be trying to turn it.

'I'll just be a second, Declan,' she said, and inserted the red key. It turned. She moved away from the door, sweating, glassy-eyed. She turned the ring, fingering each key in turn.

'Anna?'

She didn't know what to say. She stood leaning against the wall facing the door, and for a moment she was so revolted by what she had done that she thought she was going to be sick. She thought of his face, trusting, waiting for instructions. She had tricked him, and it had been incredibly easy, she hadn't even had to think how, she had just done it. Like the lying. How many times had people lied to him, tricked him? She had wanted to be different, but she was the same. It felt awful.

'Anna?' His voice was surprised, not angry, just surprised and puzzled. He rattled the door handle.

'Anna? Are you there?' He knocked on the door, a strange thing to do, she thought, to knock from the inside. Though perhaps not so strange if you were used to doors being locked, as Declan must be. She stood a moment longer, playing with her keys, like a jailer, like a guard. The sound was harsh now, metal on metal, the sound of bolts being scraped home, metal hatches in doors, metal spy-holes in doors, metal bars. Not sweet like a tambourine any more. She walked away down the corridor. She wiped her eyes with her sleeve, and the keys jangled again, merrily now, like bones rattling or chains. She put the keys on the kitchen table and sat, waiting for Luke to come home.

She heard Luke's key turn in the door, and went to hug him. He looked grey and drawn, tired. They stood and hugged in the hallway, swaying.

'Luke,' she said, and started to cry.

'What? What is it? Declan?'

She couldn't speak for a moment. All she could hear was the jangling of keys.

'Luke. He's got to go.'

Luke held onto her, wiped her tears away.

'We've got to get rid of him.'

'OK. OK. We'll get rid of him.'

'I mean it. He's got to go.'

Luke pulled her away from him, looked at her.

'What's brought all this on? Has something –'

'Nothing's happened. Not like what you're thinking . . .'

'Has he – if he's done anything –'

'It's not what you're thinking, honestly Luke, it's nothing like that –'

'Where is he –'

'Luke. Listen. It's nothing like that. He hasn't touched me.' Liar liar liar. Only to stop him going up there and hitting him, she thought, but oh she was getting good at it. It seemed to come more easily than the truth these days. She almost didn't think of the truth any more, only of what was the easiest thing to say. Lies were smoother, they seemed to fit her mouth better, they slid out more fluidly.

'He's upstairs. I had to –' she held onto him tightly, ' – I had to lock him in the darkroom.'

'Why? What's he done? Why did you have to lock him up?'

'Luke, he's supposed to have these injections, he told me, depot injections, once a month, they're for aggression, and if he doesn't have them then he gets, you know, aggressive. Well I found out that he'd missed his last one, he was due for it ten days ago but he didn't have it, and Mrs Keyes, she said he'd been round there and that he'd threatened her, Luke, apparently he threatened her, she was too upset to say exactly what he did but I thought I shouldn't take any chances, so I took him up to the darkroom, and I locked him in –' Her voice broke, lending unintended verisimilitude to the smooth, easy words that were dripping from her lips. Luke rarely spoke to Mrs Keyes, so he was unlikely to check the story. She sobbed against his shoulder for a moment. He hugged her tightly.

'I locked him in –' she continued, louder than she intended, and took a deep shuddering breath.

'When? I mean, how long has he been in there?' Luke's voice was low, appalled.

'Just a few hours. I think we've got to ring the social services people, Luke. I really think we've got to. We've tried with him, we've done our best and it just hasn't worked, we've done all we can, but we can't be responsible . . .'

Luke hugged her, shushed her, his eyes closed. This had been his feeling for some time now, he was more pleased than he could say that she was finally seeing sense.

'OK, it's OK,' he said, 'I'll ring them.'

'Declan? Can you hear me?'

'Luke? I didn't mean it, I didn't think, honestly I thought –'

'It's all right Declan, no-one's blaming you for anything, are you OK in there?'

'You see, I thought she wanted me to, I was sure she did, but then –'

'That's all right, Declan, Anna's explained everything to me and you don't have to worry about anything, everything's been straightened out now.'

'Did I do it wrong? I thought you wanted –'

'Declan? Now we're going to bring some people here to see you, just to have a look at you, see how you're doing –'

'Who? What people?'

'And if they think that you might be better off being somewhere else, then they'll arrange for you to –'

'From Rain Fields? Are they from Rain Fields Luke?'

'That's it. That's where they're from. They're going to come out here to check you over, and, Declan listen now, if they think that you'd be better off somewhere else then they'll arrange for you to go there. Is that all right?'

'Yeah OK. Luke?'

'Yes Declan?'

'Luke? I didn't – you see, what I thought –'

'Don't worry about that, Declan.'

'You're not angry with me? I didn't, well I *did* you know, but she –'

'They'll probably be here soon Declan. Do you want anything?' Luke lowered his voice a notch. 'Do you need to go to the toilet or anything?'

'No.'

'How about a cup of tea?'

'Yes. You see . . .'

'OK. I'll go and get it. Just hang on there Declan.' Something more was needed, simple courtesy required something more from him.

'Declan? I'm sorry about this.'

'Luke? See, what I thought –'

Luke retreated down the landing, Declan's voice following him.

' . . . I thought it was all right, you see, because . . .'

Luke sat in the kitchen with Anna and held her hand.

After a few minutes he became aware of a sound: Anna felt him stiffen.

'That's Declan. He's knocking on the door.'

After twenty minutes or so there was the sound of car doors slamming outside, and then a ring on the bell.

Luke hadn't rung social services, he'd rung the police. Social services, he thought, were all very well: they could deal with it when Declan was safely removed from the premises and in secure custody. They could arrive at whatever diagnosis and treatment they wanted, but Luke's priority was to get him out of here.

He opened the door to them with Anna at his shoulder. She said 'Oh,' as she saw the uniforms and the patrol car outside. 'Luke?'

The two policemen spoke to Luke, and he ushered them upstairs. Anna followed. They arrived at the door of the darkroom.

'It's OK Anna. Let them deal with him now. They'll get him sorted out.'

'Do they know he's –'

'I explained all that. They'll be careful.'

One of the policemen, a young man with a slightly podgy, slightly angelic face, tapped on the door.

'Mr Sargeant?' His voice was loud, matter-of-fact, no nonsense.

He was answered by a tapping from the other side. He looked round, puzzled.

'Let me,' said Anna, and positioned herself in front of the door.

'Declan? Are you all right?'

He muttered something, which she took to be affirmative.

'There are some people here to see you. I'm going to open the door now. OK?'

More muttering, more tapping. She recalled that she had left the keys in the kitchen and went to fetch them. The policemen stood about, talking quietly to Luke.

Anna returned and was about to unlock the door when the baby-faced policeman stopped her.

He addressed the door.

'Mr Sargeant? We're going to open the door now. I want you to make a promise with me that you're going to come out nice and quietly and not cause any commotion. Nobody's going to hurt you. Nobody wants to do that, I can assure you of that very clearly. But on the other side of the bargain you've not got to give us any reason to, you know.' The sentence ran into difficulty and went aground. He started again. 'It's a two-way-street situation, basically, you know what I'm saying here? You play fair with us and we'll – kind of thing. Am I getting through?'

Words came from behind the door, but they were not clear.

'I don't think he'll be any trouble,' Anna said, 'he's never like that is he, Luke?'

'What about Mrs Keyes though?'

Anna had forgotten about her report of the incident with Mrs Keyes. She shrugged.

'Mr Sargeant, you're not going to give us trouble now are you, when we unlock the door? Can I have your word on that please?' The baby-faced policeman leaned his ear to the door to catch Declan's reply: he couldn't make it out. Anna thought she heard the word 'beef'. Only when I'm tired. Baby-Face took the key from Anna and put it in the lock.

Declan was listening very intently to all that was said. They wanted him to do something when he came out. He heard the words 'trouble', 'commotion', 'hurt'. He knew the kind of thing they meant, he had seen a lot of it over the years. He knew pretty much how it went. His right arm swung out in a wide semicircle, fast, returned to his side. He took a few deep breaths. He heard the key being put into the lock. He cast round for a weapon of some kind. His hand closed on the plastic tongs. He was ready.

20. *Wsssssk*

Baby-Face pulled the door open. Declan stood in the doorway, still, very still. Red light darkened his skin and made his eyes retreat into his face, turned him into a devil, a maniac. He opened his mouth.

'Wsssssk.'

'Mr Sargeant?'

Declan hesitated, then lashed out, a good strong forehand, back again, and smiled. The policeman edged away from the door, unable to calculate the meaning. Declan was holding something, but he couldn't see what it was, Declan had it palmed. Anna looked, wide-eyed. Luke involuntarily took a step back, and Declan came forward.

He called out a word, or a sound like a word, and threw his head back. These are not the gentleman callers I was expecting.

'Mr Sargeant?' said Baby-Face. 'We'd like you to come with us please.' We've come to take you away, Luke thought, ha ha, ho ho, he he.

'Wait!' called Declan, and Baby-Face recoiled, held up placating hands and said:

'OK, fair comment, yeah. Yeah, we can wait a minute,' and folded his arms across his chest, looking over at his companion, who shrugged and looked at Anna.

'Declan?' Anna said, and Declan came a step forward, one arm held high, stiffly, as if in some kind of salute.

I command you, Luke thought, I command you back, this is not your place oh Christ

Declan swung again, a fast wide arc, and his face was huge, determined. People edged back as he came

167

forward down the corridor. Baby-Face led the retreat, crooning little sounds, now son, don't let's have any bother, be a sensible lad now.

More shouting from Declan, a confused mix of words and sounds, excited, passionate even. Anna thought she heard the word 'monkey'.

Only when I'm tired, Anna thought, only when I'm tired.

'Declan? Can you hear me?' she called, though he was only a few paces ahead of her. He met her eye, but he didn't see her. Whoever it was who saw her wasn't Declan.

They reached the stairs. Luke went down, muttering something like unbelievable, fucking unbelievable; the two policemen came to an agreement and took hold of Declan, one arm twisted violently behind him so that he screwed up his face and screamed and Anna called out.

'Declan? Just stop now . . .'

'OK son?' said Baby-Face through clenched teeth, 'Have you had enough now son? Eh?'

Declan struggled and writhed to the carpet and kicked his way free of Baby-Face, the other one stood in front of him and put a restraining arm round his neck, and Declan swung out at him with the plastic tongs. The policeman staggered away, fell down a few steps, grabbed at his side, checking for blood.

'Watch him, he's got a knife!' he shouted, 'get the knife off him!' Baby-Face threw himself on Declan and pinned him by the knees. He got his elbow into Declan's face, and levered his arm across his throat. Declan struggled and opened his jaw round the officer's wrist, bit down. Baby-Face banged his head against the wall and jarred his wrist as he struggled free. He tried again to pin Declan down.

'Mind his stitches!' Anna called, and ran to his side. 'He's injured for God's sake, mind his injury!' Her voice was unsteady.

Declan rolled under the policeman's body, hooked a

foot behind his knee, jerked upward, he knew the kind of thing. He was yelling, just nonsense.

Anna left him and found Luke at the bottom of the stairs. They stood together, not touching, not speaking.

There were the sounds of a tussle from above, shouts, heavy breathing, then Declan came rattling down the stairs at incredible speed, with something in his hand. He brushed past Luke and Anna as they cringed against the wall. As he passed he jabbed, fast and high, at Luke; the blunt end of the plastic tongs dug into Luke's eye and he screamed and turned away. Anna tried to pull his hands from his face to see what damage there was. Baby-Face charged past a moment later. They should be blowing whistles, thought Luke, and they should fall over each other more. The other one followed. Declan had disappeared into the front room, where Bobby Parrot sat unquietly in his cage, bright-eyed, cackling, ready for the rumpus.

Baby-Face was shouting, and there was the sound of things being turned over. Then creaking. Declan made a sound, a high rising sound, and Anna left Luke's side and ran to the door. She could see that Declan's shirt was discoloured round the waist. He was bleeding again. He must have torn open his stitches.

Baby-Face was standing an arm's span away from Declan, hands out in a calming gesture; Declan was jabbing with the tongs. Baby-Face had convinced himself that the tongs were lethal, a knife, and Declan was brandishing them in an appropriately life-threatening manner.

'OK son,' said Baby-Face, and Declan clacked the tongs together rapidly, a short staccato burst, like castanets. Anna could see Baby-Face again trying to assign some meaning to it, unsuccessfully.

Declan approached, and Baby-Face retreated; Anna could see clearly now that Declan was someone else, he held himself taller, he moved more slowly, his face was sharper. The nightmare nonsense words came out, loud, hieratic, cadenced. He was a madman.

Baby-Face and the other one rushed him again, more successfully this time: Declan's arm was braced over Baby-Face's knee, and he was disarmed. The other one looked down as the tongs clattered to the floor, not quite able to believe what he saw.

Disarmed, Declan's grand rage seemed to desert him. He folded, collapsed, allowed his arms to be pinned together in front of him, meekly permitted Baby-Face to attach the restraint belt round his wrists. The belt had special buckles with a lock. Baby-Face showed him another one too, for his feet, and a bigger one to hold his arms to his side. Baby-Face displayed them all, explaining how they fitted. But everyone agreed that Declan would be a good lad and they wouldn't need them. Bobby Parrot said hello Bob, hello Bob, cooooo.

The police led him out to the car. Anna and Luke stood at the doorway. Luke had his hands up to his face, which was streaming tears from the wounded eye. Anna stroked his neck. She saw Mrs Pelling, Mrs Armitage from number 30, others, standing at their gates or front doors, watching the show. They looked satisfactorily shocked. The police radios squawked. Declan sat in the back of the patrol car staring straight ahead. The policemen slammed the doors shut, and Declan turned his face to look at her. His mouth moved, silently: he was saying Anna, Anna. Anna thought, I should have made him sandwiches for his first day. Declan's face repeated her name as the car moved away. Anna, Anna, Anna.

1941

'At the back of the ward were seven seclusion rooms from which emanated most of the noise, confusion, and odour. One peered into these cells through narrow windows at revolting pictures of deteriorated life. There one often saw naked persons living in their own excreta, terribly hostile, repressed, or crushed . . . To enter these cells was to risk vituperation or physical attack. Upon leaving a seclusion room the physician stepped lively, fearing either his own capture or the sudden escape of the patient.'

Greenblatt, York and Brown, *From Custodial to Therapeutic Patient Care in Mental Hospitals*

21. *What Are* You *Having?*

The waitress jiggled as Luke studied the range of options on the drinks list. They were arranged in categories: wines, by glass and carafe and half-litre, beers, twelve different types, juices and coffees and four kinds of tea, including Chinese gunpowder. He wasn't sure he wanted anything, but Anna was having a grapefruit and soda so he felt obliged to order something. Coffee. Espresso, three types of mocha (mint, orange and chocolate), cappuccino, just coffee. He glanced up at Anna, back to the list. Fuck, he thought, I must be able to decide what to have to drink for God's sake, anything, it doesn't matter does it? He felt trapped. His eyes met Anna's again.

'I don't know. What are you having?'

'Grapefruit and soda.' She smiled, but it was tense.

'I'll have the same,' he said, and closed the menu.

'Same for me. Yeah. No. Wait a minute. I'll have vodka. Vodka and tonic. Please.'

Declan had been gone a week, though Anna could still smell him, or so she sometimes thought. She had washed everything in his room that was washable, aired the room, even sprayed round some filthy-smelling horror that claimed to have something to do with April meadows. She had gone on to hoover and dust the whole house, meticulously, as if Luke's mother were coming to stay. The monstrous April meadows filled the air like an eruption from some particularly ingenious corner of hell. But still she could smell him, the occasional vagrant whiff, not a strong or unpleasant smell, just a human body that wasn't her or Luke.

He intruded into her thoughts constantly, violently,

173

so that she winced, shrank back. She woke up several times a night with a jolt. She saw him in the allotment shed, his flesh bone-white under the moon. She saw him approach her, with the shears. He had picked them up to cut the twine round her legs, that was the only reason, she was certain. But she saw him with them in his hand, coming nearer, and she flinched. She saw him, weird under the red light in the darkroom, his arm extended in some kind of salute, saw his sudden slashing motions, saw his lips forming her name. Anna. She stood in front of the mirror sometimes mouthing the word. Anna, Anna. Her period was due in eight days. She tried, all the time, to behave naturally, not to carry herself like a precious vase, not to stifle every cough, every sneeze, in case, in case . . .

'How come you're not drinking?' Luke wanted to know. She shrugged.

'I might later. Not on an empty stomach though.' She had tried to talk to Luke about Declan, but he didn't want to. He's gone now, he said, just forget about him. Not so easy to do, with Luke's right eye still weeping and bruised. She had suggested a pirate's eye-patch. Actually, she thought, the slight closing of the eye didn't do him any harm at all. He looked a little like Marlon Brando.

'Why was he saluting like that, do you think?' Anna had asked. Luke had shrugged, twisted up his lip.

'Who knows.' I am come to honour you and your family. That was why. What Luke wanted to know was what the words were that Declan had been saying. What did they mean? He was reluctant to ask Anna though, or discuss it with her at all. The thought of Declan was an uneasy one. All Luke's spare time now was spent holed up in his little office, staring at his computer screen. He hadn't been back into the darkroom since Declan had gone, he didn't want to go in there. He couldn't help the thought that that was where Declan had transformed himself from a harmless head case into a raging, slashing madman who spoke in an alien language. Your tongue is not our tongue, your ways not ours. He knew perfectly well where Declan had got the salute from, what the slashing meant: he understood the developing-tongs, the clacking, the whole performance. He couldn't tell anyone. It was a knowledge that twisted and burned inside him, trying to dig its way out. Sometimes his mouth seemed full of it.

It was partly because of his endless silent vigils in front of his computer that Anna had suggested they go out for dinner. Be together, just the two of them. They had dressed up, both in black, she with silver bracelet and silver brooch in the shape of a lizard. They held hands on the way to the restaurant.

They'd passed someone in a doorway, huddled down into his sleeping-bag. He'd struggled upright as they passed and asked for something, his words weren't clear. They'd marched past, not looking. A few paces on, Anna had stopped and started rummaging in her bag. She went back – Luke stayed where he was – and handed over a small sum of money. She leaned down to whoever was in the sleeping-bag and they exchanged a few words. Luke strained his ears but couldn't hear what they said. She came back to his side and gave him a lovely, wide, carefree smile, and hooked her arm through his.

'What did you say?' he asked, but she wasn't telling. Whatever it had been it had improved her mood considerably. He would have liked a picture of her, smiling, seemingly shining in fact, not a care in the world. Full of something or other. He couldn't remember when he'd last seen her like this.

Their drinks arrived. Luke had never been a vodka man, but it tasted OK. The only thing wrong with it was that it didn't seem to last as long as a drink ought to, somehow, there just wasn't enough of it. Anna watched him as he drained the ice out of the bottom of the glass and chewed on it. He wondered how soon the waitress would return. He leaned back in his chair to see if he could see her, almost lost his balance and had to grab the edge of the table.

'Who do you have to sleep with to get another drink round here?' he said, and Anna replied: 'Me.'

'Bugger it then,' Luke said, 'I'm on the wagon.'

She opened her mouth to say something, thought better of it and didn't.

'What?' Luke wanted to know.

'Nothing. It doesn't matter.'

Something to do with Declan, Luke guessed. He himself had screened out quite a few references that evening: someone was on very active censor duty in his head. It was surprising how many things led onto, or led off from, Declan in one way or another.

'I'll get it out of you later, with my clever wiles and low cunning,' he said, and she smiled, but the mood had dissipated again. Every time they seemed to be relaxing, opening up to each other, something would pop up to separate them, a remark not made, a thought stifled. Christ let's get hammered, thought Luke, and craned round again. He saw the waitress and put up his hand, mouthing 'excuse me'. Anna laughed at him.

'It's not like school, Luke,' she said, 'you don't have to put your hand up. You just go if you have to go.'

'Too late,' he said, 'I've pissed myself.'

Anna laughed, properly this time, without reservation, and Luke laughed as well, so that when the waitress came they seemed to be enjoying themselves as much as anyone else.

She stood ready to take their order, but Luke just asked for another round of drinks. He couldn't face the menu again so soon, not with all those bloody starters and main courses and desserts. Everything was themed to within an inch of its life: the theme was classic films. Courses were called things like Monkfish Casablanca, Ribs Chaplin and so on. There was a dessert called 'Another fine mess'. It was too gruesome, Luke thought. He wondered if they had any draught Guinness on the premises. Guinness Alec, he thought. I'll have two Guinness Alecs and a bucket. My good lady wife here'll have the same, with an umbrella.

When the drinks came Luke raised his glass and said: 'To us.'

They chinked their glasses together. Screen idols looked down from the walls like deities, smiling graciously on them, guaranteeing good fortune and happiness.

The waitress was back with her little pad, all business now. It was time to order. Anna went first, unblushingly asking for a 'Some Like It Hot' starter (chilli and tortilla chips) and to follow, Rack of Lamb Vincent Price. Luke twisted, writhed in his seat. He scanned the menu from top to bottom, even turning it over to a seemingly endless list of cocktails.

'I'll have . . .'

All he really wanted was more vodka and maybe a cheese sandwich to wash it down with. He found his eye lingering amongst the seafood and dragged it away again.

'I'll have . . .'

The waitress's attention had wandered to a picture of Robert De Niro, though her pen still hung in the air over her pad. There was a burst of laughter from the other side of the room.

'OK. I'll have . . .'

Anna noticed that the waitress was moving from one foot to the other, curling her feet up to ease her arches. Her shoes were too tight.

'Would you like a few minutes to think about it?' the waitress asked, not impatiently, but Luke was adamant.

'No that's all right. I'm going to have . . .' He became aware that he was dragging the words out slightly. He was going to have, but the end of the sentence simply wasn't there, was not joined to the beginning, had been cut adrift, hacked away from its mooring.

'Yes, would you give us another moment or two

please?' Anna said finally, unable to bear it any longer. The waitress smiled and said of course.

'I'll have another vodka,' Luke heard himself calling after she'd turned away.

'Luke? Are you all right?' Anna spoke quietly but urgently to him. He shrugged, shaking his head slightly from side to side.

'I just couldn't decide,' he said. 'What are you having?'

She sat back and regarded him through narrowed eyes.

'What am I having? What difference does it make what I'm having? Just have whatever you want.'

'I don't want anything . . .'

'Luke . . .'

'I'll be right back,' he said, and stood up. The waitress was behind his chair with his drink; somehow he managed to catch her elbow and send the glass to the black and white tiled floor. He ducked away to the toilet. Anna apologized to the waitress, said he wasn't feeling well. She wanted to add, he's been under a lot of strain, but realized that that made him sound like someone recovering from a nervous breakdown.

The waitress went back to the bar in her tight new shoes to get another vodka. Luke returned from the toilet.

'OK?' Anna asked quietly, anxiously, and Luke raised his eyebrows to say, why shouldn't I be?

'Right.' He picked the menu up again. When the waitress came back he gave her his order with no hesitation at all. No starter, a Somewhere over the Rainbow Trout, with 'Another Fine Mess' to follow. That sounded about right. Oh, and more vodka. Lots more.

22. *Just a Little Bit*

'So what he did, see, he came out the forest and went to the village. And he kind of, he kind of hid the claw thing up his sleeve, he put it up his sleeve so they couldn't see it, see, and no-one knew he had it.'

Phil, the little man sitting beside Declan, twitched his leg rapidly, continuously, holding his head cocked slightly, in a gesture of mild incredulity. Every time Declan paused he leaned forward and repeated the last few words.

'No-one knew!' He laughed and rubbed his hands together. His face was chubby and amiable, with reddish ginger hair and eyelashes and thick lips.

Declan was somewhat thrown by this unexpected attention, but had to keep going because Phil so clearly expected him to. So he went on, the momentum of his words maintained by a sensation of encroaching panic, which he was keeping at bay, just, by continuing to speak. The two of them had thus reached a kind of uneasy equilibrium.

They were sitting side by side at a table where they were having Occupational Therapy. Declan's friend, Phil, was making something strange and unnecessary from thin strips of coloured plastic, which he was weaving or knotting together. Declan had a pair of scissors and larger pieces of plastic, from which he was cutting strips. When cut, he passed them to Phil who incorporated them into whatever the thing was that he was making.

'So all the people in the village, see, they let him stay there and he dug a well and cleared away the weeds round the walls and just tidied everything up for them.

And he made a kind of hut to live in. Sort of a hut. Everyone liked him.'

'Yeah! They liked him!'

'Then there was a battle, like a big war. Everyone went off to this war, all the men anyway, but the women didn't go, they stayed in their huts and swept them out and lit fires and made things to eat out of books. They had to wait, see, until the men came back.'

Declan was sweating under the fluorescent lights in the OT shop. He wasn't sure he was getting all this right. Phil, though, had no complaints as he fiddled with his coloured strips.

'The crab man didn't go to the war either, because no-one asked him to, so he stayed in the village. The thing about him was, see, that he had Special Powers because he'd had a special operation, ages ago, they'd give it him so he'd be different from everyone else, and it meant he could get the women and sleep with them in his hut. He had to tie them up first though or they ran away, because they were scared of him. But it was all right, and when he slept in the hut with them they'd have a baby after. Not right away, you had to wait for a bit.'

'You had to wait!' Phil was becoming increasingly excited, which panicked Declan more. He rushed head-long on.

'Yeah. Yeah. So then the war finished, see, and all the men came back from the war, except the ones that'd been killed, and the crab man went back to his own hut and made things.'

'Like this!' Phil shouted, and held the horrible deformed plastic thing aloft and waved it, and laughed.

'Yeah yeah. It was dark in the hut and there wasn't a window or anything, but it didn't matter really. But what happened, see, was that all the women he'd tied up and you know slept with started having the babies, and the men in the village got upset with the crab man and said that really he ought to go, and they hit him and that, there was hundreds of them. So he hit them back. They had a big fight, and the crab man said, aha!'

'Aha!' shouted Phil and waved his thing. Declan gestured too, waved his arm, and made Phil laugh.

'Aha! And he got the claw thing out from his sleeve and he cut them see with the claw thing and then he, he dragged all the bits away and the women cooked them on the fires and then they ate them!'

'Ate them! Ate them!'

Declan stopped, and Phil waited, head cocked, ready for what came next. Declan waited too, but there wasn't any more.

'Oh!' said Phil after a moment. Declan started cutting more strips, fidgeting on his seat. He twisted down his mouth at one end and tilted his head, frowning. Phil turned his attention back to his work, also looking faintly puzzled. The fluorescents buzzed quietly overhead.

It was the eighth day. Anna rang in sick to work and lay in bed, her hands clasped at her stomach. She didn't feel too good, though she didn't feel quite as bad as usual, she was certain. Slightly bloated from water retention, particularly round the eyes and in the cheeks, as if her face was filling up with honey. Her neck felt heavy, the skin dragging down over her throat, like wattles. Her legs felt heavy too, round the knees and along the insides of her thighs. Even her hair felt heavy: she imagined it hanging round her face like strings of seaweed, dripping dark, glossy oil.

Unusual, she thought, that it should be her lying in bed and Luke gone to work, and not the other way round. He was using up sick days and people's tolerance at an alarming rate. He didn't even bother making up proper excuses any more, he had an all-purpose ear infection that had flared up suddenly, inexplicably. It was mysterious in its workings, this ear infection, and the doctors were baffled! He knew it wasn't any good, as did everyone else involved. It wasn't even as if he had anyone to stay up late with since Declan had gone. He just sat up, pulling away diligently at his cans of

Guinness and his joints, staring at his computer screen. He was writing a report or something, she wasn't sure about the details. He didn't discuss it with her. The room had a strong, stale, solitary smell. What you need is a good blast of April meadows matey, Anna thought. That'll give you something to think about. She tried to persuade herself that she was indignant that he should prefer to secrete himself away like this rather than enjoy the manifold charms and palpable delights of her company, but she couldn't muster anything she was able to call convincing. She was busy, concentrating.

This morning he had managed to drag himself out in reasonable time: he didn't have a clean shirt and put one on that smelled just slightly short of gorgeous. Manna from heaven, she thought, just the perfect thing for the bored staff in the bored staff-room to talk about. And did you see, *he didn't even have a clean shirt on!* Rings round the collar! Can you *imagine*! His hair seemed to have grown suddenly, it had started to droop over his forehead in a way that, she knew, was neither intended nor foreseen. She was a little surprised to note also that his stomach was no longer even approximately flat but curved: bellied, in fact, in several folds. This couldn't have happened suddenly. She realized that she hadn't actually looked at him in any detail for some time. But she didn't care, her attentions were engaged elsewhere. Inside, not out.

She lay in bed and the birds twittered outside the window, unremarked, unattended. She was busy.

Luke had a free period mid-morning, though he felt sure someone would be only too happy to deprive him of it. He really had to catch up with some paperwork, it was mounting all round him like floodwater, box files and plastic envelopes and manila folders full of cards and sheets with numbers and names on, boxes to be ticked, remarks to be scrawled. Nor were you supposed to do it randomly, apparently, but you were supposed to consider *which* box to tick, *what* phrase to write. You got on top of it or it got on top of you. There was no other accommodation to be made. And as for collecting up the whole ungodly heap of it in both arms and pitching it fair and square into a wheelie bin, well, that would be regarded in *some* quarters as unprofessional. Unprofessional. He sang the word to himself to the tune of the Hallelujah Chorus. Uuuuuun-pro-fesh-nal! He caught a whiff of his shirt, which was expressing itself ever more piquantly as the day wore on: it smelled sweet and intimate.

He tried sitting in the staff-room but couldn't get comfortable, the chairs were too low, they sagged under the accumulated weight of stomach full of last night's Guinness and lap full of months of ignored paperwork. He gathered together the superb piles of unticked forms and boxes and went to the Audio-Visual room. He put two Formica-topped tables together and spread the papers out in their proper separate stacks. The sun came out and poured itself through the window and all over the tables. The papers were warm as he fiddled with them, the table surface was warm. His bruised eye watered gently in the sudden brilliance, and he dabbed at it with his tie. He wondered what they would do to him if he were to nip off to the toilet and make a joint. Some little sneak would undoubtedly feel obliged to report him. Sixth-form pupils were not the proud, rebellious breed that he remembered himself coming from: most of them seemed to be, if not outright Christian fundamentalists, then deeply preoccupied with right-thinking and right-doing. Inhuman little swine, he thought, and ticked viciously at a box.

The sun edged round to the bedroom window late in the morning, eleven thirty or so. There was a gap between the curtains, and a finger of sunlight came into the room, splashing against the far wall. Anna decided she would risk sitting up, and sat tracing the outline of the bright patch of light with her eyes. Her body sweltered and oozed, no longer honey and oil but trickling, tickling fluids, less viscous now. She kept her hands pressed gently against her stomach. She stared straight ahead, breathing shallowly through her nose. She clenched her thighs. She lay down again.

Luke sat in a cubicle, smoking quickly, furiously, inhaling and holding and inhaling again. It was a very different experience from his usual procedure, which was as unhurried and languorously ritualized as something from Imperial Japan. This was frantic, unpleasurable, rushed, everything he hated. The mossy sweet smell rose up, thick as incense, and he flapped his hands about in a hopeless attempt to dispel it. Drag, hold, out. What am I going to do with the roach he thought dismally, it won't flush away. He would have to pull it apart and hide it somewhere. He entertained the thought of using one of the waste-bins in the women's toilets, but fetched up against an image of a hatchet-faced female staff member storming in and finding him there, shamefaced and without viable explanation. It made the sweat break out. Drag, hold. Hold. Out. He could just throw it out of the window, of course. No-one would ever connect it with him. How could they? He tried to calm down. The blood sank inside him, away from his burning skin, slowly. He closed his eyes.

He heard someone coming in, heard a sports bag being dumped down on the floor by the urinals. Just one person. He heard someone sniffing, casually at first, then great operatic, theatrical sniffs.

'Funny smell in here,' came a voice, in that uncertain tenor of the sixteen-year-old. He didn't recognize it. He held himself as stiffly, as silently as he could. The joint burned away, little specks of burning material flickering to the floor.

Then someone banged on the door.

'Oi!'

Luke listened to his heart as it banged and rattled.

184

What if I die in here, he was thinking, what if I have a heart attack and die? What then?

'Give us a drag then.'

'Bugger off.' He tried to disguise his voice, he had no idea how successfully. He didn't think he sounded like sixteen.

'Just a drag.'

'Bugger *off*.'

More pounding. All the kid had to do was get down on the floor and look up to see that it was a teacher not a student in there. The kid might even recognize him from his footwear, it was possible. Luke held his breath.

'Smells like shite anyway. Who'd you get it off?'

'Sod off!'

'I can get you some good stuff if you want.'

Someone else came in. The kid backed away from the door, said something disgusting, went away.

Luke waited for the new arrival to start making some sort of a problem but he wasn't interested, and the door banged shut behind him less than a minute later.

Luke stood with his hand on the lock for a few moments, the roach crumpled in his other fist. He opened the door and peered out. No-one about. He chucked the roach into one of the urinals and went out. It occurred to him to worry about his breath but there was nothing he could do there. He got a can of Liptonice from the machine outside the staff-room and poured half of it down his throat in one go. Then he went back to his paperwork. He felt ragged.

By twelve thirty the finger of light had moved round so that it was touching the edge of the bed. She held out but it could no longer be denied: Declan's special powers had failed, and she was going to bleed, right on time.

There was no miracle inside her. She couldn't remember how she could ever have imagined such a possibility. It seemed insane. Yet for a few strange days she had allowed the idea to grow in her mind, like a tall weed in a garden. It made no sense, none at all. Perhaps, she thought as the sun edged ever closer to where she lay, perhaps that was why she had allowed it in, watched it shoot up amongst the immaculately tended lawns, watched it flower. The doctors had had delusions of magical potency too, but they had expressed it in different words, in computer printouts from tests, in hormone levels and probabilities. Crude names for the gods they were trying to placate. The wrong names, as it had turned out. Their magic just hadn't been powerful enough, their logic had withered and died. She had believed in them: why should she not have believed in Declan?

Declan had had no charts or syringes full of magic hormones. He had no complicated explanations, he simply had a belief in something that was impossible, and for fourteen days she had allowed herself to believe it too. The simplest kind of magic.

She reran that conversation, and the truth behind his words emerged with inescapable clarity. He had had a girlfriend, she had become pregnant, then they had given Declan an operation. They had told him that now he could sleep with any woman he wanted. To Declan this had meant that they had given him the power to impregnate anyone at will. But what they had done to him was the precise opposite: they had sterilized him.

She knew they weren't allowed to do this without proper consent. Declan's consent would not be accepted, since his understanding of the issues was obviously at best partial or confused and at worst downright wrong. Someone else would take the decision, a tribunal appointed by a court, and they would only do it for reasons they could defend in court if it came to that. It was a very serious matter, and it was taken seriously. But all the same if it was considered necessary it would be done. Declan had spoken of 'a girlfriend', but there would have to have been many, and many pregnancies. Complaints from outraged parents, demanding that something be done.

Someone would then have had to explain it to Deçlan in a way that he would accept. They had clearly done a very poor job, and, deliberately or not, they had managed to give him exactly the opposite impression from the truth, and had in fact given him a wholly new delusion about himself. Insane.

She replayed the scene in the allotment shed. She recalled how Declan had looked, standing, oddly hunched as he'd called to her, candlelight wavering behind him. Who had invented his magical potency? Not him: he held it as a simple belief, an unremarkable physical property like the ability to stand upright. No, it was she who had invented it, called it into being by her need for there to be, somewhere, a man who could do what the great doctors had failed to do, impregnate her. She had called it forth in him, as you might summon a demon. He had simply done what she asked him to. She closed her eyes as the realizations swept over her. In a way, she thought, it was worse to be let down by magic like this than by science. The disappointment was keener, sharper, less easy to bear. A great pity, for Declan, for herself, for all the confused and desperate and hopeful filled her. The fillet of sunlight reached her ankle and warmed her skin as she reached into her bedside cabinet for the little blue and white box, and the fact that it was still there, that she hadn't thrown it away, comforted her. She hadn't been completely insane after all, she thought, as tears trickled down her face. Just a little bit.

23. *Time of the Month*

Luke was back in the darkroom. He was finally getting round to the roll of film he'd taken on the photography seminar, just snapshots mostly, groups of smiling people with their arms round each other and a surprising number of pictures of Debbie. Debbie smiling, Debbie pouting. The inevitable joke shot of Debbie holding up her camera to take a picture of him taking a picture of her. A couple of fairly unsuccessful pictures of streets and buildings. He scanned the contact sheet, trying to select which ones to develop, and the answer was: none of them! A duller set of pictures, he thought, you would be hard-pressed to devise. They even lacked the studied dullness of the kind of pictures he'd taken while a student, pictures of furniture, wallpaper. Only someone who had been locked in a small room and deprived of any visual stimulation for twelve months could find anything to interest him here. Look, pictures! Of people! Look, you can see their faces and everything!

His eye lighted on a canister of film standing on the counter by a pile of boxes of paper. He hadn't marked it – it had no label. He picked it up, fiddled with it while he was scrutinizing the contact sheet.

Then he screwed up the contact sheet and turned his attention to the canister. Whatever it was, it surely couldn't be any worse than those inane pictures of happy smiling people. It might even contain pictures that were good, or at least interesting. Something better than holiday snaps anyway.

He pulled out the negative strip and cut it up into

lengths for the contact sheet. He rolled himself another joint.

Anna was sitting in the Tanners with Sal, who had managed, against the odds, to get a few hours off from looking after Ryan. Ollie had been obliged to give up a rugby training session, and was at home, righteous and resentful, with a bottle full of laboriously expressed milk and a fractious baby. Sal looked frazzled, frantic, desperately relieved to get away from her wondrous child for an hour or two, desperate for adult company, desperate to get back. Anna noticed that the conversation was oddly rushed, sentences were short and replies rapid, as if by this means Sal would be able to get back to her baby sooner. How are you, Sal? Fine yeah. How's the baby? He's fine yeah, right, well nice talking to you only I ought to be getting back now . . .

Anna mentioned Declan, but Sal didn't seem to remember who he was. Then she did.

'Oh. *Yes.*'

'Sal?' Anna was mystified. 'What does *that* mean?'

'Oh well, you know . . .' Sal looked coquettish: on her it was somehow grotesque. 'I can see what the attraction was, that's all.'

'What? What attraction?'

'Oh now. You don't mean to tell me you didn't fancy him just a little bit? Those big brown eyes and all that dark awkward stuff. Not to mention . . .'

'What? Not to mention what?'

'Well he was fairly, you know, solid. There was plenty of him.'

'How do you know that?'

'An-na! You only had to look at him for God's sake! You're not telling me you didn't even look at him.'

'He didn't strike me that way particularly,' Anna said, rather primly. She heard herself saying this, and it didn't sound as patent, as bare-faced as it was. Sally looked unconvinced though.

'Not like you to miss something like that I must say. Anyway, where is he now?'

'Oh he had to – I mean he went – he –' She stopped and looked at Sally. 'We had to get the police to take him away because he –' Her voice cracked and her image of Sally wavered as her eyes filled up. She saw the flash, heard the whirr.

'Anna?' Sally said. 'Love, whatever's happened?'

Anna shook her head, dabbed her eyes, smiled.

'It's OK.' She put on an Eastender accent. 'It's just me time of the month you know.'

Sally didn't pursue it. She found it difficult to concentrate on anything that wasn't connected with Ryan in some way, and this wasn't. She glanced at the clock behind the bar for the twelfth time in half an hour.

'Well I'm afraid I'm going to have to think about –' she started, but Anna interrupted her.

'Oh have another drink for God's sake. Let him and Ollie get acquainted. He's not going to grow up and leave home if you have another drink with me. Now is he Sal? Hm?'

'He's never going to grow up and leave home. I'm not ever going to let him,' she said, and they both laughed. Anna's eyes were still a bit runny though. She went to the toilet on her way to the bar and looked at herself in the mirror. Her mouth was moving, as if she were privately praying. Anna, her mouth said silently, Anna.

Luke had the contact sheet hanging dripping from the length of clothes-line hanging over the counter. He was unable to take his eyes away from it.

The first ten or so frames were ruined, overexposed or taken with the lens cap on, or taken in complete darkness or something, he couldn't tell what exactly had gone wrong. The next four were pictures of Declan, sitting in a chair. In the first two he was smiling, a cheesy, unsuitable expression which was plastered over his face completely unconvincingly. By the third exposure he had clearly been asked to please *stop* smiling now, and he was just sitting looking at the camera in a completely unguarded way that Luke found strangely disturbing. Usually you only got that kind of show of indifference to the camera in models, who had worked long and hard to attain it. Very young children occasionally had it, though, as they grew up they learned the habit of posing, until, by, say, age eight they were all stiffness and pose and self-consciousness. Adults were by and large hopeless, unless you could get them genuinely off guard.

But here was Declan taken, presumably, by Anna, with a face full of absolute guilelessness, just sitting nice and still for the camera. There was a trace of that restlessness in the eyes, that habitual glitter, but it was damped down by the frozen image.

Next, pictures of the house, taken from the street. The composition was erratic, and there was the odd appearance of photographer's thumb, but they were at least clear, focused, properly lit. Declan, presumably, practising.

Some more shots of Anna, in the back garden. She was sitting demurely on a low brick wall. She lacked only a floral bonnet and basket of cut roses. Anna, as seen by a madman. Luke felt the weirdness of seeing through someone else's eyes. Declan's eyes.

And then it was dark. Pictures taken with flash. It was hard to see what they were, just ground and odd bits of wall, tree trunk, a path disappearing into black nothing at the edge of the flash range.

Then an interior. A ledge, scattered, broken objects. Something in a corner. Closer in, the something was a someone, lying awkwardly on the floor, a someone whose arms were tied up with thin rope of some kind, legs too, lying on his back, spread-eagled. Clothes pulled away, the flash turning the scandalously exposed flesh to bone white and harsh inky shadows. Male.

Natural light again. A large brick building, taken from

some distance, windows broken, derelict. The edge of a coat, navy blue. Anna had one like that.

Night again. Interior. Same as before. Same disorder. Figure in the corner, tied, partially stripped. As before. But not male this time.

Female.

Anna.

There were five of these, all essentially the same, but from closer in or farther out. In the final one she seemed to have her eyes open, though her head was tilted at such an acute angle that it was hard to be certain. Nothing after that.

Luke looked long and hard. He pulled on the joint, sending wreaths of smoke up into the red light. He unstuck the appropriate strip of negative from the contact exposure sheet, and developed the five pictures, quickly, fingers trembling slightly as he adjusted the enlarger. He blew on the prints to make them dry more quickly, then he dragged out the box from under the cupboard, found the file, pushed the pictures of Anna into it, hid it again. He was still trembling. He went to the front room and put the television on. It was an alibi. He felt like he needed one.

24. *A Room Full of Smiles*

There were eight people in the room, all professionals, all highly experienced people; some of them were even highly paid. The highest-paid of all was the well-built balding man who sat beside the empty chair at the far end of the room. The empty chair was for Declan to sit in. He had to walk the whole length of the room while the highly-paid professionals watched. The others were positioned further away from this chair, in a wide ring, in descending order of remuneration. At the furthest point from the chair Declan was to sit in, at the lowest point on the money circle, was a person with the title of nursing auxiliary, and the function of guard.

Declan opened the door and was greeted by the consultant psychiatrist, Dr Fielding, was invited to come in and sit down. Eight pairs of eyes followed his path to the empty chair. Pens tapped on files and pads.

'OK. Thanks for coming in Declan. We just want to ask you a few questions, there's nothing much to it really.' He was delightfully smiley, as if he were sharing some delicious secret. He was clearly aiming for the avuncular, since he'd started balding seriously, and was actually achieving it quite well. Declan sat in the chair at the top of the clock, beside nice friendly Dr Fielding. People made little furtive notes, and whenever they looked up they smiled. The room was full of smiles. Declan smiled as well. Everyone was happy.

'OK let's see,' Dr Fielding said, 'you were admitted here six months ago, that was 12th April. Is that right?'

'Yes sir,' Declan said, but his voice just croaked and he cleared his throat and said it again.

'Yes.'

'OK. So. I wonder, would you mind telling us how you're feeling now? Compared to then I mean?' He leaned in to Declan, looking at him very hard, harder, Declan thought, than people usually do. It confused him for a moment. He didn't know what to do.

'Sorry?'

'Well, do you feel better now than then? Or worse? Or about the same? What would you say?' Dr Fielding's face was practically disappearing under the burden of concern and amiability and good humour. Declan watched him intensely out of the corner of his eye whilst looking straight ahead. A few times he caught the eye of the lowly-paid orderly. His face was much easier to read. Declan had already experienced what went on behind it, at first hand.

'Better,' he said. 'I feel better now.' Dr Fielding nodded encouragingly, and Declan added: 'Much better.'

'Good. *Good*. Now, if you wouldn't mind casting your mind back to when you were first admitted here. Now, at that time you'd got into a spot of trouble with the police, is that right? They were worried that you might hurt someone, so they brought you in to us.' Dr Fielding looked at his notes for a moment, the smile lingering faintly as he read. 'You saw my colleague Dr Teller and she put you back on your monthly depot, the fluphenazine decanoate, and a course of Haldol to be sure. And we've been tapering the Haldol, so that now you're on just 10 mgs daily. And that's been –' Dr Fielding looked up at Declan again – 'well, how has that been, would you say?'

'Fine. Thank you sir.'

'And we gave you something for the side-effects, the restlessness and so on? And that was OK?'

'Yes sir.'

Dr Fielding held Declan's eye and nodded, waiting for more.

'I feel fine now,' Declan said, and smiled.

'You *look* well, you look – well, you look a different

man. OK, well I just have a few questions for you if that's all right. Would you tell me please, what is the name of the hospital here? What's it called?'

'What, here?'

'Yes, where we are now. What's it —'

'Saddlebrook. Saddlebrook Hospital.'

'OK, good. And what is the name of the Queen of England? Her own name.' Dr Fielding smiled: just a game, his face was saying, it's just a game.

'Elizabeth,' Declan said. This is an *easy* game.

'That's right. Now would you tell me what day it is today? What—'

'Tuesday. It's the third of October. 1995. Afternoon. Sir.'

'Yes it is. You're absolutely right. OK.'

Declan became aware of a lessening of the attention focused on him. A middle-aged woman near the door had slipped off one shoe and was scratching her foot with her other shoe. Legs were crossed, papers were fiddled with. He recrossed his own legs. Without realizing it his face had taken on the benign competence of Dr Fielding's and many of the others. Someone, a young woman a few chairs away, was still looking rather hard, frowning, but otherwise they seemed to have lost interest. Should he do something to get their attention back, he thought, but decided no. They didn't want him to be interesting, he'd been a bit too interesting before. Keep it under your hat. Keep it up your sleeve. His fingers clenched and unclenched.

'Yes. That all seems fine,' Dr Fielding said. 'Is there anything you'd like to add, Declan? I mean, how would you, for instance, feel about us maybe suggesting that you're ready to leave us here and move on to the next stage, perhaps a group house or something of that sort? How would you feel about that?'

'That would be fine. Thank you.'

'Yes? OK. Well, thanks for coming in now Declan, and we'll let you know what our decision is later this afternoon. OK? Thank you.'

'Thank you sir.' Declan stood up and walked back to the door, relaxed, competent, even slightly bored now. Just like them. He smiled politely at the faces as he walked past. He kept it up his sleeve. They weren't remotely interested in him. He even smiled at the guard. The guard wasn't smiling.

The young woman who had been frowning and watching, a Community Psychiatric Nurse, had her comments noted by Dr Fielding. She was not convinced that Declan was ready for the outside world yet. She found him – well, she couldn't say exactly what, but it was something like unconvincing. Hadn't anyone else felt that? There was a quality to him that she found worrying, he seemed altogether too ready to comply with everything. Had he just been telling them what he thought they wanted to hear?

Dr Fielding listened to what she had to say, of course, but hers was a minority opinion. Obviously, he agreed, that was always a danger. Some people became so expert in being patients that it was no longer possible to separate out the role from the illness. And certainly, given the nature of Declan's condition, there was a real possibility that he was, not acting, not lying, but simply taking on a new role, the one they all wanted him to take, the recovered patient who was ready to leave. And yes, the last time he had been released he had suffered a setback.

But, Dr Fielding argued, was that a good and proper reason to detain him any longer? If he could persuade them, or at least, Dr Fielding noted correctly, the majority of them, that he was better, then he could persuade anyone. And what further proof could they require from him? What proof, indeed, could the *world* require of him? He was lucid, no longer aggressive, no longer deluded. The aphasia hadn't returned. He was a completely different man from the one who had been brought in six months ago, he had responded well to medication, he had, apparently, recovered sufficiently to persuade a review board that he had recovered. What more could he do? With the right back-up, and as long as he continued to have his monthly injections, he might be perfectly able to negotiate the outside world. There was always the danger of relapse, but that was true of every patient in the hospital. He was ready to leave, and God knew there were plenty of applicants for his bed. There was no good case for keeping him, Dr Fielding said. The young CPN demurred. It was just a feeling really, she said, she couldn't defend it, it was just the way he looked and the way he behaved. He had been too relaxed, she thought, almost smug. But she had to agree, there was no reason to keep him in any longer that could be defended at an appeal tribunal. He had every right to be released.

He just isn't himself, she thought. He isn't himself, that's all.

25. *I Won't Be a Minute*

Luke was dreaming. He was holding someone down, the person was wriggling underneath him. I just need a bit of rope, he was thinking, and we'd be all right. He pushed down harder, trying to immobilize whoever it was with the weight of his body. Someone would be along to help him in a minute, but meanwhile he really could do with some rope. He pinned the wriggling person's wrists together and reached around with his spare hand. Hold on, he said, hold on, I won't be a minute.

He woke up. He thought he could hear something. Anna lay beside him, frowning in her sleep as she often did. He stroked her hair as he waited for the dream to fade, something about a rope. He listened, but he couldn't be sure. He pulled his jeans on and padded out to the bathroom.

Declan was in Luke's cluttered little office, surrounded by the machines, the computer, the printer, the fax, the answering machine. Each with its lights, red or green, each its own sound. Buzzing, humming, clicking. He watched the pages slide out from the printer.

' . . . he twisted, fell, felt her beneath him, twisting . . . '

He'd got in through a small window at the back, which led into a room which had once been used as a pantry. He knew Luke still wanted him to do something, he just didn't know what it was. It was all connected with Luke's story, *The Revenge of the Crab People*. Declan knew he wasn't supposed to come back here, everyone had said so, the doctor, the police, everyone, but where else was he supposed to go? Anyway he was better now, they'd said so, that was why they'd let him out of the hospital again. He just needed to find out what came next, then he'd be off again. No-one could object to that. He flexed his arms as the pages slithered out.

He gathered together a sheaf and knocked them into alignment. There were forty-eight so far.

Declan had found the disk early that morning, found it in the pocket of a pair of Luke's trousers hanging in the wardrobe. Anna had been asleep as he searched. Her foot had protruded from the duvet, wriggled.

'He entered her deeply, his arm locking her claw into place above her head. She moaned, but held his eye as he probed her. Her face was different, but beautiful. His hand outlined the contours of her breast. Her eyes flashed enmity at him: he returned defiance. And her eyes softened as he moved, her sounds became rhythmic, gentle, crooning. Her eyes lost their hard glare and became unfocused. He moved inside her, felt her moving around him, over him . . .'

Declan froze: he thought he heard a sound, someone stirring. He pushed 'print' to interrupt the printer. The machine made only a slight sound, a croaking, chattering, sound, but in the dead silence of the house it seemed very loud. He held his breath as footsteps moved past the door. He heard the bathroom door open and shut. He twisted his head round so that he could read the page which he had just interrupted.

'"You have dishonoured one of our kind," called he who would avenge her, as Luc struggled against the ropes which held him against the great tree. The others stirred.

'"And there can be but one penalty!"

'Luc became still and his voice was clear and loud in the cold air. He heard the blades of the claws moving one across the other, like knives against a stone, wsssssssk.

'"There was no dishonour," he cried, "unless love itself is dishonour!"

'The crab man withdrew a few steps and donned the

ceremonial mask, with holes for eyes and a slit for the mouth. It emphasized the bony ridges of his cheeks and forehead, making him appear armoured.

'Luc flinched back as the creature raised the lethal claw above his head and, lifting his head high, spoke in the old tongue, the ancient language of his kind, a sound like bone breaking against rock. The words were dry, old, immensely heavy.

'"Dishonour is yours if you strike me, for I have no weapon," Luc called, but was silenced by the sickening hiss of the claw through the frosty air. He felt the monstrous chitinous appendage sweep past his exposed flesh, swing away to the left, describing a wide arc, then back again, gaining momentum as it swung, inches away from his cringing belly. Closer, closer . . .'

Declan heard the toilet flush, door opening, footsteps. He waited. The silence returned as the sound of the cistern gurgling and refilling diminished, until there was only a high-pitched whistle, very faint, then intermittent, then nothing. The printer came back to life with a clunk that startled him. It took up its repetitive rhythm again and Declan watched the pages as they fell onto the desk.

Luke settled back into bed, moulding his body into Anna's. Her foot was poking out of the duvet, and he rubbed her ankle with a toe. He was back in the dream almost immediately. This time there was a rope handy.

He was paying for his petrol a few days later when he saw a small item on the front page of the *Tottenham Advertiser*. It was early, he was hung-over, he couldn't focus easily, but one word caught his attention clearly enough to cut through the fog, and that word was 'photograph'. He picked the paper up and had to pay for it separately. He tucked it under his arm in a casual, young-professional kind of way and chucked it onto the passenger seat. He drove round the corner and parked illegally. He picked the paper up.

Someone had been attacked, a person described as an unemployed labourer of no fixed address. He'd been drinking with a man: this person had taken him somewhere, had tied him up and subjected him to what the paper described as an hour-long ordeal. The victim said that his attacker had seemed to change suddenly, had put on some kind of balaclava or face-mask with eyeholes, had spoken in a language not known to his victim. He'd gesticulated in a violent and threatening manner, taken photographs, then released his victim and run away. There had been no sexual component, no attempt to rob, nor had there been any injury. The assailant was described as five foot eleven, medium build, dark hair and eyes, he was wearing . . .

A language not known to his victim.

It couldn't be. It couldn't be. Luke sat in the illegally parked car and thought the same thought over and over again. Couldn't be.

Declan had been escorted away by the forces of law and order, had been removed to the dark place where the mad people raved, away from decent hard-drinking folk. How long ago now? Six months? Something like that. Couldn't be. Couldn't be. He sat in the staff-room and thought the same thought, round and round. He desperately wanted to get home and think. Couldn't be.

He remembered a drunken evening earlier in the year, remembered showing Declan photographs, then telling him some of the crab people story. How much did I tell him, Luke thought, how much?

The day passed and he was back at home. He opened a can and sat in front of his word processor. There were two ashtrays, both full, and a cup, half full. He tipped ash into the cup. The right disk was in the disk drive, ready to go. Had he left it there? He couldn't be sure, though he was aware that the habit of secrecy was growing in him all the time. He surely wouldn't have left the disk in the machine like this. But then again, by the time he was finished working these days he was so

201

out of it that he could easily forget to remove the disk. Hard to be sure.

He scrolled through the files, retrieved the one he was currently working on.

And there it was. The scene where Luc was taken prisoner by a crab man who wanted revenge for the dishonour committed on his sister by Luc. He had called for revenge in the language of his kind, a ceremonial call that would legitimize his killing of Luc. Luc had to talk his way out of it, by appealing to exactly this sense of honour that he should be allowed to fight, fair and unfettered, and with a weapon to compensate him for his lack of a claw. Justice, honour. It was a very high-sounding speech.

The crab man wore a ceremonial mask. Eyeholes and a slit for the mouth.

Luke felt a ripple of chill flutter over him, like moths. There were enough similarities between what he had written and what had been reported in the paper to make him feel sick and uneasy. Could it be some kind of strange coincidence? Could he, Luke, perhaps have read about a similar assault, perhaps weeks or months ago, and forgotten about it, but written it up as part of the story? And then whoever had done it had done it again. Yes. That would explain it. It couldn't be Declan because Declan was locked up somewhere, confined for his own safety and the safety of others.

Unless they'd let him out, of course. Unless he was out now, and had got into the house, found the right disk, the right file, read it all, then gone out and done it. Had Declan been up here, secretly, silently, reading? Luke turned the thought over and over in his head. He saw Declan walking in the dark, selecting his victim, inviting him for a drink somewhere, saw him tying him up, donning the mask, heard the voice, the nightmarish, meaningless words, he felt the terror of the other man as he tried to understand what Declan was doing, what he wanted. How far he was going to go.

How far.

Was that it? Luke turned the machine off and had a shower. He and Anna were going out with Ollie and Sal, the first time in ages. He was meeting them there. The water bounced and rolled off his head, but it didn't clear his thoughts. Maybe a joint would do it. He made a strong one.

By the time he got to the pub he was vague and smiley, tense, benign, unfocused. Anna spoke to him little. Ollie was accommodating, as always, but even through his insulation Luke could tell that he was finding it a strain. Luke found himself talking about something that had happened to him years ago, an incident in a shop, forgot quite why he was saying it. He felt Ollie's eyes, Sal's eyes. Anna's eyes. He stood up, said he wasn't feeling well. Anna offered to come with him, but he shook her off, he was fine. He lost his way slightly on the way home, though he had taken the route several hundred times. He wanted to get back in front of his computer. He had to think.

The house seemed unusually quiet when he came in. Bobby Parrot said something from the front room. Luke listened outside the door, but it didn't mean anything. He collected his papers and matches and plastic baggie and a fresh can from the fridge. Seated in front of the glowing green screen he rolled another one, as strong as it would go, as strong as his dealer made them, and started work. His fingers were stupid and inaccurate, and there were many spelling problems. But it came out, thick and fast, as he doggedly tapped away.

' . . . He felt the monstrous chitinous appendage sweep past his exposed flesh, swing away to the left, describing a wide arc, then back again, gaining momentum as it swung, inches away from his cringing belly. Closer, closer, until the air parted and the claw lashed down, and he experienced a sensation as of ice being drawn across him, felt the warm, wet trickle of his blood . . . The cut was shallow, a long fine graze. Luc regarded his rich red blood with dismay. Again the crab man swung, the air hissed and the bony claw struck again, a deeper cut this time, a warmer, wetter trickle . . .'

A little glowing ember fell onto the 'n' and burned a tiny pit. Ash dropped onto the keyboard, he blew it away, up into the air. He was finished in half an hour. By the time Anna came back he was tucked up and asleep.

He woke again with Anna beside him and the house full of darkness and quiet. There was a sound ringing somewhere, or there just had been. He lay, tense and fuddled, but again he couldn't be certain. It could have been the air banging against his ears. He lay awake for more than an hour.

26. *Russian*

'. . . by an assailant who wore a ski-mask or balaclava. He is described as being of medium build, five foot eleven or six foot . . . a Metropolitan Police spokesman said it was too early yet to say if there was any connection . . .'

Luke glanced out of the window, trying to shield the paper from anyone passing by. The early-morning light was gloomy, filtered through charcoal-coloured clouds. Luke was drinking Liptonice from the can to try to cut through the residue coating his tongue. His body throbbed with tiredness. His tongue hurt as if someone had been tugging on it.

'. . . the assailant's manner and bearing were strange, and that he spoke partly in English and partly in a language the victim identified as Russian . . .'

Russian! Luke snorted, then spoke aloud. 'Russian! For God's sake!' then realized that he was alone in his car, and thus, really, ought not to be speaking at all. He took a swig and held the paper closer to his face.

'. . . no obvious motive, no attempt was made to rob the victim nor was there any sexual element beyond the removal of the victim's shirt. The victim initially thought his attacker was unarmed, since . . .'

He kept it up his sleeve.

'. . . he did not reveal the weapon, but kept it held behind his back.'

Luke read on feverishly, the flimsy paper trembling in his hands.

'. . . in what a police source described as one of the more disturbing elements of the case, the attacker partially stripped his victim and cut him several times using a small knife, afterwards taking photographs . . .'

There it was. Luke's heart hammered against his shirt, surging up from beneath the weariness. There it was! Beyond any question there it was! He folded the paper and tossed it onto the passenger seat, then stuffed it underneath. He pulled up beside a bin outside a Greek restaurant, piled high and overflowing with vegetable refuse and collapsed cardboard boxes, and pushed the newspaper deep into the middle of it. His hand came up smeared with some rank substance: he rubbed it against his trousers. It left a mark.

Work was an endless, pointless torment, a banging chaos, a scandalously disordered place, full of terrible shrieking monsters and their distracted wardens. Luke felt like a ghost walking through the corridors full of these clamorous teenagers, or sitting restlessly amongst his coughing, fidgeting colleagues in the staff-room. He bought cans from the drinks machine and still felt dry, scorched. He smiled, exchanged pleasantries, shouted at the monsters, worked, and all the time he was feeling as insubstantial, as attenuated as a ghost, sick with a strange, deep excitement that churned inside him, like a lazy propeller in deep water. The day wore on. When it was finally over he could barely remember how to get home. He had trouble finding his car, it wasn't where he remembered leaving it.

Halfway home he had to pull up to the kerb and open the door. He thought he was going to be sick. He reached the house and parked. Mrs Keyes saw him and waved, and he managed to smile. He climbed into the house and pulled the door behind him. No sign of Anna, no coat or bag in the hall. He had to sleep. He pulled himself up to the bedroom, dragged the duvet around him, put his buzzing head on the pillow.

He had the rope attached to the wrist of whoever it was beneath him. He discovered that, not only did this disable them, but it allowed him to pull the arm to and fro, thus making it wave, like a puppet. The puppet had

206

a pair of scissors in his little fist, and Luke made him jab and feint with it, waving the arm around, like Punch. He was playing with this new-found ability when he woke up.

Anna was moving round the room; he sat up and squinted at her.

'What time is it?'

'Nine o'clock.'

'Nine o'what? Christ.'

He woke up again. It was dark. He could hear Anna talking to someone. On the phone maybe. He slept again.

In the night he woke again and the scene played itself in his head, round and round. Declan chatting to someone, feeding them with Special Brew or whatever, taking them somewhere (where?), more beer, then Declan producing his version of a claw, his knife, and a rope. The victim, drunk but sensible now of danger from this ordinary, dull-looking man, who was turning himself into something else as he watched. Tied up. Some attempt to argue, bluster. Reason, even. How far does this go? The shirt is cut open. The victim now is in terror, this is no ordinary assault, this is some derangement, some appalling madness, and who knows how far it goes. He fights his panic. He tries to flinch as Declan raises his claw, there is a wssssk, then a little cut, just a little one, a little trace of blood on arm or shoulder or belly, wherever it lands, and a sensation as of ice being drawn across the flesh. Wet. The victim stops arguing, blustering, reasoning, he falls silent, eyes wide, trying to be completely still so as not to provoke this madman any further. Declan takes his photographs. The flash is blinding. Declan approaches again, again raises the claw, another cut . . .

Luke heard a sound. He lay perfectly still while he heard the footsteps, the doors opening and closing, the click of the computer being turned on. He hadn't written any more, Declan would find nothing there. A few minutes of quiet, then doors and footsteps in reverse, going away, leaving. Luke got up when the house had again fallen silent and crept downstairs, locked the back door. Back in bed he wrapped his body round Anna's and tried to sleep. The dreadful slow churning started and stopped and started up again. Then the dreams.

27. *It's All Got to Stop*

Luke got home early on Tuesday. He should have attended a meeting after school about the possible purchase of new video equipment, but he had a migraine, he said, he'd really better just go straight home. There had been nothing in the papers that day or any of the preceding five days. Declan had stopped, because he didn't know how to continue. I can control him, Luke thought, thank God. I can control him if I can control myself.

Anna had her group supervision, so she wouldn't be back till nine, eight thirty at the earliest.

He let himself in and listened to the quietness of the house. He looked in on Bobby Parrot, who looked back at him, but had not a word to say. His cage needed cleaning, Luke noticed. Unusual for Anna to forget something like that. He made a quick tour of the room. Dust. A pair of tights, a magazine, cushions on the floor, sweet wrappers pushed inside a glass. He tidied quickly. Bobby Parrot would have to wait till later.

He stood outside the darkroom for a moment, then opened the door. He hesitated on the threshold. The room was slightly rank with neglect. He opened the window, and papers fluttered in the breeze. He found the box under the cupboard, took out the file with the pictures of Anna in.

It seemed unbelievable to him now that he had kept them like this. Developing them was bad enough, but keeping them? What for, for Christ's sake?

What had he been turning into?

He looked at them, just once each, then put them back

in the file, tucked it under his arm, left the room and went down the corridor.

He again had to nerve himself, this time to go into the office. Everything was in order. Declan had left no trace of himself on any of his nocturnal visits. Luke turned the computer on, fed it the right disk, and deleted the files one by one. When that was done he took the disk out of the disk drive and tore open the steel flap, forced the case open with the blade of a pair of scissors, exposing the black wheel of magnetic material inside. He wrenched it free of the plastic case and cut it into quarters. He swept up the dismembered fragments of the disk and went downstairs.

The garden was its usual self, messy, slightly unkempt, grass too long, edges untrimmed, borders undug. He went down to the heap at the bottom and gathered together old grass clippings, twigs and leaves. He made a small bonfire and, once it was going strongly enough, he took the pictures and fed them to the flames, one at a time, making sure each was completely consumed before he started on the next. He even burned the file itself. He chucked the plastic fragments of the disk on top, and they distorted, warped, began to emit stinking black smoke. The smoke curled upward into the deep blue of the sky. When there was nothing remaining except a few twisted shreds of blackened plastic he kicked the ashes around and spread grass clippings over the scorched patch. It's all got to stop, he told himself, all of it.

When Anna came back she found the table set and food ready. There was even wine. Luke was solemn and attentive. As they ate he cleared his throat, then formally apologized for being so distant lately. Anna was surprised: she hadn't really registered that he *had* been distant. She apologized too, she had had a lot on her mind. Luke opened another bottle. Towards the end of it he told her how much he loved her, and how he would never let any harm come to her, never, never. She ruffled his hair and said, let's go upstairs. He brought the bottle up with him.

He had the rope in place, he had the arm moving, like a puppet. There was wetness under him, warm. He relaxed his weight a fraction and tried to turn the person underneath him over, so that he could see their face. It was a difficult manoeuvre, if he was going to keep control of the person's movements and not give them any leverage. He almost managed it. Keep still, he was saying, just keep still can't you?

He woke in a sweat and went round the house, checking the locks on doors and windows. It was amazing how many ways there were of getting into a house. He was astonished at how lax he and Anna had become about security. Possibly because they had never been burgled, he thought, just about alone amongst the people they knew. Granted, this wasn't exactly a high crime area, though that meant less and less as he well knew. Anyway, this laxness, it had to stop. It was all part of the sloppy, disorganized kind of thinking that had allowed any of this to happen in the first place. It all had to stop.

He recalled his first meeting with Declan, their first collision. How could he have ever let him in? How could he have been so stupid? Everything had followed from that first moment of stupidity, and in the course of it he had allowed, not just his own safety, but Anna's to be compromised. He had allowed that madman to wander about his house at night, had left the house unsecured so that he could get in, had even heard him doing it, and had done nothing. He could barely believe it now.

He still hadn't cleaned out Bobby's cage. He did it now, as Bobby watched him sleepily, treading up and down his perch.

'Shit,' Bobby said abruptly, and Luke regarded him sourly.

'And you, friend,' he said. 'And you mate.'

211

He didn't want to go back to bed in case the dreams started up again, but it was late and he was tired. He folded himself against Anna's warm, still body and closed his eyes.

Just before dawn, Bobby Parrot heard the back door being tried, heard the handle rattle in the still, dark house. He blinked and twisted his head at the sound. Footsteps came round to the side door, then to the front. Bobby said 'Cooooo,' lifted a leg. The footsteps came to a stop at the front door, there was nothing for a minute, then they faded away again, down the garden path and out of the gate. They echoed down the length of the deserted street.

28. *With* My *Eyes?*

Anna opened the door in her dressing-gown. Mrs Keyes was standing on the doorstep.

'What is it? What's the matter?'

'I'm sure it's nothing dear,' Mrs Keyes said, trying to smile, 'but I'm fairly certain I heard something last night.'

'Something?'

But Anna's mind had already formed the two syllables of his name, had seen him, slightly hunched, moving quietly round the garden, along the paths. Perhaps jumping a back-garden fence.

'Come in,' Anna said, glancing up and down the street before she shut the door.

They sat in the kitchen amongst yesterday's newspapers and cups. Mrs Keyes unthinkingly pushed aside one of Luke's epic ashtrays.

'You heard something?' Anna said.

'Oh you know how it is in the middle of the night dear, particularly when you live alone . . .'

'Declan?' The word forced itself out from between Anna's lips. Mrs Keyes looked down at the table. 'Was it Declan?'

'I don't know dear, it could have been anything . . .'

'But you think it was Declan.'

'Well I just thought that it *might* be.'

'But you didn't see him?'

'With *my* eyes? For heaven's sake, and in the dark . . .'

'So you don't know?'

'No.'

Mrs Keyes sat back and regarded her.

'My dear, you almost sound as if you wanted it to be him.'

Anna didn't speak for a moment, her heart was jumping about too much. She made tea. Nothing bad could happen while you were in your own kitchen making tea.

'No, no,' she said after a few moments. 'No of course not. I just think that if there's someone prowling around out there in the middle of the night we should find out who it is. Don't you?'

'Anna dear, if there *is* someone prowling, *if* there is, then what we should do is call the police. It hardly matters who it is, now does it?'

'No of course it doesn't.' She pulled herself together, she shook her head, firmly. 'Of course it doesn't.' You didn't actually see him, she thought, it was dark, your eyesight's not good, he kept out of sight. You didn't actually *see* him.

A few days later she caught an eye. Quick eager eye. In a doorway. She signalled frantically, tried to change lane, horns were sounded at her. She turned left, reversed the car, pushed herself out into the oncoming traffic, forced a way through. The kind of driving she hated. Real London driving, she thought, and swerved into a side-street. There was a space a few cars down. Her parking was poor. She ran back to the intersection, turned right, ran towards the row of shops beneath a low concrete canopy. There were a few people sitting on a step. They watched her as she ran towards them, then slowed to a walk, panting. When had she last run anywhere?

'Excuse me, was there someone here just now? Five foot eleven or so, medium build . . .' She sounded like the police, she looked like a secretary having a nervous breakdown in her lunch-hour.

'Did you see him? He was here just a moment ago, I saw him.' She was accusing them, they could see that.

214

'What just a minute ago?' the girl said, 'just now you mean?'

'Yes yes,' Anna said, exasperated. 'I *saw* him!'

'No,' the girl shook her head slowly, 'no-one's been round here, have they?' Her companion shook his head. Anna stared at them. She turned, furiously, and marched back to the car. She had seen him!

She spent her lunch-hour on the phone, got nowhere. The police suggested she try Saddlebrook Hospital, Saddlebrook didn't have a file and referred her to someone at Social Services, who became very interested in why she wanted to know. 'I'm his sister,' she told the woman, her voice catching, 'please . . .' Social Services, of course, were not about to tell just anybody anything, however, and certainly not over the phone. She'd known that, really, but she'd just thought . . . Anna was given a name and an office address, somewhere out in Colindale. *If* she had a valid reason to know. She would need proofs of identity. Anna slammed the phone, enraged. The first few men in the afternoon session got short shrift. She glared at each of them, none of them the right one. She felt icy and disdainful. She took aspirins.

Luke wasn't back when she let herself into the house that evening. She felt too keyed-up to change. She boiled a kettle for tea but was already leaving the house by the time it clicked off. Her heels clacked against the pavement.

A fifteen-minute walk. The air was neutral, slightly dry. Anyone passing her on the way would have noticed only a young woman, smartly dressed, walking fast, head bowed. She didn't look up once. A few dry leaves scuttered past her feet.

Past the cemetery gate, on up the road, then across the little green and up to the allotment fences. You had to walk right along, and then cut down.

It was nearly dark as she walked up the path between the allotments, towards the shed. There was no light on inside, no candle. But he could be anywhere, hiding, lurking, ready to jump out at her. She stopped and looked around. No-one about. No sound, nothing moving. Things grew and flourished all around her in the other allotments, tough black-green leaves and fussy, straggling things attached to poles.

She approached the shed from the side, wary of being seen. She crept up to the little window. For a moment she couldn't make herself look inside. Then she did.

A clear, swept floor. Rakes and a spade and sticks and poles of various kinds stacked in a corner. No candle, no shears. She realized that someone must have taken the allotment on, decided to try and grow something other than brambles. She looked at the ground under her feet: it was partially cleared, black in patches, squares and trenches dug and turned. There were new panels in the shed, new hinges, a padlock. There was no sign of Declan. A man wheeled a bicycle along the pavement on the other side of the chain-link fence. Anna froze, waited for him to pass, clung to the shadow of the shed.

Maybe it hadn't been him that Mrs Keyes had heard creeping round the house. Maybe Anna hadn't seen him. She might have been mistaken. And even if it had been him, what would she say if she found him now? It all seemed foolish suddenly. The last time they'd spoken she had been lying about bicarbonate of soda, the time before that she was tied up on the floor of the shed and he'd been brandishing a pair of shears. Kind of hard to pick up the threads from something like that.

She'd made up the story about him attacking Mrs Keyes, but who was to say that he hadn't attacked anyone else? Anna thought, maybe I wasn't the first person he tied up, maybe he'd done it before. Maybe he's done it since. All at once the idea of coming to find him didn't seem quite so sensible. She was overwhelmingly relieved, suddenly, that he wasn't here.

When the ratcheting sound of the bike had passed she crept away from the shed and walked down to the path.

Something caught her eye, a little gleam of something amongst the weeds and grass by the side of the path. She bent down to retrieve it. A small item, about the size of a pound coin, bright white. She held it in her hand. It was a piece of paper, the kind of paper that gum is wrapped in, folded up. She unfolded it: inside was a little figure of a man, made of foil. His head was tilted all to one side, as if his neck were broken.

29. *Acceptable Design Solutions*

They both stayed up late watching a film. They didn't talk much. Luke held out for a while then made a joint. Anna watched him out of the corner of her eye. She didn't have any of the joint.

Luke stood up to go to bed before the film finished.

'You not coming up?' he said, as Anna showed no sign of moving.

'No, I'll be up in a bit. You go on.'

'OK.' He stood behind her chair for a moment, not seeming to be sure if he wanted to stay or not. The dope often made him like this, irresolute, held in thrall between simple alternatives. Stay or go. Anna watched the screen and clenched her teeth, waiting for him to go. She wanted to be alone.

'OK,' Luke said again, and went up.

Without really having decided to, Anna found that she was waiting up. The phrase crept into her head as the television chattered on: keep a watch. She was keeping a watch, for Declan. He was out there, somewhere in the great featureless sea of North London, amongst the synagogues and the Turkish bakeries, the launderettes with their faded Perspex signs, the gardens and hedges and schools. The allotments.

He was around. Sooner or later he would come back here, she was certain.

She heard the door of Luke's office open, close, heard the chair squeak under his weight.

Anna watched television until it became intolerable, a hellish, unendurable Open University programme about the launch of a new vacuum cleaner. A man who reminded her of Declan in his complete blankness said 'acceptable design solution' three times in two minutes, and she turned it off.

She went to the kitchen to make a cup of tea. There was a postcard on top of the fridge, from her parents in Portugal. The stamp was tiny, a lovely dusty pink, much marked by franking. Her mother's handwriting seemed to have broadened out somewhat since she had been there. Anna remembered it as being spiky, with angular loops and tails. But now the angles were smoothed out, the loops were broad-bellied, like plump, happy little pigs. There was a line from her father beneath her mother's porcine effusions. He called her 'squirrel'. Write soon, squirrel, all best. Dad.

Anna turned it over. It was a pink and gold picture of a church tower and window-boxes of geraniums, astonishing colours. Her mother often said how much she loved geraniums. Why she had had to go to Portugal, to some appalling retirement village, to find them, Anna didn't know. She imagined bars stuffed full of women with Versace scarves and leather hides, oiled and polished. The men would be in yachting shoes and stone-coloured slacks. Sporty little zip-up jackets for the evening. She imagined the days spent sitting on balconies avoiding the sun, then evenings in bars and restaurants. Friends. Talk about businesses, bars, tax dodges, then relatives at home. Tentative, subdued flirting later on. Her mother laughing her social laugh, bright and knowing. Anna was silently contemptuous. How could they want so little?

She wandered into the front room. Looked at the titles of books on the shelves. She saw Luke's big old school atlas and flicked through it. She found a map of Ireland. What was the name again? Ballyscally or something? She pored over the map, reading the tiny names, following the roads, like little threads that held the whole place together. Somewhere near Galway he'd said, she remembered that much. She couldn't find a name on the map that reminded her of what he'd said.

There didn't seem to be anything much near Galway. Maybe it was too small to be on a map. We were OK, he'd said. We were OK. Her eyes moved over the map vacantly. She snapped the book shut, replaced it on the shelf. She returned to her vigil in the kitchen.

Luke hadn't gone to bed yet. At least she hadn't heard him if he had. He was still in the office, doing whatever he did in there.

The light from the kitchen window fell onto the concrete path and a small patch of grass, which looked uneasy and artificial in the glare. She gazed out of the window while she waited for the kettle, and was abruptly conscious of being watched. It was a slow, cooling sensation starting in her legs and working up to her stomach. She became absolutely still. Steam blossomed behind her.

Her eyes travelled slowly across the dark garden. There was a flash, and she cried out, startled, before she realized what it was. Mrs Keyes's cat, sitting on the dividing wall, perfectly still, its head lowered, its clear green eyes fixed on her. She returned its look and it blinked, then turned its head away, casually. What *me*, looking at *you*? Do me a favour. She turned back into the kitchen to make the tea, and the cat swung its head back, its eyes again locked onto her.

She sat with her tea and tried not to think about what she would do if Declan actually did show up. She knew she wouldn't call the police. There was no way she could go through all that again. So she would have to talk to him, find out what he was doing, make him understand that he had to go away and stay away or he'd be in trouble again. What was he after anyway?

You, said a little voice, he's after you. She paused in her thoughts, brought to an uneasy halt by the idea.

Well, *if* that was it, then she would simply have to explain to him that it was quite impossible, that it had happened once and once only, because she'd temporarily lost her sense of proportion, of reason, of whatever it was that made her sane. It could never happen again, never.

She would explain that if Luke found him he might do anything, he might kill him, it was perfectly possible. Declan had, after all, tied her and photographed her. (Flash, whirr, what had happened to the film?) It was the kind of thing that men killed each other over. Honour. Dishonour. Once they got talking like that, she knew, there could only be trouble.

So you see, Declan, she said silently in the bright clean kitchen, so you see, you must just go away, at once, and never come back. You must pretend you never came here, you must forget about us, about me. You must leave Luke and me to patch things up as best we can. We have deceived each other, lied to each other, even betrayed each other, but that doesn't mean we don't still love each other. Deception, betrayal, love. They were fine, powerful words. Big words. Like honour, dishonour. But what was there to hang them onto? None of it seemed to have much to do with her any more, nor with the man upstairs.

That roll of film, she thought, and stopped. I took it out of the camera, put it into the little plastic canister. That was as far as I got. She had forgotten all about it, not forgotten what Declan had done, of course not, but forgotten that the evidence of his doing was still there, still sitting on the counter, in the darkroom. Luke had been in there, many times, had he seen it?

Of course he had. More than just seen it?

Developed it?

She stared out at the garden, bright green and grey, then shadowy, then black. A picture came to her, a picture of herself lying on that damp carpet in the allotment shed, with Declan taking his pictures. The flash had dazzled her, left brilliantly coloured after-images in her eyes, purple and yellow, but through the glare and her terrible fear (the fear was hard to remember, except as a clenched fist in the stomach and a dry mouth) he had reminded her of someone, he had moved back to frame a shot and she had been suddenly, forcibly, reminded of someone. It was Luke, of course, that was how Luke moved when he had a camera in his hands, stooped, bobbing, frowning, back and forward. Declan had been imitating Luke.

So where had Declan got the idea of taking pictures from in the first place? He would never have thought something like that up for himself, so who had put the idea into his head?

It was Luke. Of course.

The words reverberated inside her skull and took her breath away for a moment, so that she gasped.

Declan picked up all kinds of clues from all kinds of people, whoever was around. He had picked something up from Luke. That didn't mean, of course, that Luke had deliberately suggested it. Declan could simply pluck things from you, could seemingly give shape to things that you weren't even conscious of thinking. He had that ability. Luke had suggested the pictures, but he hadn't (necessarily. *Necessarily.*) done it consciously.

She shook her head. Of course he hadn't suggested it consciously, what was she thinking? If he had done that then he would be –

She pondered the man upstairs, turning him over and over in her mind, examining him from every angle, uncomfortably. She remembered the night she and Declan and Luke had drunk too much and played records, how Luke and Declan had danced, how their shadows had seemed to merge, to become one thing. They were alike, so alike. They had always got on so well, they had seemed to understand each other so easily. Because they were alike.

Were they perhaps more alike than she had at first thought? The question framed itself neatly, allowing for only two possible answers: the man I live with, the man upstairs right now. Is he insane? The words bloomed quietly in the quiet kitchen.

She shook her head again. No he was not. Of *course* he wasn't! It was absurd. This was the kind of thing you started thinking when you sat up all night in an empty kitchen, waiting for a madman (a *real* madman!) to materialize in your back garden.

So where was that film?

Luke sat in the office on the squeaking swivel chair and stared at his screen, but he wasn't writing anything.

He was reading.

'. . . it was all dark so he couldnt see anyone properly. He got out the forest all right though and then he went the village where all the people lived. They was asleep because it was the middle of the night. And the huts was all dark . . .'

Luke was sitting very upright in the swivel chair. He couldn't believe what he was reading.

'. . . he went in one of the huts and there was this man there and a lady so he got the man and he cut him all up with his arm thing, he cut him in half and there was blood everywhere! and the lady screamed so he got her mouth and . . .'

No no no, I didn't write this, Luke was thinking numbly, I didn't write any of this. This isn't how it goes.

'. . . tied her all up so she had to stay still and he had intimate relations with her with his special thing which he had . . .'

Intimate what? Special *what*?

'. . . she had a baby, not straight away, you had to wait. Then he went round the other huts, and the men screamed when he cut them up . . .'

Jesus, Luke was thinking, no, this isn't how it goes.

'. . . he hid somewhere so they couldn't find him. Then he jumped out at them with his claw thing . . .'

How did he get in, Luke thought, I locked everything up. I locked him out. How did he get in? He did a mental tour of the house, looking in rooms to check the windows. He must have missed something. He went over it again, but he couldn't think, he knew he was missing something but he couldn't think what. I'll go down in a minute, he thought, and have a proper look.

223

Not only how, of course. Why. Why has he written all this, Luke thought, why does he want me to read it? What for?

The answer came at once: he wants you to mark it. You're a teacher, you mark things. He wants your comments. He wants to know if this is what comes next. He's waiting. The last word on the page just said: Monday.

Luke deleted the file. The lights were still on downstairs, he heard small sounds from the kitchen. What was she doing down there?

He stood on the landing and called down, goodnight. Anna called back. Luke stood a few moments longer, then put himself to bed. No use checking security tonight. Declan wouldn't be back till Monday. By then Luke would be ready for him.

30. *Did you ever think of that?*

Anna had given up at three thirty and gone to bed. There
was no way she could wait up all night, she just wasn't
built for it. Her head started to buzz, her eyes stung and
watered, her brain seemed to clog up with cotton wool
and treacle. Her thoughts travelled round and round in
stupid little circles until she didn't know what they
were any more. She was only technically awake when
she finally admitted defeat and turned off the lights.

She and Luke went out the next day. It was a
Saturday, bright and cool, very busy. They had decided
to walk down the Tottenham High Road, down
Stamford Hill and as far as Stoke Newington. There was
a cemetery there that Anna liked, very shabby and
overgrown.

With no baby and no dog to slow them down, they
walked fast. Anna found that she was catching people's
eyes more than usual. She noticed particularities of
dress and manner, the varieties of complexion and
mood. She passed many that reminded her of Declan,
in one way or another. Luke strode beside her, seemingly blind. He was looking neither to left nor right, but
seemed to have his gaze fixed on some distant goal. He
looked tense, determined. Grim, even.

Someone brushed past, Luke twisted to avoid him,
knocked someone's elbow, half turned to apologize.
The propeller turning in the pit of his stomach jolted,
hitched for a second, and Luke shut his eyes, waited for
it to start up again. He was his usual weekend self,
unshaven, hung-over, bleary. Anna had had to practically push him out of the house. He looked terrible.

She waited a moment for him to catch up with her.

'Luke? Are you OK?'

He nodded. They tried to walk two abreast but the press of people was too great and they became separated again. She caught sight of him, then lost him again. She went back.

She saw him in a shop, barging his way down a narrow aisle surrounded by bunches of leafy herbs and big, white, bulbous vegetables and tins with labels in some Middle Eastern language.

'Luke?'

He was a few yards ahead of her. The shop was fairly empty and she caught him up quickly, caught hold of his arm. He shook her hand away.

'Luke? Are you all right?'

He brandished a tin at her.

'I just thought we needed some of these.'

Anna looked at the tin, a type of white beans, they looked glossy and plump and syrupy. Revolting, whatever they were. She took them from him and put them back on the shelf.

She took his hand and led him out of the shop. He baulked at the doorway, and she waited patiently as he scanned the street, his eyes screwed up as if against the glare. He saw people teeming, in all directions, like insects. He saw their hands, fingers, fingernails. Who could tell who they were, what they were? What they were maybe turning into? She felt the tension in his hand and arm.

'Let's go and get a cup of tea', she said, gently, soothingly. 'OK?'

They sat in a dark little café, the only customers apart from a late-middle-aged man with a moustache and a beautiful deep blue silk shirt.

Luke had a view through the window. His gaze was unfocused.

'I'm just not feeling very good,' he said at last. 'That's all.' Anna didn't reply. To her it had looked a lot like a panic attack.

226

Luke stared out of the window and went back over the sequence of events: someone had brushed past him, he had half turned, then someone else had *touched* him. It was a middle-aged man, short and rather heavy, and what he had done was to allow the fingers of one hand to brush over Luke's belly, just below the ribs. As he moved on his hand had rested for a moment, and the fingers and thumb had closed, just enough to exert a gentle, almost playful *squeeze*. It had been unmistakably deliberate, no casual, enforced, accidental intimacy of the sort that London life so often visited on you, but calculated, measured: *meant*. That was what had momentarily panicked him (Anna was right about that), that it was meant, that it meant something. The man was trying to tell him something by it. It was, and Luke couldn't find any way of shaking off the feeling, a warning.

'Have you ever thought,' Luke said after a minute or so of silence, 'what kind of damage the human body can do?' He looked straight at her, a peculiar little half smile on his face. 'Did you ever think of that? Just the human body itself. Teeth, fingernails –'

He broke off.

'Someone could just come for you and even if they weren't armed they could still rip you to bloody strips.' His fingers spread out on the Formica table top. 'You wouldn't even see it coming, they could just be passing you, anyone, anyone at all, and they could just lash out, just *claw* you –'

He resumed his dreamy gaze through the window. Anna watched him, appalled.

'Why would anyone do that?' she said at last, but Luke just shook his head and looked out at the street, the people. She wondered what images he had of them, what he was seeing. She was getting worried about him.

227

31. *Safe and Sound*

Anna stayed up again that night. Watched. Luke had been particularly precise, punctilious even, about locking up for the night. He had walked round twice, locking and unlocking and locking again, rattling handles.

She had gone to bed with Luke, they had lain together, not talking, for an hour or so. Luke had smoked. She had rested her hand on his leg, but with no response, and she had taken it away. When he was asleep she had risen again and washed and dressed. It was about one o'clock. The world was quiet.

Again she sat in the kitchen. When Declan came, she thought, he would come from the back of the house. She didn't know why she was so sure. She wished it would be tonight so that it could be over and done with. Luke wasn't the only one who was feeling the strain. And she wished it for another reason: she was desperate to talk to Declan, to question him. She was terribly afraid that he had done something wrong. The minutes ticked away, made hours.

It was after three when she heard a sound from upstairs, a door opening, footsteps. She heard a sound she recognized but couldn't immediately place.

She pushed her chair back and stood in the kitchen door, craning her head upward. The sound was quite clear and distinct. She stood at the bottom of the stairs: the landing light was on.

'Luke?'

The sound of her voice in the quiet house suddenly sent a thrill of unease through her. What was he doing up there? She hesitated. Suddenly she didn't want to look.

As she stood, the thought came: what if it isn't Luke? What if it's Declan? What if he'd got in somehow, crept in somehow past her and gone upstairs.

To do what exactly?

'Luke?'

Her voice sounded small and trapped, like a moth under a glass.

She went up. She reached the turn of the stairs, ascended the half-flight to the first floor, turned the corner.

There was a light at the end of the corridor, a faint light. She stood perfectly still as she looked. Luke was standing outside a door, the door to the small spare room. He was naked. In one hand he carried a torch, in the other the ring of keys, and he was slowly, calmly, trying them out, each in turn, to find the one that fitted the lock. He found the right one as she watched, turned it, rattled the handle. He unlocked it again, opened the door, looked inside, closed the door, locked it again. The keys jangled on the ring as he moved on to the next room, the room next to the bathroom. Again tried keys.

'Luke?'

He half turned towards her as she spoke, nodded politely, returned to the keys. She took a step towards him. His eyes were open but she was suddenly sure he was not awake.

'Luke? Are you awake?' No reply. 'Can you hear me?' He said nothing, but again nodded, slowly, stiffly. She came closer, a little at a time, until she was standing just a few feet behind him.

'Let's go back to bed. OK? Luke?'

He swung the door open, looked in, closed it again. Locked it. She stretched out her arm, touched his back. He stiffened but said nothing.

'Come on baby.' He allowed her to put her hand on his arm and lead him away. As she opened their bedroom door for him he muttered something, and she said, 'What?'

'All safe. All safe and sound. No-one missing.' He nodded and smiled. She guided him into bed and helped him to lie down. She took the keys out of his hand.

'All accounted for,' he said. 'Safe and sound.'

32. *It's Like This*

Luke didn't go into work on Monday morning, he rang in sick. For once 'sick' wasn't an utterly, pitifully transparent euphemism for 'hung-over'. He genuinely was not feeling tremendously perky. And he hadn't even been drinking.

He got up at eleven. There was no milk for tea. He would have to go out and get some.

He wandered round the house. There was a great deal of tidying to be done. There were cups and plates all over the place, many with traces of ash and the remains of joints smeared over them, stuffed under chairs and nestling in alcoves. There were newspapers and litter of all kinds. Poor Bobby needed doing. The cooker top was filthy, and the fridge door. He cleared everything out onto the kitchen floor, and saw how murky *that* was getting. While he was fetching the cream cleaner from the bathroom he happened to glance inside the mirrored cabinet and saw sticky, grimy deposits on the shelves under the bottles and tubes. They all needed washing. And the *bath* – !

He was looking for an old tin of Duraglit he was certain was knocking about somewhere. It wasn't in any of the kitchen cupboards. He went down the hall to the little pantry that never got used any more except as a store-room. Just a glorified cupboard really. Except that it had a window.

A window. He looked at it closely. Took hold of the sash. Opened it. It opened easily. The paint on the ledge and the wall was scuffed with shoe marks. This must have been where Declan was getting in. There was no lock. He'd just have to lock the door instead. He'd get

231

round to it later. He seemed to have so much to do suddenly.

When he looked up from scrubbing round the base of the boiler cupboard in the kitchen it was three o'clock. He still hadn't had a cup of tea. There still wasn't any milk. He would still have to go out.

He put on his denim jacket, found his house keys, dropped them into the left breast pocket. He decided to take some bottles with him to the bottle bank, and spent some time arranging them into separate plastic bags according to colour. He hesitated over different kinds of bottles, wine, beer, water. What about an empty coffee jar? Should that go as well? He rummaged in the cupboards and found jars of pickle and jam with only tiny amounts left, mere smears and crusty deposits clinging to their bottoms. They should be washed out before they went. He couldn't find anything suitable to clean them with. He glanced at the clock: nearly four.

Milk. Milk. We need a pint of milk.

Maybe there was some powdered stuff somewhere. He launched a thorough, an exhaustive search. There were all kinds of fascinating things, but milk was not one of them. He put the kettle on and went to the front door, peered out at the world.

It was a cool autumn afternoon. The big tree outside number forty-eight, which was either a plane tree or something else entirely, was starting to turn, the edges of the leaves deepening in colour and starting just perceptibly to droop. He stood for a few minutes looking at the tree, at the road beside it, at the garden path that led to the road. He would have to go past the tree to get the milk. There didn't seem to be anybody about, but there would be plenty on the main road, in the shops, everywhere. Teeming about. One of them could be Declan. He shook the thought away.

He patted his breast pocket to check that he had his keys before he left the house. They weren't there. He checked all his pockets, no trace. He went back to the kitchen, assuming that they must have fallen out while he was cleaning something. No trace. He toured the house, bedrooms, bathroom, living-room. No keys. He was becoming furious, yet the search seemed to take on a logic of its own after a while, and he found himself perfectly contentedly looking where he knew he hadn't been, where thus no keys could be, in a kind of bloody-minded trance. At this rate Anna would be home before he had a chance to go out.

He was poking down behind the big sideboard in the living-room when he realized what had happened. He had changed his jacket: he had taken the denim off when he'd started sorting the bottles and jars, and later put on his battered leather zip-up. That was why he couldn't find the keys. The denim jacket was reclining innocently on the floor in the living-room. He swapped jackets again, and again headed for the front door.

Twenty to five. The street was still deserted, the light starting to fade now. It seemed an absurd time to be going out to get milk, you did that in the morning. He hesitated on the doorstep, looking this way and that.

Then he took a step forward and the world seemed suddenly to take on weight, to lower itself, to fall, or rather to slip massively onto him, so that he almost stumbled, buckling at the knees. Then as suddenly it lifted again, and he felt light-headed, dizzy. He looked around, as if to see who was responsible for this sudden-ness, this unaccustomed sense of the immense weight of everything. Not well, he told himself, you're not well. He stepped back into the house, taking a last puzzled, scowling look round at the street and the tricksy, newly hostile world beyond it. He would go out later maybe, when he was feeling better. The moment he decided this and closed the door the dizziness left him, and the churning in his belly stepped down a notch, just turning over. He would go out later. If he felt like it. He found the ring of keys and went upstairs.

Anna came home and was on her way to the bathroom for a soak when she heard a sound from the small room

233

next to the spare bedroom, the office. Luke's office. She hadn't thought he was in.

'Luke?'

She went to the door and tapped.

'Luke? Hello?'

Nothing. She must have been mistaken. She'd thought she'd heard the sound of his word processor going, the space bar made a distinctive thud which seemed sometimes to carry through all the walls and floors of the house. She lay in her bath and stroked her firm flat belly, her breasts which, though perhaps not quite as perky as they had been say five years ago, had not yet collapsed and sagged like the breasts of some of her women friends. Sal's, for instance, had never completely recovered from the mauling little Ryan had subjected them to. She had noticed them in the changing-rooms in Warehouse a few weeks ago. Sal's breasts no longer had that bouncy playmate-of-the-month look, they were now more like a discarded piece of packaging, flattened, more triangular than round, and the nipples looked, frankly, *used*. Anna, by contrast, still had breasts that could, in the right light, pass muster as plausible objects of desire. In *someone*, anyway. It was something.

She stiffened. There it was again, that muffled thudding of the space bar, there was no mistake. She sat up in the bath, turned her face to the side, scowled. He was in there all right. So why wasn't he answering?

She got out and dripped all over the floor while she found a towel to wear. She went to the door of the office.

'Luke?'

'Yeah?'

'Oh you *are* in. I thought I could hear you. Why didn't you answer earlier on?'

'When?'

'Before. It doesn't matter. Whatcha doing?'

'Nothing.'

She dressed, slowly. It had been a long day, and she was fully determined to watch tonight for as long as she could. Luke clearly wasn't going to be taking his turn in the crow's nest, as Anna had hoped. Typically irresponsible behaviour. He appeared completely unconcerned that Declan might be out there, prowling about, with God knew what on his mind. He seemed to have decided that there was no risk of anything happening. She could waste her time sitting up half the night if she wanted to but he wasn't going to be participating in any such hysterical nonsense. In fact it was as if he *knew* something. He seemed that sure. She went to the kitchen and found scrubbed surfaces, gleaming aluminium cooker surrounds and a mopped floor.

She stood, amazed, for a moment. It took hours to do all that, she thought, hours and hours. Come to think of it, there had been evidence of similar activity in the bathroom. Unless some perverse, suburban burglar had got in and scrubbed everything instead of wrecking it, Luke must have been here all day, cleaning.

She went back up to the office door.

'Luke? Have you been to work today?'

'No. Why?'

'Just curious. You've cleaned everything.'

'Uhuh.'

'Why don't you come out for a minute?'

'I'm right in the middle of something. I'll be out soon.'

She returned to the shiny shiny kitchen and started on dinner. Every drawer she opened, every surface she touched, was clean, non-sticky, grime-free. It was amazing. It was, she reflected as she cut up an onion, as if he were preparing for something.

'Luke?' She was calling from the foot of the stairs, but she knew he could hear her.

'Luke? What are you doing up there? Dinner's ready.'

Nothing. She marched up the stairs, grabbed the door handle.

It was locked.

She twisted the knob a few times, unable to believe that he'd actually locked himself in.

'Luke?'

Nothing. She knocked a few times. She could hear him pounding away, but he wasn't going to answer her.

She ate by herself in the ridiculously clean kitchen, and when she'd finished she sat on, just sat. The thudding from upstairs started and stopped. After an hour or two she locked up and came back to her chair in the kitchen. Then she stood up again and unbolted the kitchen door, positioned her chair in the doorway and sat, half in and half out, as the cool October air stroked her. The garden was moist and scented, damp soil and leaves, wet grass. Around two o'clock the sky began to cloud over and the wind freshened slightly. She watched the stars go out.

'. . . he fled, and the dark forms pursued, through the forest, through branches that twisted and caught, leaves that dripped, roots that tried to trip him. The crab people ran clumsily, sideways, their claws trailing the ground. They were awkward, but they knew the terrain and they were still fast. Luc found that he was slowly losing ground, that they gained with every step. His breath was short and fast and painful in his chest, and more than once he thought he felt a claw at his back and lurched forward while his heart laboured and his lungs ached under his tender ribs . . .'

The office was thick with stale smoke. Luke's cleaning had stopped at the door, and the room was hugely disordered. The keyboard in particular was becoming very nasty, bits of ash and tobacco in between the keys, the keys themselves melted, burned in places, sticky overall with spilled beer. There were ashtrays everywhere, saucers, beer cans covered with ash and dog-ends.

'. . . as they called out in their deep, resonant voices, called to him to stop, to return, that they meant him no harm. He knew they lied, he knew the terrible power of their weapons. If he could regain the village, if he could but escape this forest, these dark and tangled branches . . .'

The room wasn't hot but he was sweating, and drops fell onto the keyboard, causing his fingers to become slippy. He rubbed them against his shirt frequently.

'. . . then loomed ahead of him, standing motionless in a clearing, a form he knew well. The face was hidden by its hood, but he knew at once who it was, what it was . . .'

Finally he appeared, quite suddenly, but she wasn't startled, not even surprised. He emerged from the blackness of the garden into the twilight of the area illuminated by the light from the kitchen. He didn't seem surprised to see her waiting there either. He came closer and she stood.

'. . . "I will go to my hut," Luc said to the hooded form of his foe, the avenger of the dishonour of his sister, "I will go now. Across the doorway I shall place a triple knot, and none shall enter there. I will put my house in order, I will purify my house and myself as written, then you may come to me. We will match weapon to weapon. I salute the winner!" Luc raised his hand, and the creature lifted its ancient, gnarled claw and said, "I also salute him." . . .'

He came closer and she stood.
   'Declan.'
   'Anna.'
   'What are you doing here?'
   'I just came . . .'
   His voice trailed off.
   She squinted at him. He seemed different somehow, so different that she couldn't at first say why. Then she saw it: he had grown a beard. It was closely trimmed, the kind of beard policemen are allowed to have, neat and tidy. Lighter in colour than his hair, which was also closely cropped. Almost ginger in fact. It changed the

shape of his face so completely that he could have been someone else. And he was dressed differently, neat black jeans and a jacket of some dark cloth. He looked clean and orderly. He looked good.

'You look well.'

'Thank you.'

He edged a step closer, slightly sideways, slightly hunched.

'Declan. I have to ask you something.'

'OK.'

She cleared her throat, hesitated. Now it came to it she was shy of asking him.

'Declan.' Her voice was softer, huskier. She approached him, moved closer to him, further away from the kitchen door and the bright light.

'Declan. Have you hurt anyone?'

He looked back at her inquisitively.

'Declan have you been bad? Have you hurt anyone?'

He shook his head, smiled.

'Are you sure? You're not lying, are you? You know what a lie is don't you?'

He did indeed. 'It's when you say it but it isn't true.'

'And you're not lying about this?'

'No.'

He took a step: they were less than an arm's length apart. He looked so different.

'I wanted to see you,' he said, and she shook her head.

'Look Declan, you mustn't come round here. Do you understand me? You have to go away, stay away. Don't you realize that?'

'I came to see the baby. Where's the baby?'

'What?' She stared at him. What was he saying?

'There should have been a baby, after we was in the shed, you know.'

'Declan, for God's sake. I didn't have a baby. I can't have bloody babies! Didn't you know that?'

'Oh.' For the first time he seemed unsure of himself, uncertain, more like the man she remembered. He half turned away from her, then back.

'Anyway, I wanted to see you.'

'Look, have you got any idea what Luke would do if he saw you here?'

'Is he here?'

'He's upstairs.' She was all but whispering now, they were all but touching. She had to get him away before Luke discovered him.

'You've got to go,' she said, 'you mustn't ever come back here,' and he leaned forward and put his mouth over hers, kissed her.

She stepped away from him, leaving him posed rather absurdly, slightly forward. They looked at each other. She pushed a strand of hair back behind her ear. Then his gaze left her face and moved over her shoulder. The light from the kitchen door changed. She turned round. Luke was standing in the doorway.

'Just back away from him,' he was saying, and she felt as if she were in a dream. Luke looked abstracted, he was even smiling. 'Just back away and come in.'

Luke wasn't looking at her, he was looking at Declan.

'Back away from him. He's armed.' Luke's voice was gentle, as if he were trying to talk to her without Declan hearing. She turned back to Declan. He wasn't armed.

'Luke? He hasn't got anything.'

'He's got it hidden. Just move away from him, slowly now.' She caught a movement behind her, turned again and saw that Luke was holding something in his hand, he had it palmed. She couldn't see what it was.

'Anna. Move away from him. Go to the kitchen and get some tape. There's a roll of it in the drawer.' His words were soft, uninflected, as if he were speaking through closed lips. His eyes were still fastened on Declan. She moved away from Declan, moved back until she was level with Luke at the kitchen door. He edged himself in front of her, covering her with his body. Whatever it was he had in his hand was held down at his side: she couldn't see it.

She could watch both men now. Luke edged out from the kitchen door and stood on the patio.

'Hello Declan,' he said, and smiled. Declan didn't say anything, but Anna saw that his posture underwent a sudden though subtle change when he had Luke facing him: he stood straighter, he looked less slack and empty, he looked fuller, he looked purposeful.

Luke took another step towards him, and Declan backed away a step. A delicate and complicated dance, seemingly known to both of them though not to her. She felt drained of all motive power, all she could do was lean against the door jamb and watch. Luke had said Declan was armed, she knew he wasn't, she knew that Luke was. She watched them as they moved slowly, step by step, away from the light of the kitchen into the darkness of the garden. Luke was still smiling. He was also murmuring, very softly, she thought he was saying something like 'there's a good lad now'. Declan flicked glances at her, then back to Luke. She felt detached and unreal. The two men were disappearing from her view. Luke's words echoed in her head. Get the tape. Tie him up. She thought of lying tied in the shed, thought of how Declan had reminded her of Luke, wondered about the canister of film, thought again her little question about Luke – is he insane? – thought about the tape.

The two were now some distance away; she could no longer distinguish one from the other.

'Anna,' came Luke's voice, still quiet though there was no need for caution now. 'Anna. Get the tape. Quickly now.' She leaned and waited to see what would happen next.

Declan held Luke's eye, heard the soft voice murmuring, matched him step for step. He glanced frequently at Luke's hand. Something glinted there.

'There's a good lad. Easy does it now.' Luke was hardly aware of speaking, the words seemed to come from some pre-existing pool of such things. Declan could see Anna leaning in the doorway, she seemed a long way away suddenly. He mouthed her name. She looked as if she were in a trance.

'Just hand it over now,' Luke was saying. 'Just hand it over and there'll be no trouble. There's a good lad.' Declan found himself being backed into a corner, with the rubbish heap at one side and the dividing wall with next door at his back. Luke stood in front of him. He was more than an arm's length away. Declan leaned forward, and Luke leaned back. They were locked together.

Then Declan lunged, his arm swung out in a wide arc, just missing Luke, who grunted and flinched back. The thing in Luke's hand revealed itself, a little knife, Declan could see the shiny serrated blade, it looked sharp as a razor. Luke's smile widened. 'That's the way,' he said, 'that's a good lad,' and so Declan swung again, wider this time, and Luke ducked away from the arm, which seemed to have more than just a hand at the end of it, he slashed at it with the knife, drew blood, pulled back. He was grunting, panting, still smiling. He wiped his lips with the back of his hand and blood dripped from the knife onto his face. Declan swung again, this time hooked his arm round Luke's neck, pulled him in, pulled him close to his body, held him, hugged him, and held down the hand with the knife. They stood locked together perfectly now, neither able to move, they swayed and grunted. Declan's arm dripped blood onto the soil. Luke tried to raise his arm, failed, cried out, a great, wild cry.

Anna squinted into the darkness, but couldn't see what was happening. She felt a terrible weight in her feet and legs, she was simply unable to move. Something was going on at the far end of the garden, but she couldn't see what. Someone had cried out, she couldn't tell who.

'Anna,' Luke called, his voice carrying strongly in the still air, 'for Christ's sake where's the bloody tape?' and Declan called 'Anna,' and their voices were the same.

Luke tried to transfer the knife to his other hand, and Declan without warning swung him round and banged his head against the wall, pulled it back, smashed again,

Luke saw lights and explosions, again, the lights flashed and spun. His sense of where he was and what he was doing receded slightly, and something like hilarity came to take its place. He held onto the knife, but his head was smashed again and he forgot that he had a knife to hold onto, forgot that he had a head, he tried to laugh and the lights went out.

Declan eased the knife from his fist, took it strongly in his hand and swung at Luke, connected with his belly, ripped a gash in Luke's shirt, in his skin. There was blood, it fell down in ripples and dribbles, and Declan slashed again, this time going deeper, slicing, found something tough and hooked the knife behind it, pulled, sawed. He jerked back as it popped and a huge heavy wet snake of blood leapt out at him, he ducked aside and it landed on the grass, followed by another, not so great. Luke fell onto his knees and said things, unconnected things, and Declan crouched down to listen. Blood was pumping from Luke's belly, but with less and less vigour, it jumped and started, little snakes now, dropping listlessly onto the soil, which was wet and black and slimy.

Luke lay still, panting, and a great, slow howl came to his mouth and lifted itself out into the air. It rose and rose and then broke, stopped. Anna listened and the paralysis in her legs thawed, she ran to where the two men were. A few feet away she stopped, not wanting to see what they were doing, they seemed to be hugging each other on the ground. There was a bright, strong smell.

'Luke?'

The one with the knife turned to her and she saw who it was, saw who the other one was. The one with the knife turned back to the one on the ground, and used the knife again. He sliced at the belly, pushed at it with his hand, sliced again. Blood came, but slower, thicker now, there was very little pressure left. Another howl came out and Declan watched and tested for blood pressure as Luke went into shock, howled, died. Declan was grunting, panting, he half stood, and turned to Anna, daubed and tattooed and hung about with blood, and he made a sound, 'Hrrrrgh!' looked at her with a face that seemed on the verge of tears, trembled, made the sound again. He was in mortal terror. The knife was loose and shaky in his hand.

'Hrrrrgh!'

Anna watched him. Blood was still seeping from Luke's body, leaching out quietly now onto the soil. A good year for the roses, she said to herself, it'll be a good year for the roses, and crouched down beside Declan.

'Give me the knife,' she said, but he would not allow her to pull it from his sticky fingers.

'Declan give me the knife now.'

Declan crouched by her side, still prodding, probing the body, still emitting his little cries of terror and bewilderment. The blood slipped away and as it fell Declan seemed also to shrink back, to become hollow again, quiet, as he had earlier, before Luke appeared. It was as if he were erasing himself, becoming blank again. He became himself again. Finally there was no more blood and Declan was a crouched, exhausted, humble shadow beside the body.

Anna eased the knife from him, and he turned to look at her, his face now cleared of the horror and agony. He was simply waiting for her to save him now, as she had before. She held the knife and thought for a moment, gazing at the shrunken, bloodless, bled carcass in front of her. Then she said, 'We'll have to burn your clothes. Take your clothes off.'

Declan looked at her, puzzled but obedient, and started to strip. His body emerged, unblooded, white in the darkness, a simple, innocent, human form. When he was naked she said, 'Go to the kitchen, drawer under the draining-board, there's a roll of packing tape. Go and get it.' Declan disappeared, a flash of white buttocks in the gloom. Anna stayed exactly where she was and regarded the body in front of her. She noticed Mrs Keyes's cat watching too. She guessed it had its eye on the blood. She met its eye and this time it didn't flinch from her look.

Declan was back crouching beside her with the tape in his hand.

'Tie him up,' she said. 'Tie him up like you tied me up.' Declan gave her a pleading look but she merely gestured towards the body, and he had to obey. It took him about ten minutes. Anna's legs were aching from her position and she stood up and stretched. Declan seemed to have a little difficulty with Luke's arms. There was no more blood now, so nothing got onto his skin. She was thinking very fast and clearly, more clearly, she thought, than she could ever remember thinking before.

'Now go and have a shower. Don't forget to wash your hair, and scrub under your finger-nails. Clean the bath out, then find something of Luke's to wear. Get dressed and then go to the darkroom and stay there. Don't come out until I tell you to. Do you understand all that? Say it back to me.'

He did, and she corrected some of the details. While he was gone she went to fetch petrol and made a bonfire of Declan's blood-soaked clothes. The shoes wouldn't burn, so she spent some time shredding them with the knife, then buried them deep inside the heap. It didn't actually matter if they were found, she thought, since the murderer could easily have brought a change of clothes with him and just dumped his shoes anywhere, there was nothing to connect them with Declan. But it would all look much better if there had been clear attempts to destroy them. The fire burned hot and fierce. It occurred to her to worry that Mrs Keyes or the other side might come out to see what was going on, but no-one did. She kicked the glowing embers around and mixed them up with the half-composted matter from the heap.

When she was satisfied she went back to the house and went up to the darkroom. Declan was there, good as gold, wearing Luke's chinos and polo shirt and trainers. He looked clean and scrubbed.

'Good boy,' she said, and stroked his cropped head.

'You saved me before,' he said, and she said, 'Yes. And I'll save you again, but you must do everything I say, exactly as I say.'

'I'll do anything you want,' he said, and then, 'I'll be anything you want. You know I can.'

'OK,' Anna said, 'it's like this.'

When she'd finished explaining it to him he looked at her, puzzled.

'Now say it back to me,' she said.

'You and me, we was out together, in the restaurant, and when we come back we couldn't find Luke nowhere, and then we looked in the garden and there he was, all tied up. There was no-one around, we didn't see no-one. Then we called the police.' She quizzed him repeatedly on details – the name of the restaurant, what time they had come back, what they had both eaten, how much they'd drunk. And who he was. 'But it's not true is it?' he said finally, as if he were seeking confirmation of the fact, confused by the accuracy and detail of the story.

'No,' Anna said, 'it's a story. It's a lie. You know what a lie is don't you?' She smiled benignly, the good teacher to the good pupil, and told him, 'It's what you say to stay out of the mental hospital.'

1990

'. . . patients with severe mental illness are offered comprehensive and well-documented programmes of care on discharge from hospital . . .'

NHS and Community Care Act

33. *Good as Gold*

Declan, arms across his face, ducked wildly as Bobby Parrot made another pass across the room, attempted a landing on the curtain rail, scrabbled frantically for a few seconds, and landed on the carpet.

Declan watched him, breathing heavily, eyes glittering with alarm. He'd only been trying to clean out the cage. He'd only left the door open for a second while he tried to pull out the water-dish to clean it, but as he withdrew his hand Bobby had pecked at his wrist and taken advantage of his confusion. He hadn't thought Bobby would bite. It hadn't occurred to him.

'Nice parrot, good parrot,' he said, and smiled nervously at it as he tried to approach without startling it again. Every time he tried to get near it it panicked, which panicked him, which panicked it further. They were both getting exhausted: this had been going on for nearly half an hour. Bobby's trajectories across the room were becoming shorter, less controlled, and the ratio of flapping and scrabbling to organized flight was increasing. Declan was twisting his hands together and sweating more. He'd started wiping his lips and saying 'Oh God'. Declan watched Bobby as Bobby stood on the carpet watching him, ducking his head. It was an impasse.

Ten minutes later Anna came home. Bobby cocked his head as he heard her key turn in the door.

'I didn't mean to . . .' Declan said as she opened the door. 'He just came out, I didn't . . .'

She shushed him and let him show her where Bobby was. She went to the kitchen and found a tea-towel, threw it over Bobby, scooped him up, deposited him in the cage. He hardly blinked. Declan watched her, wide-eyed. She ruffled his hair and pecked him on the cheek.

'Easy when you know how,' she said, and went upstairs. 'Big night tonight,' she called down from the landing. 'You're not nervous are you?'

'No.'

'Did you remember to pick up your suit from the dry-cleaners?'

'Yes.'

'And you collected the lobsters?'

'Yes.'

'We're eating at eight. Is everything going to be ready by then?'

'Yeah. It's all ready.'

'Just try to enjoy yourself. OK?'

'Yeah.' Declan said. He watched Bobby, who was nibbling delicately at a cuttlefish bone.

'Shit,' said Bobby.

There were four for dinner, Anna, Lauren, Paul, and Anna's brother Bernard. Anna and Bernard were celebrating living together for a year. This was the first time they had entertained, Anna said, the first time they'd felt ready to face the world again. They'd have to forgive her if she was a little bit nervous! Lauren squeezed her hand, of course they understood. She and Paul had driven down from Manchester earlier that day, both of them tight with anxiety about what they would say when they saw her. But it had been fine. She looked marvellous, happy, edgy with excitement. She wore a white silk dress, very tight, very strappy, cut low on the breast. Bernard wore a grey Kenzo suit with a Nehru collar, which was perhaps just a fraction too tight over the crotch and thighs, though it certainly brought out his shape. More than once Anna caught Lauren looking. He flattered Lauren, made her laugh, and dealt smoothly with Paul, who had had a touch too much to drink and was becoming boisterous. With Anna he was courtly, deferential, attentive. He had made an expert consommé julienne, beautifully garnished with tiny slivers of carrot and green peppers and chanterelle mushrooms, followed by a triumphant lobster Newburg, the cream sauce thick but not curdled, the paprika tickling the palette in exactly the prescribed manner. Finally there was a raspberry sorbet with kirsch. They toasted each other in expensive French wine. Bernard drank very little.

It had also been a year since that terrible thing with Luke. Anna's friends had spoken about it in whispers, appalled, unable to believe that such a thing could happen to someone they knew, whose house they'd been to, someone they'd *touched*. The police had linked it to an attacker who had been active in the area recently, some kind of maniac who tied his victims up and terrified them, though he'd never killed anyone before. Since Luke's murder, there had been nothing further from him. The police assumed he'd left the area, or was simply 'resting'. Serial offenders of this type frequently left long gaps between incidents, they'd told Anna, for any number of reasons. The police had been very good. They'd even offered her counselling.

Her friends had been endlessly willing to help, but no-one had seemed to know quite what to do. She'd seen Oliver and Sal a few times, but they were frantically preoccupied with Ryan, and anyway, they simply didn't know how to be with her. It was too awkward. Sal thought there was a problem with Anna, jealousy of the baby perhaps? Anna wouldn't talk to her about it. Sal had rung on several occasions, but had been politely rebuffed. After a while she didn't ring any more.

In fact, one way or another, Anna saw almost no-one in the year after Luke's murder. There was no shortage of sympathy and concern, but Anna seemed to withdraw, she didn't want to see anyone.

Except Bernard, of course. If it hadn't been for Bernard, she'd said to Lauren when she rang her to invite her down to London for the visit, if he hadn't happened to have been staying at the time, she didn't know what she would have done. He'd been a tower of strength, seen to everything. She'd introduced him to Mrs Keyes, who had squinted at him and smiled uncertainly. Her eyes definitely weren't improving. He'd decided not to go back to New Zealand, he'd decided to stay permanently. It had all worked out very well.

The food was precisely, exactly right, perfect, apart from the sorbet which was slightly too strongly flavoured.

'Maybe just a hint less liqueur next time, Bernard?' Anna said, and he nodded seriously.

They had mints and Bernard went out to make the coffee. He served them in the front room, and the coffee was excellent, strong and fragrant. At ten o'clock Anna looked at her watch and then at Bernard.

'Bernard?'

'It's all right,' he said, 'I'm all right, I'm not tired, honestly.'

Anna held his eye and raised an eyebrow. For a moment he looked as if he might defy her. It was just a flash of anger in the eye, then it was gone, almost before it came, and he was docile as a lamb again. Good as gold. He ducked his head and stood up.

'I have to go to go to –' he said, and stopped. 'I've gotten to bed, to go to get –' Anna stood up too and guided him to the door. She pecked him on the cheek and ruffled his hair. The sound of his footsteps faded on the stairs.

Anna turned to find Lauren and Paul exchanging a secret look, and addressed herself to Lauren, smiling serenely.

'You see, he gets tired,' Anna said. 'Poor baby.'

THE END

A SICKNESS OF THE SOUL
by Simon Maginn

'It was a bigger story than I'd imagined, and at the centre of it was Teacher. I was determined now, more than ever, to get the story, the whole story. I would do whatever was necessary.'

When Robert, an investigative journalist, tunes into a phone-in programme while driving through the Midlands, he immediately realizes he is on to something. He goes undercover to infiltrate a bizarre bikers' cult, the Sons of the New Bethlehem, led by the charismatic Teacher. It is Teacher whom Robert has heard on the radio, giving advice to distraught callers and praying for their salvation. Teacher's ministry is a fully fledged crusade, in leather. Astride their Harleys and Hondas, the gang – Spider, Loverman, Stroker, Biceps and the rest – gather in shopping centres and car parks with the aim of winning converts for Christ.

Robert's cover, however, is not as good as he'd thought, and he finds himself prisoner of the Sons, cooped up in an eerie hotel. Trying to penetrate the enigmatic facade of Teacher, and to discover what, *exactly*, is the man's method of healing his followers, he becomes involved in a series of deaths before he can escape. And when he's back in London with his partner, Fiona, he can't settle into his former life. The memories of Teacher's weird regime haunt him, and before long he's on the road to the Midlands once more . . .

0 552 14250 6

VIRGINS AND MARTYRS
by Simon Maginn

A woman's arm is found washed up on Brighton beach. The palm of the hand has been pierced, possibly by a nail. There is a wedding ring on the appropriate finger, and from the lividity of the flesh it is clear that the ring has been put on after death.

Daniel, a graduate student struggling to finish his dissertation, moves into a house in Hove owned by a polite and inscrutable skinhead. Wendy, the former occupant of his room, has vanished, leaving few traces: some shredded paper, a hank of hair. But gradually Daniel begins to feel Wendy's presence all around him, to realize that she is showing him things he'd rather not see, guiding him to shelves in the university library where crumbling books about decomposing corpses and sacrificial virgins are kept. And curiously, Daniel finds himself unable to eat, even to buy food. As he becomes thinner and weaker, his mind is dominated by sinister visions of a starving Wendy and of his own hand, wet, dead, and with a neat hole piercing its palm . . .

'A name to watch'
Ramsey Campbell

0 552 14249 2

THE LAST GIRL
Penelope Evans

'TENSE, COMPELLING, AND
PSYCHOLOGICALLY PERCEPTIVE'
Sunday Times

'They've found a new girl for the second floor.'

Larry Mann, lonely and neglected in his rooms on the top floor
of a north London house, is delighted when pale, quiet
Amanda, a young student, moves in below him. Anxious to
make her feel at home, he brings her presents, prepares meals
for her, and is always ready for a cosy chat and a drink in the
evening. Amanda's arrival makes a world of difference to
Larry, abandoned long since by his wife and daughter. And
what could be more natural than for him to help her avoid the
anger of Ethel Duck, their aged and formidable landlady, by
tidying her rooms while she's at college? Checking for faulty
plugs, looking in her cupboards to see what food supplies need
replenishing — Larry is happy to spend time serving Amanda
any way he can.

Amanda, who's shy and kind-hearted, doesn't want to hurt
Larry's feelings. But she's not always as grateful as she might
be for his attentions. And Larry, uneasy at the weekend visits
of her friend Francis, and fearful that Francis may supplant
him in Amanda's affections, broods darkly on the past . . .

Told throughout in Larry's voice, his extraordinarily eerie tale
builds to a dreadful and unexpected climax. Penelope Evans,
in her remarkable first novel, winds up the psychological
tension to an almost unbearable degree.

'TENSION HOLDS THE READER IN PAGE-TURNING
COMPULSION AND NEVER FLAGS TILL THE LAST WORD
HAS BEEN READ'
Ruth Rendell

'A VERY POWERFUL STUDY OF AN OBSESSION . . . THIS IS
A REMARKABLE FIRST NOVEL'
Penelope Fitzgerald

0 552 99602 5

BLACK SWAN

A SELECTED LIST OF FINE WRITING AVAILABLE FROM BLACK SWAN AND CORGI BOOKS

99618 1	BEHIND THE SCENES AT THE MUSEUM	Kate Atkinson	£6.99
99632 7	NATALYA, GOD'S MESSENGER	Magda Bogin	£5.99
99531 2	AFTER THE HOLE	Guy Burt	£5.99
996 28 9	THE KNIGHT OF THE FLAMING HEART	Michael Carson	£6.99
99692 0	THE PRINCE OF TIDES	Pat Conroy	£6.99
99587 8	LIKE WATER FOR CHOCOLATE	Laura Esquivel	£6.99
99602 5	THE LAST GIRL	Penelope Evans	£5.99
99599 1	SEPARATION	Dan Franck	£5.99
99616 5	SIMPLE PRAYERS	Michael Golding	£5.99
99668 8	MYSTERIOUS SKIN	Scott Heim	£6.99
99169 4	GOD KNOWS	Joseph Heller	£7.99
99605 X	A SON OF THE CIRCUS	John Irving	£7.99
99567 3	SAILOR SONG	Ken Kesey	£6.99
99542 8	SWEET THAMES	Mathew Kneale	£6.99
99659 9	THE PAINTED BIRD	Jerzy Kosinski	£6.99
99595 9	LITTLE FOLLIES	Eric Kraft	£5.99
14249 2	VIRGINS AND MARTYRS	Simon Maginn	£4.99
14250 6	A SICKNESS OF THE SOUL	Simon Maginn	£4.99
99384 0	TALES OF THE CITY	Armistead Maupin	£5.99
99502 9	THE LAST WORD	Paul Micou	£5.99
99596 7	BLOODSUCKING FIENDS	Christopher Moore	£6.99
99536 3	IN THE PLACE OF FALLEN LEAVES	Tim Pears	£5.99
99667 X	GHOSTING	John Preston	£6.99
99664 5	YELLOWHEART	Tracy Reed	£5.99
99636 X	KNOWLEDGE OF ANGELS	Jill Paton Walsh	£5.99
99673 4	DINA'S BOOK	Herbjørg Wassmo	£6.99